SOMETHING WICKED

SOMETHING WICKED

KEITH FERRARIO

GABRIEL'S HORN PRESS

This book is a work of fiction. The names, characters, places, and incidents are products of the writer's imagination or have been used fictitiously and are not to be construed as real. While the story is set in the Twin Cities area of Minnesota, the author has taken creative license with certain geographical features, street layouts, and landmarks to suit the narrative. Any resemblance to actual persons, living or dead, actual events, locales or organizations is entirely coincidental.

Revised Print Edition: Gabriel's Horn Press, LLC.
www.gabrielshornpress.com

ISBN: 979-8-88846-018-4

ACKNOWLEDGMENTS

To my early readers and trusted critics, thank you for your honesty, your insight, and your dedication to the story. Your thoughtful feedback helped me to sharpen and strengthen it throughout the process. I owe special thanks to my friends for their constant support, understanding, and flexibility during the time and attention this book required. And to the readers who have chosen to spend time with this story, thank you most of all. This is the final and most meaningful part of its journey.

ONE

"Sarah! Sarah, where are you?" Jack Railey called out into the murky void. A gray fog encompassed him—consuming him on all sides—sending a numbing chill throughout his body. He fought back the cold, clinching his teeth together to stop them from chattering as he stood listening for an answer—any answer.

"Sarah, can you hear me?" Puffs of steam rose from his mouth with each word and merged with the gloom. "It's your father! I've come to bring you home! Sarah, can you hear me?"

Jack staggered amid the thick fog—the drab mist clinging to his rugged face—a layer of dew condensed on his dark brown hair. As he stumbled forward, Jack turned his head from side to side, searching frantically—he had to find Sarah! He continued shouting out while pushing on into the heavy vapor. "Sarah…Sarah!"

Up ahead, the fog parted, revealing a childlike silhouette. It must be Sarah, he thought—he hoped. Jack ran to her. It must be—it has to be his daughter!

"Sarah?" he said. "It *is* you!" Her long blonde curls draped down to her shoulders. "I'm coming. Stay where you are!" But as he approached, Sarah slipped away. He hurried to catch up, but the faster he moved toward her, the faster she moved from him.

Jack stopped and shouted, "Please, Sarah, don't move! Stay where you are! I'm coming for you!"

Before he had the chance to take a step, a hand shot up from below, piercing the fog and grabbing Jack around the ankle. Its skin was gray and rotting. Several small pieces had been torn away, displaying the yellow bone underneath. The fingernails that hadn't already broken off were a dull purplish-red, and pus from the festering fingertips soaked into the fabric of Jack's pants.

Not having time to pull his foot loose, a second hand burst forward, seizing his other ankle. Its grip was incredibly strong—driving a sharp pain up his entire leg. Barely able to fight against the first two, a third hand grabbed hold, and a fourth, a fifth, sixth, more, and more, and more! Each climbing further up his body so that out of the dense fog, arms had shot out from all directions, ensnaring him in a mass of dead flesh.

Jack fought to untangle himself—twisting and turning, pulling and tugging at the putrid fingers and hands. Sarah was so close! If only he could get to her! Jack's eyes widened. A dark, shrouded form skulked behind his daughter, forcing her to watch his useless struggle while keeping her just out of his reach. A cruel laugh mocked him as he tried to escape.

"Who are you?" Jack roared. "What are you?" He gritted his teeth when a hand slid out from under the cloak and stroked Sarah's hair. "Let my daughter go!"

Focusing all his anger, Jack forced his right hand straight up, tearing free three of the dead digits that had held him. Immediately, he took hold of another of the decaying hands, grasping it by the index and middle fingers. He gave it a hard, single snap, splitting the hand down the center. The torn, rotten tissue splintered, then crumbled to ash. One by one, and with the speed of a man possessed, Jack tore at the other hands. The popping and snapping of brittle fingers drowned out the laughter. The broken bones fell into piles of dry, pulverized dust.

Free at last, Jack dashed through the mist to come within feet of Sarah. He jumped forward, his arms spread wide to net her. *I've got you*, Jack thought as his fingertips touched her frail shoulder. But at the very last instant, both Sarah and the shroud behind her faded to nothing in wisps of smoke, and he was left falling into an endless void with nothing except a handful of long blonde hair.

Jack jerked awake—his skull almost bouncing off the headrest. It took him no time to reorient himself to his surroundings and to the mission. He was in a stakeout car adjacent to several bombed-out buildings, one mile inside the border of Lebanon, waiting for a contact with information about which Hamas terrorist cells were currently recruiting young men to martyr themselves as living, walking bombs. A group of these radicals had recently entered the business district of Israel with ten pounds of dynamite strapped to their chests. Not showing a speck of hesitation, they destroyed themselves and as many civilians as inhumanly possible.

Next to him, in the driver's seat, was Paul Ames, an Englander. With his cleft chin and charming good looks, Paul was almost a movie cliché. He hated the slightest reference to James Bond. Jack had worked with Paul on one other mission three years earlier out of Turkey in 1992. Previous to that, Jack had heard of the Englishman's proficiency for finding informants who would sell out anyone for the right amount. And to date, Paul Ames had lived up to his reputation.

"Must've been one hell of a dream?" Paul said, slipping a stick of gum in his mouth, then offering the pack to Jack.

Jack waved it off. "Dream? No, I don't dream," he replied, believing his own words. All images had vanished—nothing remained.

"If you say so. But your timing is perfect. Our friend Behzad just showed up." Paul nodded toward the entrance to an alleyway and to a tall, scraggly man with jet-black hair and an unshaven face. He had stepped into view after a quick glance around. Despite the distance, it was possible to make out the wide, empty gap where his front teeth had been when he opened his mouth to grin.

"Why is it every time I see *our friend* there," Jack asked, "I get the feeling he would rather slit my throat than talk to me?"

"It's that charming American personality of yours." Paul laughed. "My chap's a greedy son-of-a-bitch—in it for himself and himself only.

As long as he sees the payoff, he's harmless enough. And he's been reliable so far, hasn't he?"

"Yeah. *So far*," Jack said, but also recalling the phrase, "things change." And in this part of the world, things changed with blinding speed. He made a mental note to keep a sharp eye on Behzad.

"Relax mate, this is going to be a breeze. As you Americans say—easy as pie."

At a cautious pace, Jack and Paul eased out of their car—their eyes constantly moving to detect any sign of betrayal or deception.

Behzad delayed his approach as a large dirty truck loaded down with tires drove between him and the two men—he disappeared from their sight. Jack feared the diversion may be prelude to a trap. He reached inside his jacket, gripping the handle of his M9 9-mm Beretta handgun, but held off pulling it from the holster. When the truck passed, Jack eased some, and Behzad continued his way toward them. Still, Jack didn't release the hold on his weapon quite yet.

"Easy as pie," Paul repeated.

Then Jack saw it! A dark, four-door sedan, driving slowly out of the alley, creeping into view. It was enough to start an alarm blasting in his head.

The sedan charged forward, its engine roaring and tires tearing up gravel. Out of both front and rear windows, automatic rifle barrels open-fired.

It had been a setup after all.

By pure instinct alone, Paul and Jack dived for cover alongside the relative protection of their own vehicle, but not before they witnessed Behzad's body do a death dance as the bullets tore through his soft flesh. Blood and bits of tissue sprayed out across the street. Behzad, Jack realized, was the intended victim. He and Paul were simply a bonus.

"And you said it was going to be easy," Jack shouted, bullets whizzing over their heads. The tinny sound of lead hitting the fender all but drowned out his voice.

"I was bloody well wrong, wasn't I?" Paul yelled over the gunfire, pulling his Glock 17 pistol out from under his coat.

From the other direction came more tire squealing. *Could things get any worse?* Jack thought. Like the first car, the windows were down, and guns pointed out—its occupants began shooting.

"This is not good," Paul said, dropping closer to the ground.

"You think so, Paul?" Jack scoffed. "You really think so?" He flinched. A bullet flew past his ear.

Seconds later, a loud explosion erupted into a huge fireball.

As the long shadows of the early-autumn Minnesota dusk crept through the large bay window, Anna Railey stared out at the deserted road that ran in front of the house. Anna's emerald green eyes dropped to her wristwatch. But by now, the action had become a simple reflex—the actual time meant nothing. Sounds of an engine snapped her gaze up to the road. But Anna's hope faded as the unknown car drove by without so much as a flash of brake lights.

Three hours ago, her daughter, Sarah, should have come home from school, but Anna gave no thought to the fact that she hadn't arrived as usual. Then an hour went by, then a second, and no Sarah. Even while preparing the evening's meal, Anna kept only a casual eye on the clock. For a girl of fifteen, Sarah was very responsible, Anna reminded herself, and she'd be phoning any minute now.

Anna switched on the porch light on her way back to the kitchen. The chicken had been in the oven, on warm, for an extra thirty minutes. Any longer, and she feared the bird might be too dry to be palatable. She grabbed a pair of hot pads from the counter and leaned in to extract the roasting pan. But not totally focused on her task, she pulled away. Anna made a second attempt, using great care not to burn herself.

The chicken, a roasted golden brown, sat resting on the stovetop. Its mouthwatering aroma rose into the air. Anna slipped a long, sharp carving knife out from its rack and began cutting the meat into sections—breasts, wings, legs. She stopped when the front door opened, then closed.

"Sarah?" Anna did her best to stop her voice from cracking.

"It's just me, Mom," Justin, her ten-year-old son, shouted in response. "My rear bike tire needed some air." He walked into the kitchen, rubbing his palms together, which only spread the dirt he was trying to remove. The boy had the same dark brown hair as his father, whereas Sarah and Anna shared the same shade of blonde. Both children, however, inherited Jack's sharp brown eyes.

"Go wash your hands, dear," Anna told him.

"We gonna eat soon? I'm getting sort of hungry."

"No point waiting any longer, I suppose. Wash up and get yourself a plate." Anna touched the metal bowl holding the mashed potatoes—still warm, but not for much longer.

Justin returned from the bathroom and held up his palms. "All done," he said on his way to the cupboard.

"Did your sister say anything to you?" Anna asked as Justin approached the counter with his plate.

"Does she ever? She's probably with Cindy." The boy scooped up a hefty dollop of potatoes.

"You can warm those up in the microwave."

Justin covered the white mound with gravy. "Nah, they're plenty hot," he said, taking a bite. "If Sarah doesn't come home, can I eat her chicken leg?"

"Don't say that. Of course, she'll come home."

"I didn't mean forever. I just meant tonight—for supper." He had the most serious expression on his face. "I bet she's doing some stupid after-school stuff."

"The rule is one leg apiece. I'll put hers in the fridge and reheat it for her later."

"Doesn't taste as good that way," Justin said, disappointed.

Mother and son ate their meal in silence. Anna peered out the sliding glass doors that led to a cedar deck. Night had rolled in. The large windowpanes appeared as though they'd been blotted out with black ink. A chilling dread washed over her. The house felt more isolated than usual. The nearest neighbor was half a mile away, which didn't help.

A sudden bang caused Anna to jump in her chair. The wind had kicked up, and the branches of a large oak slapped against an outer wall.

"When your father gets home, I'm going to have him prune that old tree. It should've been done years ago."

The rest of the meal passed quickly. Justin made another plea for the extra chicken leg, and to his dismay, he got the same answer: "No." As he left the table, he said something about heading up to his room to work on a new model airplane. Anna didn't catch the exact words, but nodded anyway.

Anna cleared the dishes, rinsed them, and stacked them in the dishwasher. She placed the chicken, a mound of potatoes, and a small pile of corn on a microwavable plate, snapped on its companion top, then stored the prepared meal in the refrigerator.

Following a brief cleaning of the kitchen, Anna moved to the living room. She sat on the sofa and, from the coffee table, lifted a copy of The English Patient that lay propped up against a thrice-used vanilla-scented pillar candle. The last page read was dog-eared, but she chose to restart the chapter. It had been a week since she last picked up the book.

She reread the first paragraph three separate times before putting the story down. Her attention kept drifting to Sarah, and she wished she could contact Jack. But that was impossible when he was on assignment. She didn't fault him. She knew all about his job and its consequences prior to their marriage.

The doorbell rang!

The double-chime produced a swell of mixed emotions. Relief—that it was Sarah—that she had forgotten her key. Dread—that it's the police with horrible news. Anna rushed for the door but stopped short of grasping the brass doorknob.

The bell rang!

"Who's that?" Justin asked from the top of the stairs.

Anna looked up at her son and gave him a reassuring smile, then faced the front entrance and turned the knob.

"Good evening," the woman in the Liz Claiborne suit said. "I represent Alan Keats, your State Representative for this district. Pardon the hour, but can you spare a minute?"

The two minutes the woman spoke seemed to drag on and on. Anna politely listened and agreed to read the pamphlet, then excused herself.

The canvasser departed with a head nod and political grin. As she walked away, Anna peeked past her and down the sidewalk, hoping, praying, to see Sarah coming up the concrete path.

When turning the deadbolt to lock the door, Anna came to a decision. Sarah had always been a good kid. Only once did she not call to say she'd be late. Worried then too, Anna phoned several of Sarah's friends, hunting for her. The whole thing turned out to be a misunderstanding—a mix-up of dates. Sarah was having dinner at a classmate's house, which Anna thought was scheduled for a later week. Tales of the frantic search got around school the next day. Humiliated, Sarah made her mother promise never to do that again. Anna was about to break that promise and tapped Cindy's number into the kitchen wall phone.

The other end rang twice, and a familiar voice answered—the snobby, self-important, self-absorbed voice of Leonora de Montia. Anna didn't care for the tone as she was informed that the woman had no clue to the girls' whereabouts. That news really came as no surprise. Leonora took more stock in her things than in her daughter. Anna remembered the immense diamond on the woman's finger and how she bragged about keeping the wedding ring despite divorcing her third husband.

"They'll be showing up soon," Leonora said. "You know how girls can be. I bet they're having so much fun they forgot to call. Youth is for the young." Leonora let out such a high-pitched laugh that Anna had to pull the receiver from her ear.

"You need to take this more seriously," Anna said, hearing the shrill end.

"What would you have me do, Anna, dear?"

"We should call the police. We have two missing fifteen-year-old girls."

Leonora's tone changed. "That's a little drastic, isn't it?"

Anna thought she heard fear. "Not at all," she said with a forced confidence.

"If you feel you must." The snobbishness returned. "*My daughter* will be along any time now. I give Cynthia the freedom to make her own choices. I would never stifle her growth."

Unable to stomach Leonora any further, Anna brought the conversation to an abrupt halt. She had an urge to slam down the handset, but decided not to waste the energy.

"Damn you, Leonora," Anna said to herself as doubt crept in. Was she being overly dramatic? Maybe, but sitting idle was not an option.

Anna retrieved the class phone roster from the den and began dialing Sarah's classmates. She started with Sarah's friends, then moved on to the less familiar names. Last year, Leonora "volunteered" Anna to solicit donations from the parents for the Spring Festival. At least now, she could put this list to better use.

But whoever she talked to, Anna got no good answer. "Haven't seen her since school," or "she must be with Cindy." There were a couple of "I saw her with Cindy. Did you try calling her?" and even a "I'm not her friend. Why ask me?"

Her failure to locate Sarah left Anna with one option. She wondered if she should've done it from the beginning. The hard knot in her chest told her she had no other choice.

She dialed 9-1-1.

Anna explained the situation to the dispatcher—her fifteen-year-old daughter was missing. She choked back a tear, saying the words out loud. The male voice asked if she had checked with her daughter's friends. Anna assured him she had. The officer added that teenagers often lose track of time and advised waiting a little while longer for her daughter to come home.

Angered by the suggestion, Anna clearly and loudly doubted the judgment of waiting when a young girl was involved with all the weirdoes running around.

The voice apologized and said he would dispatch a unit to take a report. He added that there was a curfew for that age, and if any patrol saw a child roaming around, they'd pick them up.

Thanking the dispatcher, Anna hung up the phone. She turned and gasped as she found Justin standing in the kitchen doorway.

"Is everything okay?" he asked.

"Yes, honey. You startled me, that's all."

"No, I mean about Sarah." A slight quiver rose in his voice. Despite all their quarrels and bickering, Justin loved his sister, even if he'd never admit it. And right now, his actions spoke volumes. "Is Sarah coming home?"

Anna's heart ached. She leaned down and gave her son a kiss on the cheek and a hug. "I'm sure she's fine, Justin." What else could she say? "She'll be home soon. You go get ready for bed."

After seeing to it that Justin had put away his airplane model, brushed his teeth, and got into bed, Anna returned to the bay window. The porch light cut twenty feet into the moonless night. The winds had died down, and the yard seemed blanketed in an eerie calm. Whenever a car drove by, she prayed it would slow down and turn into the driveway.

"Where are you, Sarah? Where are you?"

Then something stirred in the darkness—something by the corner of the house, outside the light. Anna squinted, straining to see. A large raccoon leaped out of the shadows and into full view. The mask-faced visitor stood up on its hind legs and batted its paws—its eyes illuminated with a yellow shimmer as the electric glow hit them. It stared at Anna and gave a loud, ear-splitting yelp. The furry critter sniffed the air, fell to all fours, and darted off, most likely retreating to the thick woods bordering the backyard.

TWO

Almost a week passed, and Jack Railey had a nagging hunch there was something wrong back home. He was not a man who let undue emotion or worry get the best of him, but he was also a man who listened to his hunches. In fact, he'd had the feeling for the past several days. Only now could he act on it. The clock next to the bed read 10:14 p.m.

Jack stood waiting patiently as the overseas operator opened a line to the States for a phone call long overdue. Because of the eight-hour difference, which made it 2:14 in Minnesota, it was a good time to call. And in reality, he didn't and wouldn't have any other opportunities.

The operator returned and told him the connection was going through. Seconds later, a ringing filled his ear. A spark of pleasure came along with the sound. However, that pleasure turned to concern when the ringing went unanswered. Jack convinced himself that Anna had stepped out to go to the mall or maybe the grocery store. Yet, something kept biting at him—something was wrong.

It took six rings until the answering machine picked up. He hesitated, then said, "Hi, it's me. Just called to say I'm thinking of you. Hope to be home in a few days. Miss you all. Bye."

Jack hung up the phone, disappointed that he missed the chance to talk with Anna. Where he was going, he'd be surprised to see a phone, and even then, using it was out of the question. Calling his wife in the U.S. of A. wouldn't foster trust and understanding with his new associates. Give them an ounce of doubt, and they'd return the favor with a shower of bullets, as Behzad had been reminded in the last pitiful moments of his life.

He didn't know the identity of Behzad's *friends* or which radical group they belonged to—it could have been any of a dozen. Behzad must have really pissed somebody off. And the *who* will always remain a mystery. There wasn't enough left of them to identify.

As far as Jack figured it, with all the bullets flying, one ricocheted, hitting the second car, blowing out a tire. The driver lost control and smashed headlong into the dark sedan. By the fireball produced, one car, if not both, had to be carrying explosives. Pinned down behind their vehicle, the bullet-ridden metal acted as a blast shield for him and Paul. The lucky stroke astounded Paul, but not Jack. It wasn't the first time that a fortunate twist of fate had saved his ass.

A knock at the door broke Jack's thoughts.

"It's open."

Paul entered. "You about ready, mate?"

Jack's eyes lingered on the phone. "Sure," he said, "sure thing." He checked his gun before he and Paul left the room.

For half an hour, Anna stood on the corner of Hennepin Avenue and West Twenty-sixth Street, waiting. *How did this happen?* She kept asking herself that question over and over—each time her heart ached. Sarah had disappeared, and no one could or would help find her. She tried talking to the police. They sent her on to Juvenile Services. Juvenile Services referred her to Social Aid. Social Aid sent her back to the police. She'd been going around and around for days—hallway after hallway—office after office. None of those alleged professionals said it to her face, but a couple alluded to the possibility that Sarah might be dead. She refused to believe it.

Anna was out of options when a phone call told her where to locate Sarah. At first, she hesitated, unsure whether the caller was serious or setting her up for some sick joke. Anna asked the caller for his name, but the response was a loud click. Prank or not, she jumped at the chance to bring Sarah home.

But with hope fading by the minute, Anna felt foolish for even considering the words of some anonymous voice and angry that anyone would perpetrate such a cruel hoax. She decided to leave for her car. Anna got only three steps when she froze—an odd music filled the air. It was a collection of rhythms and chants coming from a band of children wearing white robes and dancing down the sidewalk. All the boys had their heads shaved bald—the girls were fashioned in short pixie cuts. Two girls, poorly shaking tambourines, tried to keep with the beat of a chubby boy pounding on a drum. The rest of the children asked passing strangers for money.

A tall man handed a boy some change, which he, in turn, placed in a large bowl held by one of the girls. Stunned, Anna did a double take at what she saw—at who she saw. The girl holding the bowl was Sarah. With her long blonde hair trimmed up to her ears, Anna didn't recognize her until now.

Anna tried to yell out, but the shock had muted her. She stepped off the curb to cross the street at the very instant a hand seized her by the upper arm. Anna let out a gasp as she spun around to confront her captor. In her current state of exhaustion, she didn't have the strength to put up much of a fight, though screaming was always an option.

Before she opened her mouth, the man spoke in a soft tone. "Please," he said, "do not be alarmed." He was short, balding, and wearing a tailored charcoal-gray suit. His non-threatening appearance calmed Anna enough to listen. "I can't let you go any farther."

"Excuse me?" Anna said, turning her head, staring at the man's hand still touching her arm.

"Forgive me." He released his grip. "My name is Anthony Bane, and you must not disturb those children."

"But my daughter..."

"Believe me, madam, I sympathize." Bane's face revealed his own anguish. "My son is also among their number."

"Then why—?" Her question hadn't even escaped her lips when she received her answer. The screech of hard-braking tires made her turn back to the group of kids. She watched as two large men bolted out of a silver Buick. Anna feared someone had hit a child. But then, the biggest of the two grabbed a tall, thin boy while the other blocked the remaining juveniles, strategically cutting them off from their comrade. Anna realized she was witnessing a kidnapping.

"That's Tony—my son," Anthony Bane told her. "I've had this planned for over a week. Now you see why I stopped you. I couldn't risk you scaring them from this spot."

Anna watched as the children fought with the blocker. Her eyes widened as Sarah began acting like an animal—clawing at the man—biting his forearm. He pushed her aside. The bigger man had his own hands full, shoving Bane's son into the backseat of the car.

She tried to move forward, but again, Bane grabbed her.

"You can do nothing," he said. "It will all be over soon."

The men, both finally in the Buick, signaled to the driver. He gunned the engine, and the tire squealed in a trail of white smoke. The driver swerved to miss a tiny red-haired girl, but then they were gone.

Anna broke free from Bane's grasp. "Sarah!" She ran toward her daughter but got to the other side too late. The children, including Sarah, had scattered. Anna was alone on the walkway, fighting not to cry.

"I'm sorry," Bane said, coming up behind her. "It was the only way to retrieve Tony."

"Will I have to do the same thing to get my daughter home?"

Bane gave her a sad smile. "I'm afraid it won't be so easy next time."

"It didn't look so easy this time," Anna said, staring down the empty street.

"I just meant that they'll be on guard. They won't allow any more of their group to be taken in such a manner."

"You've obviously given this some serious consideration, Mr. Bane."

"It pains me to have to agree with you…ahh…Ms.?"

"Anna…Anna Railey."

"Railey? You're Sarah Railey's mother?" His reaction at hearing her name surprised Anna. He studied her as if she wasn't what he expected.

"Do you know my daughter?"

Bane's expression brightened. "Not exactly. I'm head of a small group of parents. Your daughter's name came up in connection with the daughter of a member. I understand your husband is out of town on business and can't be reached."

"Yes, but…" Anna paused. *This man seems to know a lot. Maybe too much.*

"We need to talk, Mrs. Railey," Bane said. "I can help you save Sarah."

While Anna Railey talked with Anthony Bane, across town, another stranger, a man she would never meet, also anguished over his daughter. But his torment had taken on a much different and immediate form.

"I didn't do it! It's all a lie! He made her say those things about me. You don't understand!"

The police officers ignored Harry Reid's plea as they led the skinny man to the lockup area. Approaching the steel bars, frightened and desperate, Harry pulled away to run, but a harsh blow knocked him down, forcing a loud gasp from his mouth.

"Sickos like you make me wanna puke," the cop said, standing over Harry, baton still in hand.

"Easy, Mike," his partner told him. "Let's put 'im in the cage."

As Harry lay doubled over, both officers pulled him up by an arm. Harry tried to speak but found it difficult to catch his breath. They carried their prisoner into the cell and dumped him on the bunk.

Mike leered down at him. "Too bad we couldn't arrange a roommate for you. These guys are scum, but they know how to handle child molesters. God, you're a piece of shit! Your own daughter…"

"I didn't do it!" Harry coughed. "He made her lie! He's evil! I have proof."

"You're gonna need it," Mike said as he slammed Harry in. The officer glanced down the hall, making certain he was out of earshot of the others. "I hope they throw your ass in prison for twenty years. And if there's anything I can do to make it happen, I will."

Harry staggered over to the locked door. "Please, please, you have to believe me. I did nothing wrong. Will someone please believe me?" From between the bars, his words were answered with a baton-tip hard to the stomach. This time, he grabbed a rung, preventing himself from hitting the floor. "I never hurt my daughter," Harry wheezed out.

"Tell it to the chaplain." The officer left the man to his pain.

Harry clutched the cold metal until he regained enough strength to return to the bunk. He eased his butt onto the thin mattress and forced several deep breaths. His mind reeled—he had been on the verge of getting his daughter back. Three days after filing the paperwork with family court to gain sole custody, the police showed up at his house. In his most horrid dreams, he couldn't fathom her telling such lies about him. It could only mean he was close to learning the secret of that evil man, though it gave him no solace. He sat in silence, resting his forehead in his open hands. Harry closed his eyes, losing himself in his despair—if he had just had a little more time.

A strange sound compelled Harry to lift his head. He looked and saw nothing. But then he heard it again. A sound that shouldn't be there. A sound that started his heart to pound.

Hiss-s-s-s.

An enormous snake slithered past the bars and into Harry's jail cell. It slid across the white tiles along the edge of the concrete wall. *Hiss-s-s-s.* The reptile rose high off the floor. Its tongue darted in and out, seeking its prey. When those dark eyes met Harry's, he felt the blood drain from his face—his insides turned to jelly. The fear of snakes plagued him since childhood. They always terrified him. He thought he'd pass out.

But somehow, Harry got himself to move—to jump off the bunk and to the door. He pulled at the bars. "Help me." He barely managed a whisper. "Help me."

As if directed by some outside influence, the serpent turned toward Harry. *Hiss-s-s-s.*

Harry slammed his body hard against the unyielding steel. The snake slithered closer, and closer, and closer, forcing Harry into a corner. His labored breath caused his lungs to burn as the reptile crawled over his foot and climbed his leg. He wanted to cry out, but only a feeble gasp left his throat. Harry's eyeballs strained in their sockets, and the sweat dripped down his face, watching the serpent inch up his torso. *Hiss-s-s-s.* Then, with blinding speed, the snake twisted up over his shoulder, its cool scales rubbing on his skin. The creature wrapped itself around his neck. Harry clawed at the living noose—his fingers dug into thick flesh but were useless against the viselike hold. As he fought to break free, the powerful tail thrashed through the air and encircled the highest crossbar.

Then the snake recoiled, pulling Harry up. His feet kicked out, and he struggled to regain a foothold. Dangling midair, he gave one last attempt to scream. No whine, no whimper, not even a single breath escaped the tight coil. The room spun, then went black. Harry's life drained away. He hung motionless, alone in the emptiness of his cage.

Twenty minutes later, the officers found Harry and cut him down.

"The sicko was guilty all right," Mike said, smirking. "Why else would he have hung himself?"

But a second officer asked, "Where'd he get the goddamn rope?!"

The hallway echoed with the clatter of footsteps on a wooden floor. A short, stocky, robed figure moved through the dim corridor. He approached a large door, which had an exquisite brass knob and matching etched hinges.

Rajak softly knocked.

No response.

On a second knock, he turned the doorknob but did not enter. The scent of burning sage wafted out into the hall. "Master?" he called out. The room was as black as a starless night. The small amount of light from the hall shot forward, splitting the void in two. "Master, a situation has arisen," the man said into the darkness.

"Speak."

The servant turned his face to the voice. "The children have returned from their gathering," he said with a quiver.

"You disturb my meditation with such a mundane event?"

"I beg your forgiveness, Master," Rajak said. "There is more…"

"Get on with it!" Shallow, raspy coughs followed the words.

"The boy, Tony Bane, did not return with the others." The robed man took a deep breath. "Two unknown men attacked the children. They grabbed the Bane boy off the street. A third drove them away before the other children could—"

"Enough," the voice said, but devoid of any anger. "This is not unexpected."

Silence lasting several seconds compelled Rajak to speak. "Master, what shall we do?"

"This matter will resolve itself. I have already seen to it." The shadow coughed once more, which ended with a series of painfully sounding gasps for air.

The servant wanted to spring to his master's side, but the resulting consequences would be severe—he stood his ground. "May I aid you?"

"Summon the children to the chamber."

Rajak bowed and backed out, pulling the door shut behind him.

THREE

Jack Railey was exhausted. His mission had been nonstop since he first reached his drop point in Syria. He hadn't been able to relax —really relax—for the past month until now. He fell asleep almost the instant the airplane took off from Heathrow. Paul suggested he stick around for a day or so, but Jack left England hours after the two of them gave their debriefings. He always looked forward to going home, away from the guns and bombs, the undercover surveillance, and, most importantly, from people trying to kill him. He accepted those hazards as part of his job—so far, and contrary to some fine efforts, he was still kickin'.

As he slept, images of his daughter intruded into his subconscious, disturbing his peaceful bliss. The evil shape had a hold on Sarah, and no matter what he tried, he was unable to free her. He felt so powerless, so weak—she needed him, and he could do nothing.

A shaking pulled him out of his nightmare. He jumped in his seat, not knowing where he was. His dream vanished as he awoke. His eyes focused on the face hovering above him, and he sat up, remembering the woman from when he boarded the plane.

"Good morning, sir," the flight attendant said, leaning across the empty seat next to him. “We’re entering our landing pattern into Minneapolis-St. Paul, please fasten your seatbelt.”

He looked down, and sure enough, his buckle had been undone.

“What time is it?” he asked, fighting a yawn.

“Ten-o-five local time. We’re right on schedule.”

Just as Jack put his seat in the upright position, the pilot came on the intercom. “Attention, passengers. They’re having problems down below clearing a runway for us. We’ve been placed in a holding pattern for approximately thirty to forty-five minutes. The crew apologizes for any inconvenience.”

“So much for being on schedule,” the flight attendant told him. “It seems we have a wait. Can I get you a sandwich? Or a piece of fruit? There’s a few apples left.”

“Isn’t it against the rules to serve food this late in the flight?”

“Usually,” she said, “but you slept through mealtime.”

“Thanks, but no. I’m never hungry when I first wake up.”

“Are you certain? It’s no bother.”

Jack smiled. “That’s very considerate, but I’m fine.”

“If you’re sure,” the attendant said, returning his smile. “The pilot will announce our clearance to land.” She concluded with, “I hope you had a pleasant flight.”

“Restful, at least,” Jack said. The attendant moved on to her other passengers, double-checking that all was secure for them as well. Jack adjusted his wristwatch, hoping things got squared away quickly down below. He hated flying in circles, knowing Anna and the kids were waiting for him.

“I’m afraid it’s my fault you missed your lunch,” a voice spoke from the window seat. A tad groggy, Jack had forgotten he wasn’t alone. The voice belonged to an attractive woman with long black hair, dark brown eyes, and perfect skin.

“Pardon?” Jack said.

“You appeared to be on weary legs as you came aboard. I didn’t have the heart to let them wake you when the food cart came along. I should’ve minded my own business.”

“Trust me, I appreciate the extra sleep.”

"Tough business trip?" she asked.

"Something like that. Is it obvious?"

She grinned. "Doing a few years of the job-related traveling thing myself, I'm pretty good at recognizing the signs."

"Then thank you for your keen observation. I needed sleep more than I needed food."

"Still, I feel bad," the woman said, gently touching Jack's arm. "Perhaps we could grab a bite together after we land. You should have an appetite by then."

"A kind offer, but probably not such a—"

"I'm sorry," the woman said before Jack finished speaking. "I've put you in an awkward situation. I'm normally not so forward. Really—I'm not."

"That never crossed my mind," Jack said. "It's just that my wife hates it when I date other women. She's funny that way."

"Wife, huh? She's a lucky woman."

"I'm the lucky one," Jack told her.

Thirty-five minutes later, the aircraft touched down with a soft jolt. Upon disembarking, Jack was glad to be on friendly ground, not having to worry about anyone shooting at him. It had been a hell of a mission, from start to finish, and he missed Anna—he missed his children. His job kept him away much too long. Jack knew in his heart that if Anna weren't such a loving wife, she would have left him years ago. She never asked too many questions about his assignments and was always tolerant of him having to leave, sometimes with less than an hour's notice.

Jack grabbed his case off the customs counter. The inspector gave him a nod. But that was a mere formality. Thanks to the papers Jack had handed the man, the bag wasn't checked all that closely.

Jack snaked through the airport terminal, keeping a lookout for his family. His height allowed him a good view of the crowd. He saw a young couple in a tight embrace, kissing—an older woman bending down to greet a small child—and a large fellow eating a half-wrapped sandwich while pulling a suitcase behind him like an obedient dog. Similar scenes repeated themselves up and down the concourse, but he saw no Anna.

He considered the possibility that the agency hadn't informed her of his arrival time, or worse, she had no clue he was en route. But then he spotted her and Justin. Jack looked from one to the other. Something was wrong. He quickened his pace.

As he drew closer, Anna's familiar glowing smile had been replaced with a frown. Jack walked faster. Her eyes were red and puffy. She'd been crying, and they were not tears of joy.

Once he reached her, Jack kissed his wife. His hands held her trembling shoulders.

"Where's Sarah?" he asked.

"Gone," Anna said, crying again. She strained to tell Jack what had happened. Her words and sobs spilled out together as the weeks of frustration broke down her fragile mental state.

Jack watched his wife struggle to regain her composure. The main terminal corridor was no place for this. Jack wrapped his arms around her, and she wept on his shoulder. He led his family to a nearby airport café, where they sat in the farthest booth from the entrance. Jack ordered two coffees and a chocolate milk.

"Now," he said calmly, "what do you mean 'gone'?"

"She's with this group, Jack. It's some sort of cult. She won't come home." Anna dug into her purse for a tissue to dab away the new tears welling up. "The leader, he has control of her. He controls them all." She gently ran the tissue along her lower lashes.

"All?"

Anna took a deep breath to steady her words. "There's over a dozen children under his power. He sends them out to collect money. They're begging on the streets."

"Our daughter is begging?" In no way, shape, or form did Jack ever imagine he'd ask that question about his child. Sarah was a strong girl who did extra chores to earn money rather than ask for freebies from him or her mother. He couldn't even conceive of her begging for a dime. "It's not possible Sarah would've come up with that herself," he said. "She wouldn't get involved with a cult on her own volition."

"It's so insane, Jack," Anna sobbed into her tissue. "I tried to find someone to listen to me, but nobody seemed to give a damn."

"I'm here now. We'll see how long she stays in that cult." His mind reeled, and a sharp pang of anger swelled in his chest—he gave Anna a reassuring smile. The names of all the people who owed him a favor scrolled in his head. *I promise, hell or high water, Sarah will be back with her family.*

"The police can't or won't help," Anna said. Her voice cracked slightly. "But there are some parents—they're banding together. They all have children in the cult. A man named Anthony Bane—he's a friend of Leonora de Montia—his son was the first taken. He started the group. Anthony wants to meet with you. I told him you'd be gone for a few days. He gave me his business card and said it's important that you two meet as soon as possible."

"Me? I've never heard of the man. Why is it so critical he meets me?"

"He didn't say, but I could tell by his tone it was to him." She touched her husband's arm. "He kidnapped his own son to rescue him. He'll help us too. Please, go speak with him. For our daughter's sake."

"And for yours," Jack said, kissing her forehead.

It was a quiet drive home. Anna rested against Jack's shoulder. He thought she was sleeping, but as the silver Pontiac Firebird stopped, she spoke.

"I'm so glad you're here," she told him.

"Me too." Jack turned to Justin, who was sitting in the backseat, not saying a word. In listening to his wife, Jack had practically ignored his son. "How about you, buddy-boy? How are you holding up? Bet you've been busy with your model planes."

"I painted my Cessna L80 last night. It looks great."

"One of these days, I'm going to have to make arrangements to bring you flying. Who knows, maybe you'll become a pilot."

"Not just maybe," the boy scoffed. "Models are fun, but I want to fly the real thing."

"Someday you will," Jack said.

Mother and son got out of the car, but Jack stayed behind the wheel. "I realize this is bad timing," he told Anna, "but I need to stop by the office. You know how Gordon Brigham gets if he's not briefed. I could end up assigned to the Arctic for six months." Jack gave her a concerned glance. "Will you be all right?"

Anna nodded.

"I'll finish with Brigham, then pay a visit to this Anthony Bane and find out what he has in mind." Though Jack had his own ideas brewing, he'd talk to the man for his wife's sake. And it did interest him to know why Bane was so intent on speaking with him. "I shouldn't be long. Go in the house and relax. It may be difficult, but try not to worry. When I return, we'll sit and discuss our options."

"Options?" Anna said in dismay.

"There are always options—be sure of that." He leaned over to Justin and squeezed the boy's shoulder. "I'm counting on you to keep your mother safe while I'm gone, buddy-boy."

Jack's gaze met Anna's. His heart ached as more tears formed. "Don't cry," he said. "I'll do whatever it takes to bring Sarah home. I promise."

She leaned down and kissed her husband. "Please hurry."

"I will." Before driving off, he mussed his son's hair.

Outside the blue glass building, Jack Railey stood collecting himself. He needed to put on his game face. On the drive over, he had been plagued by the thought of his missing daughter and the anguish he saw in his wife's eyes. In his profession, he had to learn detachment, but he figured when it came to his family, detachment comes with a lot more effort.

Just as he was about to grab the door handle, Jack heard a rustling from a nearby bush, followed by a high-pitched squeal. A second squeal had Jack leaning down for a better look. The overgrowth of landscaping around the building's base forced him to bend a shrub out of the way.

"What the hell…?" he said, not knowing what he was seeing—some type of little, brown creature. Several short, leafy branches blocked his line of sight, making a clear view impossible, but he knew he had seen nothing like it before. Jack stared for a few seconds and concluded the thing couldn't be alive—it had to be a rubber toy—that was until he saw it move. And it moved at great speeds. It darted along the concrete foundation, stopped, and then, as quickly, changed directions. In a blur, the creature made another turn—a turn toward him.

"Hey, buddy," a voice said from behind Jack, "can ya spare any loose change?"

Those words caused Jack to snap to attention. He turned his head and stared at the grungy man for a long minute. A sudden uneasiness overcame him, and for a moment, Jack felt nauseous. This man asking for money had him imagining his own sweet Sarah out panhandling on street corners. Both sadness and a deep anger hit him hard.

"Whatcha say, buddy?" the beggar added with his hand out. "A buck for a cup of coffee? Sure could use a cup of coffee." The grimy glove he wore had all the fingers, except the pinkie, torn off.

Jack didn't speak. Instead, he stuck his hand in his pocket, pulled out a twenty-dollar bill, and handed it to the beggar, whose eyes lit up as he snatched the money. "God bless, sir. God bless." The man tipped his hat and ran off as if afraid Jack would change his mind and ask for the bill back.

The beggar disappeared around the corner of the building, and Jack's focus returned to the bushes. But by then, there was no sign of the strange animal. It was likely a mole digging itself up from the damp earth or a rabbit rooting in the rotting leaves. The turned-up rocks combined with the decaying vegetation, add in the shadows under the bush, all contributed to its peculiar appearance. He listened and heard nothing. Jack pushed aside the shrub, but the critter had vanished, probably down the same hole it had crawled up.

Jack wasted no more time or attention rummaging along the shaggy plants and took the final few steps into the building. After an elevator ride to the ninth floor, Jack made a left and continued down a short hall. A locked door blocked his way. Above the doorknob was a black and silver number pad. He hit four of the digits, and the first of three green buttons illuminated. Jack slid a card into the side slot, causing a second light to come on. Jack tapped in four additional digits. A third light lit up, then all three blinked in unison.

Jack pulled the knob, and the door opened. Down the corridor, he passed several people who greeted him by first name. Not having to stop, Jack walked through a second door and into a plush office.

"Welcome home, Commander," a thin redhead said upon seeing him —her smile sincere. "Go right in. You're expected."

"Thanks, Carol," Jack said as he moved across the room to the open inner office door. Gordon Brigham, sitting behind his oak desk, stood up as Jack entered. The older man extended his hand. "You did an excellent job, Jack, as usual." Both men sat down. "I hate to put the rush on you…"

"But…?" Jack understood Brigham's tone all too well.

"We've received some distressing news." Brigham opened a folder lying on his desktop. "A situation has developed." He removed a single page and handed it to Jack. "Markus Radford and his team have been exposed."

Markus Radford—that was a name Jack hadn't thought of in years. And that fact shamed him. Markus was the closest thing to a mentor he could have in this business. The man had even saved his life, getting shot in the process.

Reading the mission summary, Jack asked, "What happened?"

"What *ever* happens? A leak somewhere. A stupid slip-up. Who knows? What matters is that all six of them are in danger. If the Iraqis find them, they'll most certainly be killed, and their bodies will be used as a banner against American imperialism or some such garbage." Brigham leaned back in his chair. "You have to go in and bring 'em out."

"I just left that part of the world," Jack said, remembering the bullet whizzing by his ear. "Can't you give them an exit plan?"

"I wish that was possible, but we lost contact five days ago, and we have no idea where they're holding up."

"You lost contact?!" Jack said, his anger spiking. "Sorry," he said for his outburst. "And you're sure they're still alive?" Jack asked in a much calmer voice.

"All current indications say yes. If that wasn't the case, Saddam Hussein would invite CNN, and anyone else who'd listen, to his palace for a giant press party."

"No arguing that. But why me?"

"Your experience and contacts in the Middle East. I can think of no one better."

"My money's on Tom Blair. He's smart, quick on his feet, and he knows the area."

Brigham handed Jack the complete file. A glance inside and Jack's face went stern. "Terrific. He's a member of Markus's team."

Brigham nodded and added, "You were busy, which now seems fortuitous."

"What kind of timeline are we working with?"

"We'll require at least forty-eight hours to set things up. You'll be going by an indirect route. Entry into Saudi Arabia is much less complicated than Iraq. Journalists are being scrutinized more than ever. Our inside man will have you added to the approval list. That will allow you easy access at the border checkpoints."

"Once I'm in, how long do I have to get them out?"

"A week—ten days tops," Brigham said. "Our sources tell us their position was overtaken, and they're on the run. All normal means of exit are under tight surveillance. The Iraqis are closing in on them."

"I'm glad you're giving me plenty of time," Jack said sarcastically. "That's a lot of sand to search."

"Can't be helped. It's our best estimate. We don't…"

Sarah begging for dollars and coins popped into Jack's head. If only he had been home more. He should've been here. He let Sarah down. He let Anna down.

"Jack," Brigham said, "you okay?" The man's expression was one of puzzlement.

"Sure, yeah. I guess." Jack looked at Brigham. "No, I'm not. My daughter's in some trouble. It's something I have to deal with before I go anywhere." Jack suddenly felt paranoid—he had to be careful of what he told Brigham.

"Like I said, you got two days. That time's yours. Do what you need to do."

Jack shook his head. "I'll need a week, maybe more."

"Markus and his team could be dead in a week."

"They could be dead now." Jack didn't mean his words and apologized. "Anna has been dealing with the situation alone. With me gone months on end…I can't leave her again."

"If I had someone else to send," Brigham said, "I would, but there is no one else. You're it. Finish this assignment, and you can take whatever break you want."

"Ten days? That's all?"

"At the most. If it's necessary, I can have Colin Reeves replace you. He's scheduled to return next week. But realistically, if you don't locate the team by then, it may be too late."

Jack stood up. "All right. Ten days. Not eleven. Not twelve. Ten. I'll think of a way to explain it to Anna." *I've lost a daughter*, Jack thought. *It's even odds I'll be losing a wife too.*

Brigham also stood up. "You've got my word on it."

The two men shook hands.

"If we're done here," Jack said, "I have an appointment to keep. And after that, I need to get some chow. Slept right through my lunch."

"Be prepared to leave in two days. Things should be tied down by then."

"Should be?" Jack said, smothering a tiny smirk. Brigham's orders were going to be carried out to the letter. There was no "should be" about it. He had no doubt all arrangements would be completed and ready in forty-eight hours. That bought him a couple of days to get Sarah home where she belonged. And Jack knew where to start, but he had always been leery about accepting help from strangers, especially when they ask for him by name.

FOUR

A half-an-hour later, Jack stood in the office of Anthony Bane. The short, balding man met him at the door as he entered and introduced himself with a soft handshake.

"I'm pleased to meet you, Mr. Railey. I only wish the circumstances were better." The well-dressed man guided Jack to the other side of the room and signaled him to take the seat positioned off-center of his desk. "How is your wife?" Anthony asked, hurrying to his high-back leather chair. His tone sounded sincere.

"Frazzled," Jack said, still standing, "Angry. Scared. Pick a word."

"Understandable. Your daughter's in the hands of a dangerous man."

Jack pulled the chair out and sat.

Anthony Bane kept the space neat and tidy. Behind him, on the far wall, a set of large windows looked down onto the street—the view covered quite a distance. On the desk were two computer monitors, and on a small table off to the side was a third, which was in constant motion. It scrolled screen upon screen of information. Jack wondered how anyone could process that much data that fast.

"What is it you do here?" Jack asked.

"Stocks and investments—financial planning. Basically, I make other people money."

"It must keep you rather busy."

"I enjoy the challenge, but I have to admit to some long days. As with anything worth doing, it requires work. I'm sure we can agree on that."

"And I'm sure," Jack said, "we can also agree on being direct with each other, so I'm not gonna pussyfoot around. I don't know you. And until three hours ago, I've never heard your name spoken out loud."

"But I've heard of you. And to paraphrase Charles Dudley Warner, necessity makes strange bedfellows." Anthony's face turned straight. "You and I have a common enemy."

Jack half-grinned. "Warner also said, 'Everybody complains about the weather, but nobody does anything about it.' My wife tells me you kidnapped your son."

"Touché, Jack. May I call you Jack?"

Jack returned a slight nod.

"And yes, damn right I did. Not more than four blocks away from this very building. An incident I wish she hadn't witnessed."

"It made quite an impression on her. She's not easily shaken, even in the worst situations."

"But what could be worse?" Bane asked. "To have a child ripped from a parent's grasp."

"Nothing," Jack said, "except maybe not being able to stop it."

Anthony glanced down at the desktop and spoke in a tone that revealed that he was neither proud nor happy about what he had done. "The event has an ironic twist, wouldn't you say? I kidnapped my boy from those who kidnapped him from me."

"Exactly how does a stockbroker arrange a kidnapping?" Jack asked. "Thugs-R-Us?"

Anthony chuckled. "A client of mine is a psychiatrist—an expert in deprogramming cult victims. He arranged everything. Fortunately, or unfortunately—depending on your point of view—he's had to do that sort of thing on more than one occasion. He employs some men to assist him. They're professional and excellent at what they do. Three of them did a coordinated strike and grabbed my boy in front of his group—and in broad daylight. Sweet as you please—the other cult members never saw it coming. Once they wrestled him into the backseat of a car, it was a simple matter of driving away." Anthony's brow furrowed. "You should've seen him—my son—one of the chosen. Wearing bed sheets, head shaved bald—the whole bit."

"And now your son is home?"

"No. It pains me to say he's not. After a week of telling the doctor what he wanted to hear, my son was gone again."

"You'd think a psychiatrist would be tough to fool."

"Oh, he was snowed and snowed good. My boy, Tony—his demeanor didn't change right away—that would've been too obvious. During the first couple of days, his attitude improved. By the end of the week, he acted like his old self—he even cried and said he loved me. All of it performed so subtly, so smoothly. He must have been given a lot of coaching." The man slammed his hand against the desktop, shaking a monitor. "Please forgive my outburst," Bane said. "It's so damned frustrating. That bastard is utilizing some kind of mind control on those poor helpless kids."

"Mind control? You can't be serious."

"As serious as a dead man."

An odd choice, Jack thought.

"Let's say, for the sake of argument, he possesses some power to control human minds." The words caught in Jack's throat. They reminded him of something right out of the rebroadcasts of the 1930s *The Shadow* radio shows he listened to years ago in his college days. This entire conversation was really off the wall. This little man, who he'd known for barely fifteen minutes, wants him to believe Sarah's being held by someone yielding mystical powers. What next?

"Understand with absolute certainty," Bane said, "that the fiend who has your daughter is incredibly powerful."

"If he's all that powerful," Jack conceded for the moment, "then I have to ask—why children?"

"Excuse me?"

"Why control children? Why not the mayor, the governor? Hell, why not the president? What's his angle in manipulating children?"

"I've been trying to piece that together. It may hold the key to stopping him. But I haven't been all that successful. And while his reasons remain unknown, the results are not. Several children under Kahir's *care* have gone missing—vanished without a trace."

"Kahir?"

"Abhaya Kahir—our mutual foe. Or at least that's what he calls himself now." Bane reached across his desk to a collection of papers preserved in a manila folder. "It's important you understand, twenty years ago, Kahir did not exist."

"Aren't you exaggerating some?"

"Afraid not. Prior to 1975, there was no *Abhaya Kahir* on planet Earth."

"So he's using an alias," Jack said with a tone of indifference.

"Not merely an alias, a new life. In France, a man named Daksha Yamuna died under suspicious circumstances—a fire. His body was never recovered. Six weeks pass and Kahir shows up in England. And before Yamuna, a man living on the coast of Greece—Tandu Vasin—also had a suspicious mishap. A boating accident, presumed drowned—body not found. When one man's history ends, another starts, each spanning twenty years or so. There are other names in other countries, but I'm sure I've made my point."

"How did you obtain this information? Tracing any person's past can be challenging enough these days. But covering six decades and across an ocean to boot?" Jack cocked his head to the side, watching Bane carefully. "What convinces you those men have any connection?"

"My sources are impeccable." Bane handed over the folder, an action all too familiar for Jack. "Check for yourself," Bane said. "Names, dates, photos—it's all there. Some pictures aren't the most flattering, but if you compare the faces closely, you'll see they are indeed the same man."

Jack studied the images. What he found surprised him. He expected a withering, frail man in the twilight of his life, but each depicted a person of vigor and strength. "How is this possible?" Jack asked, looking up at Anthony, who had a smirk on his face as if he read Jack's mind.

"Put your reservations aside," Anthony said. "For now, let it be enough that I say all these men are one and the same."

Jack continued his study of the documents. Not that Jack doubted

Bane's claim that Kahir had past lives under different names and identities. The U.S. government did the same thing with the witness protection program, though the alleged time span gave plenty of room for skepticism. That fact notwithstanding, his original question to Bane, which he noticed was skillfully dodged, remained unanswered. *How did a stockbroker in Minneapolis gather intelligence on a man's life with such accuracy? How would he know where to start?*

Jack's own eyes confirmed that the men in the photographs were the same person. He then unfolded the newspaper story attached to the picture of Yamuna. The piece was written in French with a title line: *Chef de secte recherché en cas d'adeptes manquants*, which he translated as *Cult leader wanted in case of missing followers.* Jack scanned the article. It corroborated what Bane had told him.

"Did the French police ever find this Yamuna character?"

"Didn't have to—he turned himself in for questioning. But on concluding their investigation, not finding a shred of evidence, the Police Nationale released him, satisfied that he had nothing to do with the disappearances."

"And that was that?" Jack asked, returning the small pile of photos and clippings to the desk. "They never gave him a second look?"

"Not so much as a glance. Then, years later, on cue, Yamuna *dies*, and Kahir appears in London."

"Now he's here," Jack said. "But with the same name. If what you say is true, it doesn't follow his past patterns. What triggered the change?"

Anthony shifted his weight. "Who knows?"

"In my experience, a person doesn't alter their behavior without reason." Jack caught the man shifting his position again. He recognized the signs of growing anxiety. Anthony Bane was holding something back.

"Maybe fear of exposure. As before, wherever Kahir went, children disappeared. Not all at once, and spread out over years—and with no apparent ties to him."

"You said 'apparent.'"

"He slipped up. I have evidence linking Kahir to three of the missing children."

"If you have proof, then bring it to the police."

"Not yet. There's more coming. I expect the last piece I need to nail things down sometime tonight."

Jack couldn't fault the man for his cautiousness. From what he'd surmised, Anthony Bane would get only one shot, and he didn't want to waste it. Jack shared the man's frustration. "How did your son fall in with Kahir?"

"I have to share some of the blame, I'm afraid. I missed the warning signs. Tony was an easy mark for Kahir's prattle. He has always been high-strung—looking for quick answers. But then, aren't all young people?"

"No," Jack said, blank-faced. "Sarah is a level-headed girl. She'd never run away and join a cult. It's not in her nature."

"Yes, of course. I'm sorry your family had to get entangled in our problem."

"Our problem?"

"Your daughter's friend Cynthia de Montia. Cindy…"

"What about her?"

"Sarah and Cindy were together."

"Not surprising. They usually are."

"They were together when Kahir took them. Cindy's mother, Leonora, is part of my group of *interested* parents."

Jack let the words pass.

"Don't you see? Kahir has taken our children in an attempt to stop us. And your daughter got mixed up in it all. Kahir thinks that if he has them, we are powerless. But he is wrong, so very wrong."

"The law can't help?"

"Let me tell you about the law. After I reported my boy as a runaway, a social worker came to my home to investigate me. Can you imagine that—investigate me!" Bane's face tightened. "This gray-haired woman acted as if I was some criminal—like I abused my kid, as if I'd hit him… or worse.

"She asked how many hours a week I worked, suggesting I wasn't giving Tony enough of my attention. Food, clothing, and shelter meant nothing. And to top it off, this public servant had the gall to ask me how often I brought women home. I could only guess what she was implying. After advising her to stuff the questions, I threw her out of my house. I should have turned the dogs on her."

Jack had to fight off a chuckle.

"It gets better," Bane said, the sarcasm coming through loud and clear. "In the short while he's been in town, Kahir has crafted a reputation for himself with the city as a philanthropist who so generously helps runaways get off the streets. He has manipulated them to turn a blind eye to the begging since the money is for *feeding the poor* in third world countries."

"Nothing was ever done?" Jack asked, astounded by the casual attitude of the authorities described by this man.

"At first, the police returned some children to their families. I was there with an associate, hoping to recover his daughter. It was an Oscar-winning performance. Kahir kept telling her, 'It was all for the best.' He stood there with concern dripping off his face, but under that glowing facade, he was laughing at us. The next day, my friend's little girl was back with Kahir. That same story played out multiple times with multiple children. The police grew tired of having to retrieve runaways.

"They said, 'With all the missing children cases on the books, we should feel grateful to such a generous individual as Kahir.' Grateful to Kahir…? Bullshit! They don't realize how evil he is. To them, he is saving the children from the streets and paperwork for themselves.

"A very surly detective made it clear that with all the gangs and murders, they can't waste the manpower on…how did he put it? 'On a man who is providing clean rooms, warm clothes, and nutritious food to children. Children who would most likely be stealing, selling and using drugs, or end up prostituting themselves.' He told me, 'All the juvenile centers are full, and here's a place where runaways can live in safety.' The fool."

"The other parents couldn't have possibly accepted that," Jack said.

"You're right, they didn't. In response to multiple complaints, the county sent another group of bleeding-heart social workers to the house, only to be fed the lies Kahir had brewed up. The children began making accusations of sexual abuse and that they were afraid to return home. Under that evil man's influence, the children believe they're telling the truth. Kahir's mind control has the parents as the enemy."

"But the social workers, the police—somebody had to see through the lies."

"Don't be so sure. Through my connections, I'm aware of two fathers arrested on those charges. One of them supposedly committed suicide in his cell."

"Sounds like you think otherwise."

"You bet I do. I know the dark power of Kahir."

"The police aren't stupid. They had to suspect something if all the kids were parroting the same allegations."

"It doesn't matter. The damage is done. I've spoken with other families who *were* willing to demand that Kahir be shut down. But following the arrests, they grew afraid. And I can't say I blame them. They fear Kahir will turn their children against them. Be warned, Jack, your daughter can be as easily turned as my son."

Not my Sarah, Jack thought, but rather than debate the issue with the man, he simply nodded.

"Will you join our group, Jack? I can arrange a meeting for tonight. You can meet the other members."

"Give me a time and place, and I'll be there." Jack rose from the chair and extended his hand.

"Seven o'clock," Anthony said. "On your way out, my secretary will give you directions." And as it began, Anthony Bane ended the conversation with a soft handshake.

FIVE

Anthony Bane's secretary handed Jack a folded slip of paper containing hand-printed directions to the evening's meeting. The text was written on Bane Financial Consulting letterhead. Jack had a hunch that Bane knew he would agree to meet with him and his confederates. Bane had clearly prepared the instructions in advance, figuring that, as a father, he'd do anything to get Sarah back from the stranger holding her—and the man was right.

The woman wearing large round glasses behind the reception desk watched Jack with bored eyes as he stuffed the paper in his pocket. Jack smiled at her, then left the office and headed to the elevator. He passed several people in the hall—most in a hurry and chatting as they scurried along. Some guy in a three-piece suit burst into a belly laugh that produced more than a few stares. Jack quickened his pace and caught the elevator before the doors closed. He rode down with a thin man holding a white cardboard box—the stranger's scowl made it obvious he had received some bad news.

Once outside, Jack inhaled deeply and let it all out in one long exhale. He needed to clear his head and started to walk. Just walk. It seemed the right thing to do. This whole situation had caught him off guard. Less than five hours ago, he woke up on an airplane, happily expecting nothing but to land and see his family after a long mission, never imagining that his daughter Sarah was now in a cult.

Venturing further into the Uptown area of Minneapolis, Jack heard a faint bang of a drum. Drowned out at times by passing cars, as he continued on, the banging became louder and clearer. The rhythm had a steady but slow, melodic, almost hypnotic beat.

Jack slowed his pace, then stopped altogether when an odd sensation struck him. Sarah's image popped into his mind's eye, but more than that, he felt his daughter's presence. Then Bane's voice replayed for Jack: "*Not more than four blocks away from this very building.*" He must be near where Bane's hired thugs grabbed the man's son—if he followed the bangs, he'd find Sarah.

But Jack's thoughts drifted to Anna. He had been gone longer than planned—the worry of leaving her for the extra hours weighed heavy on him. But here, he had an opportunity he couldn't pass by. Jack closed his eyes. *Why is this so difficult?* Even at the worst of times, while under a barrage of gunfire or chased through bombed-out buildings—in the searing desert or a war-torn town—he never lost the ability to make snap decisions—this should be no different.

"Anna, darling," Jack said aloud, "I hope you can forgive me."

By habit, Jack took a casual stride, resisting the urge to run, careful to avoid arousing curiosity or suspicion in others. Adolescent chants joined the low beats—the children had to be close. Still unable to see them, Jack only had to track the thumping. He made several wrong turns, but the drums always returned him to the correct path. Jack worried they'd be shooed off by the police or simply get tired and stop. He didn't have any idea what to do when he found them, but first things first.

Jack moved between buildings and across parking lots. His ears tracked the children until finally spotting them coming up on the far side of Hennepin Avenue, all dressed in white. He understood why Anthony Bane referred to the clothing as bed sheets.

Wanting to observe and not be seen, Jack mingled with a cluster of men and women bunched up at a bus stop. Even from that distance, he could make out faces—the oldest, not over sixteen. They chanted with the rhythm, holding out wooden bowls to passersby. Some people dropped in a few coins or a dollar bill. Most, however, ignored them.

Several of the bus-goers commented on how disgusting the way some children act. A woman wearing a tan beret and matching scarf remarked that the parents were at fault. "Such behavior comes only from neglect," she said.

A wave of guilt smashed Jack in the chest. Those words hit a little too close to home. *Is she right? Have I been neglecting my kids—always running off on missions?* It wasn't like him to second guess himself. He knew Anna was there for Sarah and Justin when he couldn't be. And during his time off, he always gave his family his total attention.

Jack let the harsh statement drop. He had to remain calm and concentrate on the situation at hand. A tall boy in the lead directed the others by pounding out a steady pace. At his side, a chubby lad held out a bowl to passersby. The girls banged their tambourines and danced close behind.

It took Jack a moment to recognize Sarah. As Anna told him, all the girls' hair had been cut to the napes of their necks, and all the boys were shaved bald. Jack's memories of his daughter with long, flowing blonde locks faded—the short strands made quite a change. He also recognized Sarah's friend Cindy, who stood away from Sarah and alongside a girl with jet-black hair cropped in the same style. Jack wondered which boy was Anthony Bane's son.

The children drew closer, and Jack studied their expressions one by one. They seemed to be staring off into space, dancing and chanting without feeling. When begging for money, their gaze rarely met the person giving the handout. They dragged themselves along the walkway, only slowing to collect donations. The drummer stopped and waited for an elderly gentleman to pull a couple of bills out of his wallet. Two of the smaller girls stood next to the boy, stiffly swaying to and fro to the beat. The old man said something to one girl, which produced a huge smile. That was the first real emotion Jack saw from any of the children.

Seeing Sarah just across the roadway, he wanted to go to her. But that might make matters worse after what happened to Tony Bane. They'd be on guard, skittish—they'd probably scatter like cockroaches at the flick of a light.

The old man gave the little girl a short wave and moved on. The group started off in the opposite direction. Jack gave them some leeway and then left the cover of the bus stop. He shadowed the kids to West Twenty-seventh Street, where at the corner, they took up a new position and resumed banging drums, shaking tambourines, and chanting. The girls danced, and the boys pushed money bowls toward passing pedestrians. Most people walked by with barely a glance.

Jack noticed how forced, almost mechanical, their movements appeared, resembling puppets on a tight string. But as more children joined in, the motions grew fluid and choreographed. As Sarah began to dance, Jack looked to detect any signs of what Anthony Bane called "mind control." Except for Anna, he knew his daughter's mannerisms, her behavior, the way she carried herself better than anyone. If some outside force controlled her actions, he was sure he'd know it.

She circled the other girls, her movements relaxed, graceful, and smooth. Sarah's natural ability for dance had been apparent at the age of seven while attending her first ballet class. Jack maintained a safe distance to avoid being perceived as a threat by his quarry, but the frolicking caught someone else's eye besides his own. A patrol car pulled up, letting out a single siren blast. The solicitation of dollars and coins persisted uninterrupted until the officer got out of his vehicle and spoke.

All dancing stopped. The band of children gathered together and started walking along the cracked sidewalks. The cruiser trailed for six blocks, out of the main section of Uptown, until turning the corner at Lyndale Ave. Jack tagged along, figuring now out of sight of the law, the begging would resume. To his surprise, the children proceeded in a straight line.

The winds picked up as evening rolled in. A shiver ran down Jack's neck and shoulders. He zipped his jacket to his chin, then checked his wristwatch. More time had passed than he realized. He promised himself he'd make his family whole—this madness must end.

Jack looked up. Sarah and her *friends* were getting farther away. Never had he suffered such difficulty staying focused on a mission, but then again, this wasn't a mission—it was personal. So much for detachment!

He hurried to close the distance, trailing the group as they turned onto Grand Avenue. A few minutes later, their destination became clear—an enormous Queen Anne-style house, tower-like turret included, surrounded by eight-foot-high walls of mortared gray stone, and accessed by a broad, black iron rung gate.

The lead boy walked up to a metal box attached to the thick bars and pressed a red intercom button. He spoke. A loud buzz sounded, and the boy pulled open the pedestrian section, letting his companions go through first. Once the last child entered, Jack rushed up to the gate, keeping his body tight against the rock and concrete, giving him a clear view of the grounds. The lawn, short and green, sprawled out until meeting a narrow flower garden of white, slightly wilting Mums running the full length of the southern side of the house, which sat a good hundred yards off the street. On the ground floor, lights shot out from the windows, but the second story appeared dark and lifeless—as did the corner tower. The stone barrier that ran around the entire estate had no visible breaks other than the front entrance, and with the lack of trees for cover, no one could approach the house unobserved by those within.

In complete silence, the children made their way up a concrete path towards the gabled porch. It reminded Jack of a funeral march. All that was missing were the hand-held white candles. The boy signaled for the others to halt, and they obeyed his unspoken order. When the door opened, a short, stocky man appeared. Similar to the boys, his scalp was clean-shaven. He stood at the entrance with a wide bowl, and each child passed him, unloading money from their smaller bowls or pockets. The coins clattered and rattled as they filled the wooden receptacle.

That's certainly not Kahir, Jack thought. He'd never forget the face from the clippings in Anthony Bane's office. The odd man had to be a servant. By what Bane said, Jack doubted Kahir would soil his hands with the collection of money—he'd leave that to underlings.

A sudden black fluttering caught the corner of Jack's eye. From the top of the wall, a large raven cawed. Jack froze. He hated birds like ravens and crows—dirty scavengers! Three days after his eleventh birthday, he accidentally came upon a raven's nest while exploring some cliffs and was immediately and viciously attacked by the big black bird. Angry shrieks were followed by the ebony feathers flapping atop his head and talons pulling at his hair. Jack tried to defend himself, holding on to the ledge with one arm and swinging the other. But the creature was too fast —it was something straight out of his worst nightmare. With labored breath and a pounding heart, he climbed off the rocks, almost falling twice. Young Jack ran, hoping to escape, but the raven kept dive-bombing him. Jack's body shook, remembering the sharp beak biting and pecking at the back of his neck. The memory caused his right hand to move up and rub the jagged scar. No matter how many years had passed since that horrid day, ravens still gave him the creeps. He didn't fear bullets whizzing past his ear or bombs blowing up close enough to throw him to the ground but show him one of those disgusting creatures, and his stomach would churn. Fear is a hard thing to explain sometimes.

Through glossy, solid black orbs, the raven stared down at him and squawked again, then stretched its wings and soared toward the house, landing on the overhang of the porch. The sight of that tremendous wing-span shot an icy current down Jack's spine. The children continued dropping their money, oblivious to the screeches of the ugly bird.

Sarah was the last in line. Jack wanted to call out. He opened his mouth to shout her name but held his tongue, thinking it best not to reveal his presence to her. Even if he had to remain silent, Jack wished Sarah would turn his way. It would have meant the world to him to see her face.

The raven let out one more caw. Sarah approached the short man and released her handful of coins over the bowl before disappearing into the dark house. The servant trailed behind the child and shut the door.

Jack stepped out into full view—his expression firm but calm. The children, the man, and the raven were gone. He stood alone.

Yet, Jack felt eyes upon him. He saw nothing—no movement in the windows or elsewhere on the grounds, but the sensation persisted—there was no shaking it. He'd been in the field too many times not to recognize the difference between these feelings and simple paranoia. It would be pointless to go back into hiding. Somehow, Jack sensed the name of his silent observer: Abhaya Kahir. And if Kahir was watching him, Jack wanted Kahir to know he was watching, too.

Several lights on the far end of the second floor snapped on. "Bingo," Jack said, reasoning those must be the kids' rooms. And that information could prove useful.

SIX

When Jack got home, he made two phone calls, then sat down with his wife and son for a much-needed meal of spaghetti and meatballs with a side of homemade garlic bread. On the go since stepping off the plane, his stomach had been complaining about its emptiness. One thing he loved about returning from a tough mission was Anna's cooking. He often joked that was the main reason he married her. But peering into her green eyes, the jest always crumbled.

Anna appeared to be doing better since he had dropped her and Justin off preceding his meeting with Gordon Brigham. Despite the obvious pain, she held herself together, talking and listening and even smiling once, all without letting a single tear slip. Jack kept his anger in check as he spoke—showing his true emotions wasn't going to help the situation. He needed to reassure Anna while also preventing her from wanting to do something rash.

Jack knew he could end this nightmare by calling in a few favors—a quick raid of Kahir's compound and Sarah's in her own bed tonight. But with what consequences? A daughter who tells filthy lies about her parents. A daughter who hates her mother and father. In Anna's present state, she wasn't equipped to handle that ordeal—it would destroy her.

And what about the other children? If he got Sarah out, he'd be leaving them with Kahir. No, Kahir had to be defeated totally and with finality. He must answer for all the suffering he had caused.

With his wife sitting across from him, Jack chose his words carefully. "I saw Sarah," he said. "She looks fine." He decided it was wiser not to bring up the girl's hair. Such a small thing, but Anna adored her daughter's flowing blonde curls, so why remind her they had been chopped off? "You could almost say content." *A good a word as any.* "Her color was good, and she appeared well fed. And she was the best dancer."

"Jack," Anna said, "I can't believe you said that."

"Well, it's true." He gently interlocked his fingers with hers. "We have to keep our spirits up. Like I said, she looks fine. Her friend Cindy seemed okay too." Jack gave Anna a slight grin. "But with her, it's tough to know for certain."

"Why doesn't Sarah come home?" Anna asked. "She hates being away from us. We barely talked her into camp last summer."

"Yeah," Justin said with a giggle. "She wrote every day how miserable she was. Camp was a blast for me. Remember the garter snake I snuck back in my duffle bag?" The boy giggled again.

Jack signaled to his son not to laugh, then said, "If you're done eating, buddy-boy, help your mom out and put your dishes in the dishwasher."

"Then can I go work on my models?"

Father nodded to son, which caused a large smile to form on the young face. Justin gathered his plate, glass, knife, fork, and spoon, and brought them to the kitchen before he dashed up to his room.

"What is it you have to tell me?" Anna said, releasing Jack's fingers and squaring up her shoulders.

Jack held up his hand to stop her from speaking. Then came the thud of Justin's bedroom door closing, after which Jack spoke. "Anthony Bane has some rather unorthodox views about the man holding Sarah." He took a breath. "As crazy as it may sound, he's convinced this Kahir is using some form of mind control on the children—all the children, not just Sarah."

"Did you hear him right?" Anna asked. "He didn't seem nuts when I met him."

"There's no mistaking what he said. He's also sure that Kahir has manipulated the police, social services, or anyone else able to remove the kids from his keeping."

"Don't remind me. That evil bastard steals our little girl, and the so-called authorities do nothing."

"Anthony says he has a plan," Jack told her. "I'm guessing he'll try to discredit Kahir—to give them proof he's not the humanitarian he portrays himself to be. Anthony showed me an extensive file, quite impressive actually, but my gut tells me he's somewhat hesitant to reveal everything. Let's pray that afterward, whatever power Kahir has over those kids is broken."

Anna looked down at the table. Jack saw a tiny tear reappear.

"Let's give him a chance, Anna. We mustn't lose hope."

She wiped the corner of her eye. "But how long until Sarah's home? A week? A month? A year? I want my baby home now."

"We'll get her back," Jack said. "Have faith." His wristwatch beeped twice. "I told Anthony I'd be at his place at seven, and there's a stop I have to make first."

"That only gives you an hour. It's not your job, is it? Can't it wait until tomorrow? Anthony Bane was such a support while you were gone. Please, don't be late."

"It's not my job. And I have plenty of time." He caressed her cheek. "Trust me." Deep down, Jack had a hunch that Bane had been more than just vague—Jack suspected him of deliberately concealing information. This first meeting might clear up a few questions prior to heading over to Bane's house.

"I wish I could see her," Anna said.

"You will soon. We'll break the grip that man has on our daughter." And if Bane's plan failed—there was always his way! Jack remembered the strange feeling when observing Kahir's estate—the feeling of something hiding in the darkness—a predator waiting for its prey. But Kahir would learn that prey can bite too.

The guard at the desk looked over Jack's signature, then directed him to the elevator. Jack rode up to the eighteenth floor. When the elevator arrived, it opened to a hallway of subdued lighting. The corridor had an eerie tint, and his shoes on the ceramic tiles clicked out each of his steps. He searched for office 1832 and was surprised to see the black and white plaque above the number: *Biopsy Lab*.

He knocked once. The door opened, filling the hall with a yellow glow.

"Dr. Edward Manahan?" Jack asked.

"You must be Jack Railey." The older gentleman, wearing glasses and a lab coat, held out his hand.

Jack returned the gesture. "I appreciate you seeing me on such short notice." *Just don't ask me how I got your number.* Jack didn't feel good about using work resources to track down this man, but the minutes were ticking away. Brigham did say, 'Do what you need to do,' so really, it's a gray area, and it was only a phone call.

"Don't mention it. If you're in the same pickle as Anthony Bane, I'm happy to help. I regret however, I can't give you much of my time."

"I'll take any you can spare. I hope now is convenient."

"Now is perfect. I'm preparing a tissue sample in the centrifuge. It has to spin for about fifteen minutes."

"Tissue sample? I was told you were a psychologist."

"I am, but I also hold PhDs in biochemistry and neurophysiology. My research involves the physical and chemical properties of the human brain and how it functions. Think of me as an all-around brain doctor." Using his thumb, Dr. Manahan pointed down the hallway. "Can I interest you in some coffee?"

Jack couldn't possibly express the pleasure those words gave him. The day was closing in on him. "Sounds great."

"Hope you don't mind it strong." Manahan led his guest to a small lounge. "Probably the one single perk of working late—got the coffee maker all to myself. I like my juice supercharged."

After filling two Styrofoam cups to the near edge, they sat at the closest table. Both men preferred their coffee black.

Jack took a quick slug as Dr. Manahan spoke. "Did your daughter know or have any contact with Tony Bane before she joined Kahir's little band?"

"Not that I'm aware of. We live on the opposite side of town from the Banes. Both kids go to different schools."

"Most often, teens are drawn in by their peers—friends, cousins—others their own age they trust."

"Sorry to disappoint, but my Sarah had no connection to Tony Bane."

"Maybe some other cult member then?"

"I saw their group earlier today. I'm familiar with my daughter's friends, and I didn't recognize any of the kids, except for Cindy, but she *joined* the same night as Sarah."

Manahan shrugged in a conceding manner. "It's unusual, but not unheard of."

"Please, Doctor," Jack said in frustration. "All I want is information. How do I get my daughter home? You call it deprogramming."

"That's not something I can teach you—well, perhaps if we had a year. I can explain the technique, but it wouldn't do you any good without the practical training. When a person is indoctrinated into a cult, the process is extensive and has many layers. For instance, I'm sure you noticed the similar haircuts and the matching robes."

Jack nodded.

"Their purpose is to strip away all individuality to make he *or she* a part of *the group*. Your daughter, if I may use her as an example, is no longer an individual. She is a piece in the cult and belongs to the cult, both physically, by the clothes she wears, and mentally by…well, to be honest, I'm rather stumped on that bit."

"Then you don't know how Kahir is controlling those kids?"

"I only wish I did, Mr. Railey." He sipped his coffee. "And I'm in company with the Russians, the Chinese, the Brits, a whole list of countries—both enemies and allies. There's not a scientist engaged in the study of the mind who wouldn't love to get their hands on the secret of total mind control. It's akin to turning base metals to gold."

"Alchemy," Jack said. "Are you talking about magic?"

Dr. Manahan snickered but saw Jack Railey was not amused. "Excuse my laughter. It was a terrible choice of phrase. There was no magic or mysticism in the 1974 case of Patty Hearst. The girl was coerced to join the Symbionese Liberation Army—the very terrorists who kidnapped and kept her against her will. She even helped her captors to rob banks, which cost her almost three years of her life in prison—and that was commuted down from seven by President Carter."

"My daughter won't be robbing banks anytime soon," Jack assured the doctor.

"All I'm saying, as with Patty Hearst, your daughter is a victim of brainwashing."

"But I've never heard of brainwashing at this level and done this quickly." He had been involved in a case that dealt with brainwashing during an assignment in Paris. "It can take weeks—months. My daughter hasn't been gone that long, and she was seen asking strangers for money days after she disappeared. That's too little time for brainwashing." Thinking of Sarah begging caused Jack's anger to swell. Jack forced himself to calm down—he had never had such trouble controlling his emotions.

"You obviously grasp the theory more than the usual layman. Then you must also comprehend that the most common method is to alter a subject's base memories."

"Whoa. Slow down a bit, Doc. I understand the basic concept but not the specifics—not how it's done. That's why I came to you."

"There are several methods," Dr. Manahan told Jack, "including the use of drugs or hypnosis. All can be employed to change a person's perception of the world, making the subject suggestible to any implanted information or false memory."

"You examined Tony Bane," Jack said. "Were there any drugs in his system?"

"None. In a way, I hoped we would've found some. It might have explained his behavior. The control over the boy was complete. I interviewed him, and he fooled me. It was so perfect—he set the hook and reeled me in like a trout. He ran right back to Kahir."

"Sounds more than your run-of-the-mill brainwashing."

"Whatever Kahir's technique, it's cutting edge. It's nothing I've ever seen or read about." Dr. Manahan leaned forward in his chair. "He must be laughing at us eggheads."

"You sound bitter."

"Nobody should have the power to control others. Not us, not them!"

Jack gripped his cup with both hands. Any more pressure and the Styrofoam would have collapsed inward. "I'm curious, Doctor. What can you tell me about Anthony Bane? Have you known him long?"

Manahan's brow furled slightly. "Does that matter?"

"Humor me. What kind of man is he?"

"Anthony has been my financial adviser for years. He's brilliant at what he does. Made me a pile of money—the man's a whiz with stocks and bonds. He appears to be a good father. He's certainly gone to extreme measures to retrieve his son."

"As well as that went," Jack said, and instantly regretted it. "Sorry, please go on."

"That's about it. Until of late, our interactions have focused primarily on business." Dr. Manahan gave Jack a questioning look. "Is anything wrong? Why are you asking about Anthony?"

"I just want to know who I'm dealing with."

Jack thanked Dr. Manahan for his time and left the lounge. He had gotten what he needed. When Jack reached the lobby, a different security guard was behind the desk, who nodded at him as he signed out. Jack walked to his Firebird, key ring spinning on his middle finger. The cool air on his face helped him to relax. The urge to smash his fist through a table was gone. He had an easy twenty minutes to get to the Bane place, so he'd keep his promise to Anna and not be late. His anger might have subsided, but his gut was still sending up flares. More than ever, Jack looked forward to his next talk with Anthony Bane. He had questions—he'd get answers.

Far off, in the dark house of Abhaya Kahir, Rajak, his servant, entered the meditation chamber carrying a tray of bread and broth.

"Master, please eat something," the short man said.

Kahir swatted the food out of his servant's hands. "Take it away." The metal tray hit the floor with a loud clang. The bowl dumped its contents, splashing over Rajak's robe, then landed top-down and empty. "I will summon you if I hunger for food."

Rajak retrieved the overturned dish and started for the round loaf of wheat bread.

"Leave it!" Kahir ordered.

Rajak, still holding the bowl, bowed and hurried to vacate the room.

Alone, Kahir sat, concentrating inward—his mind commanding his body to stop shaking from pains that most closely resembled withdrawal symptoms. But Kahir craved no drugs, no alcohol. He had depleted himself and his energies further than at any other point in the past.

His enemies forced him to act—to put events into play that left him dangerously weak. And though those seeds would soon bear fruit, he had to be very cautious. If they knew of his current state of vulnerability, they'd seize the advantage and revel in his defeat. He no longer possessed the strength to go against them directly, but that was never his intention—he'd vanquish them from within—he'd destroy the infidels, or they'd destroy him.

"They're coming through as we speak," Anthony Bane said into the mouthpiece. "I'll wire your final payment in the morning." He hung up the phone, then rose from his desk and approached the fax machine spitting out six pages per minute. "Knowledge is the real power," he said aloud to an empty office. He removed a sheet from the stack and scanned it. "Perfect."

He had gathered all the material required to indict Kahir without implicating himself or the others. "Try using your *magic* on this. Betray me, will you? We'll see which of us survives."

Twenty years ago, Abhaya Kahir arrived in the slums of London. He appeared from nowhere—a man with no past. On that day, he opened his home for runaways, similar to the shelter he set up across town. But back then, he only took in street rats—the children of the London ghetto. Children with no one to miss them and no one to care.

In Anthony's possession were documents confirming that the London police had suspicions regarding Kahir's role in the disappearances of those very children. He had lists of names, ages, descriptions, and, in some cases, photographs. And now, finally, he received the most damning piece of evidence—eyewitnesses. Affidavits from Kahir's previous cult members left back in England, willing to come forward and testify against their former leader. It required his personal funds to identify those ragtag people, many of whom were homeless, but after long last, he had the proof to expose Kahir.

Anthony threw the papers into his leather case and started toward the office door when a thud came from his window, followed by a second. He turned to find a pair of birds fighting on the ledge. One bird had a scrap of food in his beak. The other bird wanted it.

"Scram!" Both birds flew off. The short man grinned.

Locking the door behind him, Anthony walked down the long, deserted hall to the elevator. He pressed the down button. The illuminated digit above the elevator told him it rested on the first floor. He kept his eyes on the numbers. They didn't change. He pushed the button again, harder this time. Still, the light didn't budge. "Come on! Come on!" Anthony jabbed the button repeatedly with his finger until the hum of the powerful lift motors kicked in. Muffled by all the daily noises of people coming and going, office doors opening and closing, the metallic whine was usually undetectable, but standing alone in the barren corridor, it was quite clear.

Anthony saw the numbers move. "Halle-fuckin'-lujah." It switched to *two*, then *three*. Anthony glanced at his Rolex. *Six*, *seven*, *eight*. He never noticed how quiet this place could get. Like a tomb. *Ten*, *eleven*. The elevator dinged its arrival.

Anthony half-stepped forward, waiting for the steel doors to slide open. A few seconds later, he entered and hit the garage-level button. The elevator started with a slight lurch, and he rode it down, thinking it was moving slower than usual. He checked his Rolex for second time. Getting so close to contending with Kahir was making him impatient.

He was the one who persuaded the others to bring Kahir to this country, so it was up to him to deal with this viper. Under his approval, a vast amount of time and money had been exerted, and he himself pulled a lot of strings to provide Kahir with the necessary papers. In repayment, Kahir agreed to use his powers to their benefit—for their goals and purposes. Or that was how they intended it to be.

But Kahir had his own agenda. And when Anthony tried to control him—dictate his actions—he rebelled and broke away from the group. They attempted to contain him, but his power proved too great, resulting in the need to employ other means.

The elevator came to a halt, and the doors opened. The garage was void of people, but his Lincoln Continental wasn't the only vehicle in a stall.

Anthony got behind the wheel, put the key in the ignition, and fired up the engine. The guard waved goodbye as Anthony passed the booth out of the underground garage—a gesture Anthony did not return. He watched in his rearview mirror as the security gate lowered, but his mind locked on revenge and on Kahir's betrayal ending in dismal failure.

Part one of the plan was nearing completion. All that remained was to slip this information to a hungry reporter he met several months ago—someone unknown to Kahir—someone he couldn't get to. When the press released the story, the Minneapolis police would have no choice but to take a closer look at both Kahir and the local kids who went missing. They'd be forced to shut down Kahir's shelter during the investigation, separating him from the remaining children.

Anthony Bane's foot pressed hard on the gas pedal. His car picked up speed, as did his feelings of self-gloating. Kahir abducted his son, convinced he'd have the upper hand, but he was wrong. At the meeting tonight, Anthony would reassure the others that the first phase to defeat Kahir was on track—flawlessly on track. Then, he'd introduce them to part two of the plan: Jack Railey.

SEVEN

Traffic along I-94 wasn't too bad—Jack Railey made better time than he expected. Exiting on Snelling Avenue, he traveled less than a mile to his turn onto Summit. Once on Summit, the street numbers got higher, and the elaborate estates got larger and farther apart. Jack drove until he found the address written out in his directions. By the size and architecture of the Bane house, the investment business must pay very well.

A granite cobblestone driveway guided Jack through the main gate, left wide open in preparation for the night's meeting. Atop the pillars on either side of the entrance sat two ominous gray gargoyles, each detailed down to the stone horns, bulbous eyes, and curved beak mouths. The ten-foot-high security fence stretching out from the gateway was fashioned with matching granite pillars every three yards, with rustic iron bars filling in the gaps every six inches, each tipped with a spearhead. When closed, the entire property would seem secure as a fortress. He surmised that was the desired effect.

Jack rode by the swinging section and noticed the sign attached to the metal bars: "Dogs on Patrol." *Nice touch*, he thought. Despite the gate being ajar and knowing that the dogs had to be penned up somewhere, Jack still scanned the vast grounds.

He followed the circular driveway up to the house as one half of the double doors swung inward, and Anthony Bane stepped out onto the stoop. Jack got out of the Firebird, and sure enough, he was greeted by the relentless barking of dogs. For an instant, Jack felt lightheaded and needed several deep breaths of fresh air—how he hated having jet lag. But his recovery would have to wait for now.

Bane walked forward to meet him with his hand extended. "Welcome," he said. "You're the first to arrive." Another soft handshake.

On the surface, Bane seemed sincere enough, but in Jack's book, appearances were always deceiving. Dr. Manahan trusted him. Anna trusted him. He, however, did not. Something about this guy bothered him. Maybe he had been out in the field too many times and was seeing danger where there was none.

"The first?" Jack asked. "I worried I'd be late."

"No, right on time. Come in. Let me fix you a drink."

The dogs' barks grew louder and more intense. They must have caught a good whiff of him—an invader in their territory. Even for guard dogs, they sounded almost wild.

Jack stepped through the front door and was impressed by the grandeur of the foyer, with its intricate moldings, high vaulted ceiling, and a sweeping staircase that curved up to the second floor, where a broad balcony overlooked the space below.

Bane led Jack to a room just right of the main entrance. By the number of shelves laden with books, it had to be a study. The brick fireplace on the far wall must be a great comfort during the long, frigid winters.

"Your poison?" Bane asked. "Scotch, Brandy, Vodka? I have it all."

"I'll have whatever you're having."

"Please take a seat," Bane said over the clinking of glassware. Jack chose the overstuffed wingback chair closest to the patio door, which offered a view of a fine garden.

"It shouldn't be long until the others join us." Bane placed the drinks on coasters already set out on the oak coffee table between Jack's chair and his own. Bane sat, then drank from his glass and sighed. "Russian Vodka—that country's one true gift to mankind."

Jack brought the shot of alcohol to his lips and took a sip.

"You have questions," Bane said, rubbing the glass between his palms.

"That's an understatement."

"I assure you, after tonight, all your hesitations and concerns will be satisfied."

I really doubt that, Jack thought. He studied the man sitting opposite him. He watched his eyes, tracked his body language, and looked for any signs of deception or deceit.

Bane glanced at the large black and silver clock above the mantel. "My associates should be here soon."

"Who exactly are your associates?" Jack asked.

"Like myself—parents willing to pool their talents to bring down a madman."

Jack imagined Bane would be well suited for politics—he spoke without saying anything. "Talents?" Jack put his drink down. "What kind of talents?"

Bane didn't get a chance to answer. The patio door exploded, sending glass and wood shards shooting across the study. Jack dove out of the way of the flying projectiles, shielding himself with his well-padded chair. He reached inside his jacket, only to curse his decision never to carry a gun while not on a job. It's too hard to keep up a believable cover as the average family man when you're toting a weapon.

Anthony Bane let out a terrifying scream!

Jack jumped up to find a gate gargoyle standing in the middle of the shattered mess. The stone creature made no sound except for tapping its claws together in a grasping motion, producing the distinct clicking of rock hitting rock.

Bane picked up a bronze horse bookend and launched it with all his strength. The statuette smacked the monster hard on the beak. The gargoyle didn't flinch or falter. It lumbered forward, stiff and clumsy, leaving deep imprints in the carpeting. It pushed over the oak table, crushing the fine wood and drinking glasses with its next step.

"Get away!" Bane yelled, grabbing anything—books, golf trophies, a heavy crystal ashtray—and threw them to fend off the gray horror. "Get away from me!"

Jack ran past the fireplace, closing in on the gargoyle. It was then that he realized the creature wasn't aware of his presence. Jack snatched the iron fire poker from its stand and slammed it down on the gargoyle's shoulder. Composed of stone exposed to the stresses of raw Minnesota sub-zero winters and hot, humid summers, the creature was somewhat brittle—a chunk broke off and crumbled.

The gargoyle showed no signs of pain, though it did turn and, with a motion swifter than previously observed, walloped Jack on the upper arm with a rock fist, which sent Jack hurling backward. He tumbled to the floor but rolled with the impact, avoiding any real injury. The world spun as he staggered to his feet, bracing himself on a nearby bookshelf. Jack's sight focused enough to see Bane dash from the study, pursued by the monster. He shook his head, clearing out the remaining cobwebs, and trailed man and beast with the poker tight in his grasp and no idea of his next move.

Still a little dizzy, Jack leaned on the study's doorframe. He witnessed Bane soaring up the staircase with the gargoyle close behind him—its weight cracked each step. He was about to take the stairs himself when the front doors burst open. Jack raised his weapon, preparing to strike if the second gargoyle had joined his friend. But instead of a monster, two men entered.

"What the fuck is going on in here?" the largest one asked.

"We heard banging from outside," an older, bearded gent added.

"Stay there," was all that Jack said. Both men stood befuddled as the events played out.

Jack pulled himself up the long staircase at the same instant Anthony Bane charged out from an upper-level room holding a pistol—barrel at arm's length. He shot at the gargoyle. His hand shook, hitting nothing more than the creature's left horn, blowing it to pieces.

Bane's face grew stern. He carefully aimed, then fired again. And again. And again. The bullets struck the monster in the chest, creating tiny craters and spraying out circles of dust.

The gun clicked empty, and the gargoyle seized Bane around the ribs.

With a single hard squeeze and a loud snap from his spine, he went limp in the monster's arms. Only then did the gargoyle drop the lifeless body.

As the living stone spun toward him, Jack performed a perfect low flying tackle, knocking the gargoyle off balance. The thing tumbled backward against the railing, but the wooden banister couldn't hold the moving weight and gave way. The creature plummeted twenty feet down to the foyer and smashed into several pieces, both large and small.

Jack crawled to the edge of the balcony, ignoring the throbbing in his shoulder. He stared down at the broken gargoyle. The two strangers were examining the rubble, which moments ago moved under its own power.

The heavier-set man looked up at Jack. "Do you need help?" he asked.

The stairwell reverberated with the sounds of young voices chanting as they marched in single file up to a spacious, open attic. The lead boy, Tony Bane, carried a brass lantern that lit up the entire level. He stopped at a set of sliding doors and silently gestured to the others.

The rhythmic tones ceased, and the children removed their sandals. Tony stationed himself by the doorway as they dropped their footwear and entered the large room. The darkness within had been cut by a lantern, which was the mate to the one Tony held. He waited until the last child found a position on mats spread out in a half circle.

Before Tony could step inside, Rajak slipped out of the shadows. The servant whispered in the boy's ear that Kahir wished to speak with him after the sacrament. Tony simply nodded his acknowledgment.

In the sacramental chamber, Tony hung his lantern. The light doubled, and he saw his companions all in place, facing an oversized cushion a foot from the farthest wall. Next to the cushion was a brazier etched with the same patterns as on the lanterns and filled with burning coals. He made his way to the front, scooped out a handful of ground incense from a nearby canister, and tossed the powder on the embers. A greenish-blue flame erupted but quickly died down, releasing a puff of white, sweet-smelling smoke. Tony took his seat on the center mat.

Everyone sat in silence until an interior door unlocked, and a cloaked figure stepped into view. The children chanted his name: "Kahir, Kahir, Kahir." None could see the man's features—the hood of his red robe covered his face.

Kahir sat on the cushion as the worship continued. He raised a hand and lowered it. The chanting stopped.

Facing the brazier, Kahir spoke words of a long-forgotten language. The embers glowed bright red, then transmuted across the color spectrum: orange, yellow, green, blue, violet, and back to red. He passed his palm over the brazier and spoke but a single word.

All responded to the action with: "Kahir."

The brazier smoke snaked into the air with a life of its own. Kahir added to his incantation, and the heavy white vapor swirled and swayed. It rippled out in a wave, surrounding and covering all those who sat.

The hooded figure spoke once more.

On cue, the children shouted, "Kahir!"

More strange words.

"Kahir."

And again.

"Kahir."

The smoke rose up and off the children. A charge of electricity rode on top, crackling and popping in streamers of blue light. It drifted to Kahir, and inhaling deeply, he drew the smoke into his body, which then shimmered with a silver-blue aura.

Many minutes passed until Kahir stood. And with no other sign or signal, his worshipers did the same. At a slow, sluggish pace, they departed—except for Tony. From the hall, Rajak closed the door.

Tony stayed motionless. He waited. His legs ached. He waited. Finally, Kahir turned to him. That was his permission to approach his beloved leader. "You wanted to see me, sir?" he asked, keeping his eyes down. His words were whispers of respect and reverence.

"Please, look at me," Kahir said, his arms tucked into the wide sleeves of his robe and his hood still up.

Tony obeyed and lifted his gaze to a man he freely and willingly called father. This was a man who understood him, cared for him, kept him safe, unlike his real father, who was more interested in business and money than his own flesh and blood. Tony would do anything for Kahir —Kahir was his world.

"I have been watching you, my son."

"Me?" Tony said, thrilled by Kahir's personal attention.

"Don't sound so surprised. You are very important to me. Despite your capture by those who seek to destroy me, you returned. Others would not have accomplished that, but you are special. You are one of my chosen."

"Thank you, sir." Tony beamed with a new vitality of joy.

But that joy surrendered to shock when Kahir moaned and dropped to one knee.

"Master," Tony yelled, grabbing his robed arm.

"Fighting our enemies has taken much from me."

"My father," the boy said with anger and hatred.

"And his allies." Kahir placed his hand on the young disciple's shoulder to steady himself.

Tony choked down a gasp. The fingers touching him were thin and wrinkled. The bones seemed to be tearing through the withered skin. "You need rest," he said, aiding Kahir to stand.

"Rest would mean my destruction—our destruction. I require your assistance."

"I'll do whatever you ask. Let me help you."

"I knew you to be worthy." Kahir held Tony's head in both hands. His dried palms felt rough on Tony's cheeks and suddenly became hot. Blue sparks ran across Kahir's fingertips and penetrated the boy's temples.

Tony's whole body shook. "It hurts," he said, his voice just above a whimper.

"Your pain will be brief, my son."

Blue bolts shot out of Tony's eye sockets—the soft tissue within boiled away in seconds. The massive discharge intensified, pouring out from his nostrils and mouth. Kahir absorbed the energy the same way it left Tony. The two were linked in the flow of life force.

Kahir bathed in the raw, untainted essence, relieving the many days of struggle and agony. The meager amounts he reaped during each harvest ritual kept the hunger at bay, but this feast filled him with what he had truly craved. He released his hold on Tony Bane.

The desiccated corpse fell. One brittle arm snapped off on impact. Thin plumes of dark smoke smoldered from the empty eye sockets and open mouth of the now skeletal face.

Kahir flexed his fingers. His strong hands had returned. His body surged with the boundless energy of youth, rejuvenating every fiber of his being.

Jack staggered down the long staircase. His feet felt so very heavy, and his head spun. The steps curved to the foyer, and a cool breeze blew against his sweat-heavy brow as he hit the landing. From that short distance, he glanced into the study. The smashed patio door and the broken furniture reminded him of a war zone.

He cautiously went over to the pile of rubble embedded in the floorboards. The debris covered a wide area, and Jack bent down to examine the fragments. His hand eased forward to touch the jagged stone when a claw shot up, grabbing him by the wrist. The weight of the talon pinned his arm down as the other broken bits, both large and small, quivered. Like a bewitched jigsaw puzzle, the pieces snapped together, merging and rejoining.

The claws and arms reunited, followed by the shoulders, then the chest and head. The legs and hips fused with the torso. Jack pulled in vain to free himself, seeing the gargoyle rising to its feet. His wrist twisted slightly in the fierce, stony grip, which only tore his flesh. He yanked and tugged, straining every muscle. Jack fought the pain until the rock fingers broke—but at a cost—blood trickled down his arm.

Jack dropped low and slid across the floor, hoping to escape. But no matter how fast he moved, the creature kept right on his heels. He didn't know how, but he got the front door open without the gargoyle snatching him.

Jack ran down a narrow path cut down the center of a dense forest with loud stone footfalls booming behind him. He hadn't gone far when he first heard the laughter. Jack stopped, trying to locate its source. He spun in circles. The taunting surrounded him.

A thunderous crash drowned out the wicked cackling. Jack turned as a gray barkless tree splintered and tore free from its roots. The gargoyle threw the trunk as easy as throwing a rolled-up newspaper. The woodland closed in on Jack, and the pathway disappeared.

"You cannot stop me," a gravelly voice said.

Kahir's face floated above Jack, laughing, and the gargoyle grabbed for his throat.

Jack shifted to his side, gasping for air. Something had a hold of him. He groped in the dark, expecting to find a stone claw, not a soft, smooth human hand.

"It's all right, honey. It's me. It's me."

Jack recognized the voice. It was Anna. He was home—home in his bed.

"Great first night home." She gently touched his shoulder.

He flinched at the sharp pain.

"Oh, I'm sorry," Anna said. "Still sore?"

The intense throbbing kicked in. "Just a twinge."

"You need more aspirin?"

"Maybe." He sat upright with his feet on the floor. "Yes."

"You stay there," Anna said. "I'll get it." She put on her slippers and walked to the bathroom. The light illuminated only a corner of the bedroom. Anna reappeared with two white tablets and a glass of water, which she handed her husband. "Must've been some dream. Wanna talk about it?"

Images flashed through his mind, but nothing coherent. A second later, everything was gone. "You know I don't dream." He popped the pills in his mouth, and with a gulp, they were down his throat. "Sorry I woke you," he said, putting the untouched water on the nightstand.

"I wasn't sleeping, really." Anna slipped back into their bed. "I haven't slept well since—since that night Sarah didn't come home."

Jack returned his head to his pillow and, with some soreness, wrapped his arms around his wife. He pulled her close. "I'm sorry I wasn't here for you."

"Between the two of us," Anna said, "how many more times are we going to apologize?"

"I'm serious. I should have been here."

"How on Earth could you've known something like this would happen? Sarah's a good girl. No one saw this coming. Don't blame yourself."

Jack said nothing. What could he say?

EIGHT

The next day, a small group assembled in the office of the late Anthony Bane. The meeting time had been set for eleven o'clock, though the clock on the wall showed it was eleven-thirty-three. Jack thought it somewhat morbid to gather in this place, considering what had occurred at the Bane house. It was Benjamin Abrams, an older man with a heavy gray beard, who believed it to be ultimately safer than anywhere else. Thaddeus Blackburn agreed with his colleague. Still incomplete, they waited on one last member, Leonora de Montia.

Besides the customary cordial greetings, Jack had hardly spoken since his arrival—he had only met these two men yesterday. But then, the same was also true of Anthony Bane.

Jack's eyes examined every inch of the room. It revealed little of Anthony, except for a single picture on the desktop of a thin boy with a beaming smile holding a sizable bowling trophy. Otherwise, there were no other pictures, statues, or knickknacks around to give Jack any more clues to the man who rented—had rented—the space.

And these other men, he knew nothing about them. When they suggested the meeting, it was out of sheer curiosity that he agreed. Jack had no idea what he was getting himself into, but it didn't escape his notice that both took what they had seen the previous night with an easy acceptance.

“I hope Leonora gets here soon,” Thaddeus Blackburn said. “I’ve a busy day ahead of me.” The heavyset man strained to cross his legs. Resting his shoulders squarely against the chair’s backrest, he brought his hands to chest level and interlocked his round fingers. “She’s probably not coming at all.”

“Patience has never been counted among your virtues,” Abrams said to Blackburn from behind the desk. Unlike Jack’s first visit, all the computer monitors were black and lifeless. “Do yourself a favor. Learn to relax.”

“What the hell was that shit show last night?” Jack blurted out, stopping what had all the makings of an argument.

“Explain,” Abrams said.

The word astounded Jack. “Explain?! You’ve got to be kidding! Let’s start with how a chunk of stone can move on its own and kill a man.”

“By the pricking of my thumbs, something—”

“Enough, Thaddeus”, Abrams said, cutting the man off. “I’m sure Mr. Railey isn’t interested in some obscure quote.”

“Macbeth,” Jack said, “Act 4, Scene 1.”

Blackburn blinked, caught off guard. His lips parted like he might say something, then pressed into a thin line. Abrams allowed himself a brief smirk, eyes briefly flicking to Thaddeus before settling back on Jack.

Jack didn’t wait. “If we’re done with the bullshit. I ask again—how did a stone kill Anthony Bane? Things like that don’t happen. Things like that aren’t real.”

“Enlighten us,” Blackburn said. “What’s *your* theory?”

“Hypnosis, maybe. A drug-induced group hallucination. There are plenty of ways to mess with your mind. Even nerve gas—you name it.”

“What kind of business did you say you were in?” Abrams asked, raising a brow.

“I’m a freelance journalist.” That was his cover story, anyway. It got him in and out of a lot of countries. No matter how sinister a dictator, they never passed on press coverage. Jack’s cover included several recent bylines to maintain the façade. But if the truth be known, he couldn't string enough sentences together for a readable article to save his life.

Apparently satisfied with that answer, Benjamin Abrams said, "May I remind you, sir, that the attack began *before* we joined you. How could we have been affected by drugs or a gas?"

"And how could we all have the same hallucination?" Blackburn added.

Jack shook his head. "It had to be a trick of some kind." He studied the faces of both men. Just like Anthony Bane, they were holding something back—and it was starting to piss him off. "I've seen some weird stuff, but that was a new one. Rock can't spring to life and go on a murderous rampage. Nobody has that power. Not even this Kahir guy. It had to be an illusion. It couldn't've really happened."

"How's your shoulder?" Abrams asked.

Not thinking, Jack rotated the top of his arm in tiny circles and said, "A little sore." He caught himself. "Point taken. But how?"

Blackburn snickered. "There are more things in Heaven and Earth, Horatio," the man recited, "than are dreamt of in your philosophy."

"Stop quoting Shakespeare," Jack snapped.

"Excuse my friend, Mr. Railey. He loves to show off. The critical issue is not what tragedy transpired, but what we do about it."

"Now that Anthony's gone," Blackburn said, "is there still anything we can do?"

"He showed me a file he was building on Kahir," Jack said. "It's a good guess he was planning to use the information to discredit him."

"Discredit?" Blackburn asked.

Abrams immediately spoke up. "Anthony and I had discussed this many times. Kahir's greatest strength is his secrecy. Expose him, and he is vastly weakened. He'll go to great lengths to hide his true nature. Kahir draws his power from the ignorance of the innocent."

"It may have been Bane's idea," Jack said, "but why can't we continue without him?" That suggestion brought different reactions from the two men. Jack detected fright in Thaddeus Blackburn's eyes but detached calmness in Benjamin's.

"The same plan?" Blackburn asked, glancing across the room at his friend.

"Why not?" Abrams said. "You act as if it's doomed to failure."

"Isn't it?!" Blackburn stood up. "It didn't do Anthony a damned bit of good. He's dead! I refuse to be next."

"Sit down, Thaddeus," Abrams said. "No one is asking you to lay down your life." Despite his stern tone, Abrams was composed—obviously a man who didn't let his emotions rule him. Blackburn, on the other hand, seemed almost driven by emotions—at least by his fear.

"We should leave Kahir be," Blackburn told them both while pulling a white handkerchief from his pocket to mop his forehead.

"Wait just a damn minute," Jack said. "I didn't come here to listen to you bicker. And I didn't come here to give up. I realize I'm the new kid in the band—and before last night, I wouldn't know you guys if I saw you on the street—but I have no intention of letting some mad man keep my daughter. Sarah belongs home with her mother and brother. And that's exactly what I intend to do—get her home—by any means necessary."

At a loss for anything else to say, Blackburn retreated to his chair.

"Of that, Mr. Railey, we have no doubt," Abrams said. "It is that attitude that makes you a worthy addition to our ragtag troop."

"Pardon me for asking," Jack said to the older man, carefully choosing his phrasing to avoid any offense, "but you don't seem the sort of person to have a teenage child."

"Grandchild," Abrams replied. "Grandson, to be precise. Shawn came to live with me after his parents died in a tragic car accident when he was five years old."

"And you?" Jack asked, shifting his attention to Thaddeus Blackburn.

"Krissy, *my* daughter."

For the first time, Jack felt a kinship with this man. To have a child taken is tough enough, but a daughter is especially hard.

"With Anthony's help," Thaddeus said, "I retrieved her, but Kahir's control of her was too strong. She snuck back to his lair in less than twenty-four hours."

"Bane told me something about that when I first met him," Jack said. "But it doesn't weaken my resolve when it comes to my family."

"We'll free *all* our children," Abrams said. "And reunite the others with their families as well. We are the only ones who are willing—or stupid enough—to try to stop him. I'm sure Kahir also realizes that fact. Eliminate us, and that's that. There will be nobody else to trouble him."

Jack watched Abrams with a steely-eyed intensity. "Would Kahir attempt to kill you to keep his hold on those kids?"

Abrams returned the look. "There's no question."

"And you, too, are in that same danger," Blackburn told Jack. "Being here makes that so."

"Let him come," Jack said. "If it's a fight to save Sarah, then so be it."

"Brave words," Blackburn said.

"They're not just words. Trust me when I say I'll do whatever it takes to succeed." *Ask the Iranians*, he thought.

Blackburn was about to speak, but Abrams spoke over him. "It seems, Mr. Railey, you'll make a strong ally."

"Then it's all a matter of choosing which of us will face the lions," Jack said. "Who has Bane's papers?"

"Anthony's notes and photographs are safe and stored away," Abrams said.

The sudden sound of the office door opening turned all heads. Leonora de Montia stood in the doorway with a stern expression on her gently wrinkled face, which was surrounded by long curls of salon-dyed brown hair.

"You started without me?" Leonora asked, then walked in without another word. Her attire seemed better suited for someone going out to dinner than to a meeting to discuss their lost children and the bizarre death of a friend. She wore a full-length coat and green gown-like dress, accented by a string of perfect pearls. Jack peeked at her hand and the large diamond ring Anna had spoken of once or twice. He had to admit it was an impressive rock—he couldn't say the same for its bearer.

"Far from it, Leonora," Blackburn said. "Just passing the time until you got here."

"Good morning," Benjamin Abrams said, standing up. "Please, Leonora, take my seat. I'll stand." Jack followed the elder's lead. Blackburn did too, after a few uneasy moments.

The woman sat. "Any news from the front?"

"Not since we last talked," Blackburn said.

Leonora set her purse alongside the desk. "We need to do more about Kahir. Even from that first day, I told you he—"

Blackburn cleared his throat. "Leonora, you know our guest, Mr. Railey."

The startled woman turned towards Jack. "Oh, yes. Sarah's father. Benjamin said you'd be here." She lifted her bag from the floor and opened it to retrieve a small bottle of aspirin. While tapping out three of the white caplets, she complained about having a headache and asked Blackburn to fetch her some water. After downing the pills, she continued speaking with Jack. "It's too bad your sweet daughter was dragged into this mess. Your lovely wife must be at her wits' end."

"She's been better."

"That comes as no surprise. I remember the night she called my house looking for Sarah. You should have heard the worry in her voice. If only I could've warned her."

"You knew this would happen?" Jack asked, moving his body to the edge of his seat, almost on the verge of springing up.

"Of course not," Abrams said. "We were all caught off guard and foresaw none of this."

"If that's true, you severely underestimated Kahir," Jack said. His shoulder began to throb. He considered asking Leonora for a couple of her aspirin, but changed his mind. "I can't explain the killer gargoyle, but it's clear he's a dangerous man."

Blackburn scoffed. "He thinks his little trick will scare us."

Jack shot the big man a look, then glanced over to Leonora—surely she was the reason for Blackburn's newfound bravado. "Some trick. You didn't have to fight that...that thing. And let's not overlook the lie we told the police."

"Lie?" Leonora asked.

"We suggested Anthony had blundered in on a burglary," Abrams explained, "and in the ensuing struggle, he was thrown from the second floor and killed."

"But it's my neck if they suspect differently," Jack said. "I was having drinks with the guy. My prints are on the goddamn glass, the chair, the fire poker—"

"We certainly couldn't tell them the truth," Blackburn said. "And since the three of us corroborated the story, the police were satisfied."

"Until they begin investigating," Jack snapped.

"We mustn't fight among ourselves," Abrams said, seeing tempers flaring again. "We're all under a great deal of stress, but we have to remember why we're here. Remember who our common enemy is."

Blackburn, leaning back in his chair, his posture eased somewhat. "I agree," he said. "The question, then, is very simple. What do we do now?"

"We better act soon," Leonora said. "Kahir must not win." She said the words so dispassionately that Jack thought she approached this situation akin to a game. He had heard that the woman was cold when it came to her daughter. The way she showed no emotion, it appeared true.

"Prior to your arrival, Leonora," Abrams said, "we decided to proceed with Anthony's plan. Right now, it's all we've got. The one decision left, as Mr. Railey so colorfully put it, is who will play the part of Daniel and step into the lions' den."

Blackburn stared down at the floor, which did not go unnoticed by his older friend.

"There is but a single choice," Benjamin Abrams continued. "I volunteer."

"You're putting yourself in harm's way," Jack said. "If I may be blunt…maybe a younger man."

Abrams smiled. "Youth wouldn't guarantee success in this case, Mr. Railey. Experience can play—"

"I didn't mean it as a criticism," Jack said, interrupting the gentleman. "Rather a concern for your safety."

"I possess the means to protect myself. I'll be quite safe."

"Shouldn't we wait for the rest before you make such a commitment?"

Benjamin, Leonora, and Thaddeus all looked at each other in bewilderment.

"The rest of the parents."

"There is no 'the rest,'" Blackburn said. "Minus Anthony, it's just us four."

"I saw the children," Jack said. "I trailed them to a house on Grand Avenue." That revelation sent waves of shock across Blackburn's and Leonora's faces, but Abrams' expression remained stoic. "There were well over a dozen of them. It's hard to believe other parents didn't join your cause. Bane told me he had been in contact with several families."

"He must've also told you that many are afraid of Kahir," Abrams said, "and their own children's accusations."

"But you three are moving against him—regardless of the consequences. Others could feel the same way."

"And they may have," Leonora said, her eyes narrowing and her voice harsh. "If we bothered to contact any of them to tell them what we're trying to do. You two are so pigheaded!"

"We've discussed that option," Abrams said, directing his comments to Leonora. "It would be too dangerous involving others."

"And we can't have others involved in our business," Blackburn said. Those words produced a stern gaze from Abrams.

"Then why include me?" Jack asked. "I'm an 'other.' Of you all, I'm only familiar with Leonora, and only because of her daughter, Cindy."

"You've answered your own question," Blackburn said.

"I insisted we get help," Leonora told Jack. "You were all they would agree to."

"Please don't misunderstand," Abrams said. "Our intentions are to rescue all the children from Kahir. If we defeat him, they will be saved."

"That's a pretty big if," Jack said. "He has all the earmarks of a petty dictator doing anything and everything to maintain power."

"Your apprehension is reasonable—"

"Kahir's cult is a snake," Blackburn interrupted. "Cut off the head, and the body dies."

"Some snake," Jack said, noticing Leonora's strained expression—she wanted to speak but was holding her tongue. "One thing keeps bugging me," he added. "How did Bane collect so much information on Kahir?"

"Anthony had detectives investigating him," Abrams answered.

"Know thy enemy," Blackburn said. "That was Anthony's favorite saying. I'll miss him."

Abrams nodded. "I will too." The elderly man adjourned the meeting.

Jack Railey came out of the building, his brain racing as he took each step to the street. Once more, he couldn't shake the feeling that these people were keeping secrets. The whole encounter stirred up memories of his last assignment in Lebanon and his dealings with Behzad. Every time Behzad spoke, Jack listened to the words, but his gut told him not to trust them. And right now, his gut was kicking him—kicking him with a steel-toed boot.

He started down the walk when he heard, "Jack! Jack Railey." He turned to find Leonora waving him back. Jack stopped but figured he had heard wrong.

She gave him a second wave.

This time, he was sure. He reversed direction. Leonora made a weak attempt at a grin as he approached.

"Is it possible for us to have a drink together? We should talk…" Her eyes shifted slightly to the main entrance, double-checking that Abrams or Blackburn hadn't come out behind her. "…without the others present."

Well, this is new, Jack thought, seeing an opportunity to get some real information. Not wanting to appear anxious, he glanced at his wristwatch. "I can spare a few minutes. There's a place around the corner."

The start of the lunch hour found the Wayward Hive Restaurant nearing capacity. Jack and Leonora waited for a table in silence until a pretty blonde wearing a short red dress seated them. Leonora commented on how sickening it was for someone to be so bubbly that early in the day.

Jack thanked the young woman as they settled into the booth.

Leonora ordered a Long Island Iced Tea before the girl had a chance to escape. Jack asked for coffee—black. As Leonora slipped off her coat, Jack imagined she must have been a real looker several years and many gallons of alcohol ago. It explained how she had landed all her rich husbands. Only her third had died during the marriage. Husband one and two, she divorced with large settlements, keeping her first husband's name.

"It would be a terrible mistake for you to involve yourself in the battle with Kahir," Leonora said.

"You think so?" Jack said, somewhat amused by the woman's sharp frankness.

The waitress returned with Leonora's drink and Jack's coffee. She smiled at him and practically ignored her.

Jack sipped from his cup, then stared Leonora dead square in the eyes. "I'm already involved." The tone of his voice made her shudder in her seat.

She recovered quickly. "You're in over your head. You just don't know it."

"Trust me, I've been there."

"I doubt you've ever been in this much danger."

"Oh, I wouldn't quite say that." The eight-inch scar on the right side of Jack's abdomen reminded him of past dangers after every shower.

"Use your common sense." She drank from her glass. "Kahir killed Anthony Bane."

"That's what Abrams and Blackburn tell me. But to be honest, I'm not convinced."

"It was Kahir," Leonora said, straining to keep her voice down. "He murdered Anthony."

"Okay, fine. Kahir killed Anthony Bane."

"And we are all in jeopardy. We could be attacked at any time. You. Me. Benjamin. Thaddeus. All of us."

"You're not telling me anything new," Jack said. "We hashed all this out up in Bane's office."

Leonora glanced down at the table. In that brief moment, she almost looked ashamed. "But none of this is your fault. You shouldn't be involved."

"I repeat, I'm already involved!"

A hint of concern colored her tone. "Please, you've got me wrong. It may not seem so, but I have your best interests at heart. As well as Anna's…and your son. Justin, isn't that his name?"

"Yes. Justin." The woman hit a nerve. *Anna*, he thought. *Justin. How can I put them in danger?* This wasn't a job in the Middle East. His actions could directly affect his family in a very real and fatal way.

"Gather your wife and son, and get out of town. Just go. Tell them you've decided it's best if you all went on vacation. There must be relatives you can stay with. Or travel somewhere you've always dreamed of visiting."

The suggestion shocked Jack. *Leave now when Sarah needs me? Run, hoping to avoid the so-called wrath of her captor? Not fuckin' likely!*

"If money is the problem." She reached into her purse and pulled out an envelope. "This might help." She slid it across the booth toward him.

Jack's shock morphed into anger, and he pushed the envelope away. "Let's stop playing games. What am I missing?"

"I don't understand."

"Bullshit! You're trying to bribe me. Why?"

"Bribe? Don't be silly." She lightly touched the packet of money. "I feel somewhat responsible for your daughter's predicament. If it wasn't for my Cynthia, Sarah would be home."

"Keep your money," Jack said flatly.

"No one would blame you. I've given some consideration to leaving town myself."

"And your daughter? You can't abandon her."

"There's no guarantee I'll ever see Cynthia again. If we defeat Kahir, and that's slim, nothing says she'll come home—that Cynthia will be the same girl that left. Even with his death, Kahir's hold may prove too strong."

"What was all that crap about not letting Kahir win?"

"I didn't want Benjamin to know my true feelings." Leonora's hand shook as she removed the envelope from the tabletop. She tried to hide it by leaving both the money and her hand out of sight.

Jack had hit his fill of coffee, but he had to do something besides sit there. He took another short sip and watched as Leonora gulped the Long Island Iced Tea. She had consumed over half. He hadn't realized she was downing such big swallows.

Leonora set her drink down. "Sarah is a sweet child." Her whole body trembled as if hit by a sudden chill. "She takes after you."

"Thank you," Jack said, astounded by the abrupt transition. He wondered if it was the alcohol talking. "I always thought she was more like her mother than me."

"For now, perhaps. But as she grows older, the similarities will grow. She'll take after you."

Jack held back a smirk. Fortune telling was clearly not the woman's strong suit. Sarah following in his footsteps as a spy? Running around the desert, getting shot at? No chance! He wanted much more for his daughter.

"You need to be careful," Leonora added. "If you free Sarah from Kahir, it's still not over until he's defeated. And as I said, I'm not sure even then."

"You're forgetting the plan to expose him. Abrams will continue where Bane left off, and when the police learn what Kahir is—"

"I can't make it any plainer," Leonora interrupted. "If you stick with them, you'll get yourself killed. And you won't be able to help anyone, especially your daughter. While Kahir is out there, we all have to find a way to protect ourselves. Yours is the simplest. Collect what's left of your family and leave town—go somewhere safe."

"Not an option," he said.

"You're a foolish man, Jack Railey."

NINE

Leonora de Montia decided to stay in the booth and order another drink. But for Jack Railey, the time had definitely come for him to go. He left the woman to the comfort that came from a bottle. The blonde waitress smiled warmly at Jack on the way out, adding, "Have a great day."

Outside, the weather had turned from sunny with a few clouds to a gray, overcast sky. "How quickly things change," Jack said aloud—the last twenty-four hours coursed through his brain. So much had happened—arriving at the airport to discover his wife in tears and his daughter in a cult, begging for money—the meeting with Anthony Bane and the man's death by stone statue—all culminating with him joining Bane's questionable friends to thwart a madman. But the one thought he couldn't shake—this was just the beginning.

Then, like a faint echo, Jack heard a boom. It reminded him of a far-off thunderclap one hears on a dark, starless night, and when you wait for the lightning, it never comes. He assumed at first it was the rumble of distant construction work or maybe a truck backfiring, but the boom was followed by a second boom and a third boom.

A hard knot formed in Jack's stomach, recognizing the drum beat. Up the block and across four lanes of traffic, he caught sight of the robed children, dancing and chanting and singing. Most people walked by without a notice—to them, they didn't exist. But every so often, someone did drop a few coins in the money bowl.

The distance made it a challenge to distinguish faces, and they were all dressed alike, but with the boys bald and the girls with cropped hair, Jack only needed to focus on half the teens to pinpoint Sarah. He eased closer, stepping into the parking lane to obtain an unobstructed view. The children weren't as energetic today—their action seemed strained, except for a short boy who dashed about. Jack stayed hidden between a dirty black Ford Bronco and a shiny red Dodge Viper, which gave him a clear line of sight. The boy grabbed a nearby girl and swung her at arm's length with such a polished move, an onlooker might think the youth had taken many hours of ballroom dance. Jack wondered if the boy understood the suffering and anguish his parents must be feeling.

Jack didn't know the girl, but from his vantage point, she looked quite pretty, which explained why the boy had picked her out to be his impromptu partner. Jack's gaze moved to the next girl, then the next. He feared Sarah might be with a different group. Nothing prevented Kahir from scattering his crew to cover separate parts of town. To canvas more sections meant collecting more cash.

Sarah stepped out from behind two of the boys. Jack's pulse quickened, and he was flooded by an odd surge of emotion—a mixture of happiness and anger, relief and frustration. Before Jack realized it, he was on the other side of the street, skulking in the darkened doorway of Malone's Liquor—his actions driven by pure instinct.

The band of children approached his position. The girl who had been dancing moments earlier had moved up front, holding out the bowl to indifferent passersby. Her ex-partner secured a new victim in Cindy de Montia, but the combination wasn't as graceful.

When the single file line marched past Jack, they paid him no mind—not a glance, not a word. He studied their faces. Their expressions were empty—no emotions, no pain, no pleasure. *The lights are on, but there's no one home.*

As a yellow taxicab drove by, Jack recalled Anthony Bane's story about how he hired three men to kidnap his son—how they wrestled the boy into the backseat of a sedan. He could grab Sarah, but his car sat four blocks away, and he didn't see any other taxis in the vicinity.

He imagined the visuals of him running down the sidewalk, carrying a kicking and screaming child over his shoulder. And it wouldn't be long until some hero-type swooped in for the rescue. Unaware of the circumstances, they'd assume they'd be stopping a pervert from kidnapping a little girl.

Jack had no time to adjust his plan when a adolescent wail filled his ears. Cindy stood screeching, her arm extended with a finger pointing at him.

The children split into two packs. The closest shoved Jack backward—the other surrounded Sarah and pulled her away. Kahir obviously trained his disciples on how to defend themselves if confronted again. They moved swiftly and with purpose. It had all been performed to perfect execution.

"Sarah," Jack called out, struggling against the many hands shoving him. "Sarah, please. Come with me!"

The only response to his calls were the mocking words from kids stalling his advance. They shouted and spit. They cursed, and they hit. Jack was overpowered. He could fight forward and trample over them, but they weren't to blame. He refused to injure innocents for Kahir's doings. Jack stood and watched Sarah disappear around the corner. As she went out of sight, her eyes met his.

Leonora coddled her drink, not emptying the glass until the waitress brought over its replacement. An adjacent booth must have ordered lasagna or spaghetti—the odor of garlic and tomato suddenly hung heavy in the air and smacked her hard. The thought of food made Leonora sick. On the waitress's return to query her about a third drink, Leonora asked for the check. A swipe of her platinum American Express credit card and she was gone.

On the pavement outside the restaurant, Leonora held the top of her coat closed with one hand and flagged down a yellow taxicab with the other. The driver, a man in his late twenties with a thin beard, gave her the once-over through blue plastic-rim glasses before admitting he was available. Leonora got in, told the man her address, then stared out the side window.

During the ride, she spotted Jack Railey standing in the recessed doorway of a liquor store. He appeared very determined and a little angry. Then she saw the children coming toward him—including her Cynthia. Leonora tried to grip the window crank, but her unsteady hand missed—twice. When she finally grabbed hold of the plastic knob, the taxi was well out of range to call out to her daughter.

"Anything wrong?" the taxi driver asked.

"No," Leonora answered. "Nothing at all," she added, trying to convince herself.

Cynthia was lost to her. Deep down, she couldn't blame the girl. Heaven knows she hadn't been much of a mother. In fits of rage, she would yell out how Cynthia had been a "damn accident." Even without Kahir, Leonora knew Cynthia wanted to leave home. She had stumbled upon letters written between Cynthia and her father—several asking, begging really, if she could live with him. Leonora sent her own letter to her ex-husband, setting him straight regarding their daughter and her future—it was blunt and to the point.

The smooth ride and the hum of the tires on the blacktop had a hypnotic effect on Leonora, and she passed out. The next thing she knew, the taxi driver had stretched over his seat and was shaking her by the shoulder. She looked up at the large house—she was home. Whatever "home" meant.

The man offered to help her up to the front entrance, but she declined and handed him three twenties. His mouth dropped open, and he repeated his offer. Leonora exited the vehicle and waved the driver on his way.

She staggered up the walk while rummaging in her purse for the key. All the windows were dark and lifeless. Entering an empty house had never bothered her, but now that emptiness seemed so permanent.

With Cynthia gone, there was something more concrete about this darkness—her quest for riches and power had destroyed her life. She had foolishly let Thaddeus Blackburn sway her. And together, they both persuaded Benjamin Abrams. But getting entangled with Kahir was a mistake—a tragic mistake. They all learned that lesson much, much too late, and when they acted to rein him in, it made matters worse. Anthony Bane was dead, and she sensed Kahir's long, evil fingers reaching out for the rest of them.

Leonora's house key struggled to find the lock, though eventually, with a turn and a loud click, the heavy door swung open. A cold chill blew past her as she entered. She groped down the drywall to the light switch and flipped it on. Leonora dropped her purse where she stood, not noticing the door slowly closing. She zombied her way across the foyer—the silence swallowing her up. It reflected her life—it was a void—a giant hole. She wouldn't have believed it possible, but she missed Cynthia. After years of berating the girl and regretting her decision not to have an abortion, she only now realized the truth—the truth that she had been lying to herself—that she loved her daughter and would do whatever it took to get her back.

The telephone rang.

Leonora jumped at the sharp tone, then ran to answer the call—it might be Cynthia. "My baby wants to come home," she shouted out. Leonora grabbed the handset. "Cynthia?!" she said into the mouthpiece. "It's Mommy!"

The base of the phone rang again. Leonora tapped down on the cradle buttons, fearing they were stuck in place.

"Hello," she yelled. "Hello!" The base rang once more, but twice as loud. Leonora knocked the telephone off the table onto the hardwood floorboards, where it rang still louder.

Along the living room wall, the antique grandfather clock she had inherited from her grand-aunt Dorothy boomed out the hour in thunderous gongs.

The TV snapped on at full volume, then the stereo.

From the kitchen came the growl of the garbage disposal and the whine of the blender.

The ringing, the gongs, the voices, music, grinding, whirling, all mixed and merged into a chorus of electronic chaos.

Leonora moved from device to device, yanking their plugs from their sockets, which only caused the racket to grow more and more intense. It all became an agonizing wail, piercing her head like a red-hot metal spike tearing apart flesh and bone. She screamed and covered her ears. Her eardrums throbbed, and the copper taste of blood seeped into her mouth as her nose began to bleed.

The pain made walking difficult, but she dragged herself up the stairs, hoping to escape the hellish roar. On the upper level, she fell against the wall and forced herself onward until she got to the master bedroom, slamming the door behind her. The heavy wood filtered the noise somewhat, and Leonora pushed her body tight to the panels in a vain attempt to hold the clamor at bay.

From the table alongside the king-size bed, the alarm clock went off. The buzzing bore into her temples. Leonora crumbled to her hands and knees. She cried while crawling into the connecting bathroom. Even unplugged, the hair dryer on the countertop started up with painful results.

The nightmarish shrill of the entire house poured into that small, isolated room. “S-st-ooop,” Leonora yelled. A warm, sticky wetness dripped between her fingers as she cupped her ears. “Please-e-e stop!” Tears of blood streamed down her cheeks. The trickle from her nostrils turned to a gush. The woman gave a final howl and fell with a sharp thud when her skull struck the marble floor. A pool of crimson seeped out onto the white tiles.

The blaring sounds ceased, plunging the house back into silence.

Jack Railey read the file of his upcoming mission, and he welcomed the distraction. He hated feeling so helpless, and being outmaneuvered by a bunch of brainwashed children didn’t foster confidence. At least going over the preliminaries of the assignment restored some semblance of usefulness.

The folder was stamped SECRET and EYES ONLY and contained a detailed dossier of the missing team who he’d be sent into Iraq for search and rescue—two women and four men. Two members, Markus Radford and Tom Blair, Jack knew all too well. He had worked with both before and would trust either man with his life—and he had. The rest were names and faces unknown to him. The agency wasn't in the habit of revealing its operatives, even to its own people. Unless you've served with them, you could sit next to a fellow agent in a movie theater and never realize it.

According to their profiles, the four strangers had two things in common. First, they were all well-trained and qualified, and second, they were all young. None over twenty-three, but that played into their cover. *They're practically teenagers*, Jack thought.

Sarah's face briefly popped into Jack's mind. He had been so close, but he made the cardinal mistake of focusing on his target to such an extent he forgot about his surroundings. In other situations, that would have gotten him killed. And on one occasion, it almost did.

How ironic—he had just gone over the splash page of the man who had saved his life that day in 1980. Five months had passed since Iranian militants stormed the U.S. Embassy in Tehran, taking some 90 hostages, 66 of which were Americans. Only his fourth year as a field agent, Jack partnered with Markus Radford—they were to learn the exact location of those hostages in prelude to the failed rescue attempt of April 24th that same year. Some higher-ups in the chain of command objected that a relative rookie be put on such an important job. Markus had used his pull to quench their doubts.

During the mission, he and Markus were to meet with an Iranian student who said he had information on each hostage, right down to the floor and room number where they were held. As they approached the prearranged meeting place, Jack missed seeing the rifle barrel poking out from the open balcony window. Luckily for Jack, Markus didn't and shoved him clear. Though not so lucky for Markus, who took a bullet in the back and suffered a collapsed lung and a fractured rib. Following hours of surgery and months of rest, Markus recovered with a fifth scar added to his collection—battle kisses—he called them.

"Something unclear?" a voice said from the office door, forcing Jack's return to the present.

"No," Jack replied, turning to face Gordon Brigham. "The file is as complete as always. I was just thinking about…ancient history."

Brigham walked to the opposite end of the large desk, passing an oil painting of an old man fishing with the initials G.B. in the corner. He sat. "Ancient history?"

"It seems ancient—to me, anyway. This report about Markus and his team stirred up some old memories." Jack closed the mission packet. "He's a good man. And a good friend."

"You know him, you know how he thinks." Brigham leaned back in his chair. "You're the best agent to locate Markus, and extract him and his crew." Brigham saw the hesitation in Jack's expression. "Something you want to say?" he asked.

"To speak frankly, this couldn't have happened at a worse time."

"Is there a better time for our agents to be lost in hostile territory?"

"I don't mean that. My daughter…"

"Last we spoke, you were rather vague on the details. Is she sick?"

"*That* I could deal with." He tossed the folder on the desktop and slid it across. "She's gotten mixed up with some people—a cult. And getting her out is proving more difficult than I first expected."

"If that's all there is to it…" Brigham reached for the phone. "I can have a retrieval team ready in five minutes."

"I've already considered that," Jack said. "I made a stupid attempt on my way in." He shrugged. "I didn't think it out—plan it through. And I shouldn't have tried. The whole thing was pointless. Even if I got her to the house, at first chance, she'd run off."

"Once she's in your custody, you can take steps to ensure she stays put."

"I'm not going to lock up my daughter—keep her a prisoner in her own home. Besides, there are other children in the picture. I can't stage a retrieval for all of them—there has to be another way. The problem needs to be dealt with at the source. I'm working with some other parents. We're all in the same boat."

Jack immediately detected that disapproving stare. Brigham had a knack for making his stance known without saying a word.

"Don't worry." Jack smiled. "I won't reveal any national secrets."

"I'm not worried—about that. My concern is if your plan fails and someone gets hurt. That would put you under the spotlight and possibly affect our operation. A lot goes into maintaining your cover."

"It's not my plan," Jack said. "It's all them. I'll see how well they do before I come up with a strategy myself."

Brigham pushed the file toward Jack. "I'm sorry about your daughter, but we have to discuss your trip to Saudi Arabia. You're scheduled to leave the day after tomorrow."

Jack's eyes widened. "I'll need a week…minimum."

"Markus Radford and his entire team need you now. If it wasn't for the touchy arrangements we have to make, you'd be on the plane tonight."

"But—"

"No buts, Commander. It's your job. Must I remind you of the seriousness of this situation? Those people will die without help. Not might die—will die."

"You're not leaving me any choice," Jack said, staring down at the mission folder.

TEN

Anna sat in the kitchen of her empty house. With Justin in school and Jack away doing who knows what, she had only her half-filled coffee mug for company. If she listened carefully, she could almost detect the echoes of past happiness—of birthdays and picnics, of Christmas mornings and Easter egg hunts. All that had changed. All that had ended. She feared her family would never be the same.

"Where are you, Jack?" Anna said aloud, fighting a tear. She needed her husband, but like so many times, he wasn't there for her. *That isn't fair.* A shiver of shame hit her hard. Before they married, Jack told her exactly what he was and what he did. She entered this marriage with her eyes wide open.

Her mind slipped back to the day she first saw Jack Railey. It was in Bethesda, Maryland, during her stint as a nurse at the National Naval Medical Center. An emergency case was coming in, and the doctors were all scrambling to prepare for the patient's arrival.

An ambulance roared up to the sliding glass doors, and within seconds, medics, screaming to clear the way, pushed a heavily laden gurney into the emergency room. It wasn't Anna's normal station, but fate stepped in—the surgeon on duty commandeered her to assist. Upon graduating from nursing school, she spent her early years in an ER, so it was all old hat. The doctors stabilized the critically wounded man and rushed him into an operating room.

She remembered that even with all the blood, the man's face looked so calm, so peaceful. The clear plastic oxygen mask strapped over his nose and mouth hadn't taken away his quiet strength.

After thirteen and a half hours on the table utilizing two surgical teams, they moved Jack to intensive care. The doctors feared he wouldn't outlive the night and were amazed when he did. A verifiable miracle, they all thought, surviving such massive wounds. Still not out of the woods, they measured Jack's life by the hour. For Anna, he became her charge. She monitored his progress and made her reports directly to the chief surgeon. But those hours turned to days, then weeks, and though remaining unconscious, he had beaten the odds.

Anna worked extra shifts to ensure Jack's care. Even off-duty, she'd check on his status. Sometimes, she'd come in just to sit with him. And she was there as Jack regained consciousness. Hers was the first face he saw. Jack mumbled about being dead—that he must be in heaven. Anna blushed at the word "angel."

Jack spent another six weeks recovering, not needing the minute-by-minute attention. He was transferred out of the ICU, but Anna made it a point to visit him as often as possible. On the day of his release, her heart broke.

For the next five months, she tried to put the man out of her head until a mysterious bouquet of roses showed up at the nurses' station. For some unknown reason, she knew who sent them. That night, Jack called. But Anna was beyond annoyed. It had been so long without a note, a letter, a phone call—nothing. He did his best to convince her to meet him. She reluctantly accepted his offer of dinner.

The instant she spotted him in the restaurant, a flood of feelings churned up, almost overwhelming her. Anna beamed as she took her seat. The meal was wonderful! They talked and laughed as if no time had elapsed since they last saw each other. During dessert, Jack confessed he'd been having some trouble focusing on his job. He kept thinking about her. She admitted to the same problem.

Their relationship bloomed, and she had never experienced such joy *until* Anna received a message that Jack had left town on an emergency. She wasn't happy learning via a third party and by a very sexy-sounding female voice. But Jack did return, and she couldn't stay mad. She asked for an explanation, and he said something about work. Later, Anna realized how smoothly he had changed the subject, not answering her question.

Then it happened again. Jack departed for parts unknown. Barely for three weeks, but he came home with a broken arm. Anna was so concerned about him that she forgot to ask where he had gone.

Over half a year flew by, and the moments they spent together were perfect. Anna had to use all her willpower to concentrate on her work. Her thoughts often drifted to Jack. She wondered what he did during the daytime, but at night, her questions vanished in his arms.

Their bliss shattered, however, one early evening over drinks when Jack revealed he had to go away. He couldn't say for how long and was vague about the place and what he'd be doing.

For days, guilt ate at Anna for how she yelled at him before he left. Deep down, she hoped showing her pain would convince him to stay. Weeks slipped by, then months, and she suffered through a cycle of emotions—anger, next remorse, on to loneliness, past worry, back to anger.

When Jack did phone, she hung up. But undeterred, he sent her flowers and cards. He convinced other nurses to deliver little gifts to her during her breaks. This continued until she agreed to see him.

Outside the coffee shop, Jack Railey said, "Hello," then reached into his pocket and pulled out a ring box. "Will you marry me?"

Anna didn't have to think twice about her reply, and she was about to speak, but he stopped her. First, he had to tell her the truth—tell her what she'd be in for. And he told her all of it—about the assignments, the reasons for his abrupt departures, the unexplained injuries. He joked he could only divulge what her security clearance allowed—she was still a naval officer.

They had a quiet, intimate wedding. A year later, Sarah was born—seven weeks after Jack's return from a mission in Iran. Anna resigned her commission, and to her surprise, Jack took a position behind a desk. She didn't miss the rank that came with the post—she was a nurse, not a soldier. For Jack, the sacrifice seemed greater, but Anna knew he'd try to make the best of his new duties of gathering and evaluating information and handing the assignments off to other men. It did mean a promotion and a heavy pay increase. He assured her he had made the right decision.

Over the next year, Anna noticed a change in her husband. The hours he kept, the way he spoke about interesting bits of intel. He never said it outright, but it was clear he wanted to get out into the field. Six more months passed until at last Jack came to her—he didn't have to go into any great detail. She kissed him and told him to be safe. The following morning, Jack was on a plane to Europe.

A buzzing caught Anna off guard. She jumped in her chair and whacked the kitchen table leg with her shin. "Damn it!" She rubbed the sore spot and limped to the dryer to unload the clothes, not wanting them to wrinkle. It had been her third load—finding every piece of laundry that needed washing—down to the last dirty sock.

Earlier, she had cleaned the entire house from stem to stern, washed all the dishes, emptied the garbage cans from each room, and scrubbed both kitchen and bathroom floors—she welcomed the distraction.

As Anna hung Jack's shirts in the closet, a piercing ring filled the master bedroom. She gasped. Anna clenched her teeth and took a deep breath through her nose, then headed over to the bedside table, where she answered the telephone.

"Hello."

"Anna?" Jack said.

"I'm here." A definite pleasure accompanied his voice, but that was about to change.

"Anna, listen closely. Pack enough clothes for a week. Pack for Justin too."

"Jack, what's happened? Does this have anything to do with Sarah?"

"I think it's best if you and Justin weren't so easy to locate."

"Where are we going?"

"I'd rather not say over the phone. Be ready to leave once I get there. I'll pick Justin up at school."

"Don't hang up!" Anna said. "Someone named Benjamin Abrams called. He was adamant about talking with you."

"Did he give you a number?"

"No, an address."

"Give it to me."

Anna relayed the house number and street, then asked, "Do we really have to abandon our home? What is it you're not telling me?"

His pause spoke volumes. "Please," Jack finally said. "Please be ready."

Replacing the receiver on its base, she stood alone in their bedroom. The house felt so small—it was closing in around her. The walls of her life were collapsing.

Anna suddenly found herself standing in the doorway to Sarah's room. It stunned her, having no recollection of walking there or opening the door. The dark space within had a faint but stale odor. Anna moved to the window and propped it open, letting in the light. The curtains danced while the breeze pushed in fresh air.

When Anna turned, a pair of eyes caught her gaze—eyes of paint and plastic. A worn toy clown sat up high in silence as if keeping a secret. Its acrylic smile mocked her with the memories of innocence, happiness, and joy. She remembered the glee on Sarah's face as, at ten, she tore open the birthday present that held the clown, a jester with a three-pointed cap with bells on each tip. The jester watched over Sarah from the special spot on the center shelf where she kept it. Anna wondered if Sarah would ever be home to see the toy again.

Anna cried.

Jack reread the scrap of paper, confirming the address he had written down. He scratched his head, wondering if he had heard Anna wrong. The building in front of him had seven columns and detailed exterior stonework. Above the columns was the inscription, *Templi Argenteum Noctem*. His Latin was rusty, but he read it as *Temple of the*

Silver Night. It was not a residence, and he doubted the strange structure was used for business.

He walked up the seven steps to the pointed, arched wooden double door, unsure if he should knock or go in. He pulled on the oversized brass handle, reasoning that if he was supposed to knock, the entrance would be locked.

It opened, and he entered.

"Benjamin Abrams is expecting me," Jack told the two young but rather large men standing inside. They both remained silent and glared at him as though they were searching for something specific. It dawned on Jack that perhaps these men didn't speak English. He considered trying some other language—maybe he'd get lucky. He was about to explain in French when—

"Benjamin Abrams?" the burly man sporting a crewcut asked, not easing his suspicious stare.

"Yes," Jack said, "Benjamin Abrams. He called my home and left a message for me to come to this address. I'm Jack Railey."

On hearing the name, the man disappeared around a corner. The other gestured for Jack to hold where he was. *Not a problem*, Jack thought. While young, both men looked like they could tear his arms off at the shoulders if given the slightest provocation.

Crewcut reappeared and, saying nothing, waved Jack forward. This whole thing was too weird for his taste. Turning around and leaving had crossed his mind more than once.

Instead, Jack followed. Down a long stairway, down a hall, then a second stairway. Passing through a door that he figured must lead to the basement, it surprised Jack to find two additional men, each sitting on either side of yet another door. This lower, outer chamber was chilly, but the men ignored any discomfort. And as before, no one spoke.

The guard to the right, seeing Jack, knocked twice, producing a metallic twang. A moment later came the scrape of a bolt drawing back. As the inner hatch slid open three feet, the guard signaled Jack to enter. His curiosity now aroused, he obeyed.

Inside, Benjamin Abrams waited by the opening, sealing it upon Jack's entry. The room was sparse except for a cozy-looking sitting chair. Next to it was a side table topped with several books. Both pieces of furniture faced a roaring fire, which heated the space quite well. The walls had no pictures, no shelves, no hangings of any kind. In place of those usual trappings were symbols painted in red, white, and black. Jack couldn't even give a guess to their meaning. In the farthest corner, he spotted a second, much longer table laden with more books—stacks and stacks of books. By their bindings and yellowed pages, it was obvious some were very old.

"I'd offer you a chair," Benjamin said, "but as you can see, the accommodations are designed for single occupancy."

"I remember you saying you had a way to protect yourself, but isn't this taking it to an extreme?"

"Would Anthony Bane say that?"

Jack nodded his head to the side, conceding the point.

"What can I do for you?" Benjamin asked.

"I've come as you asked. You left me a message."

"No. I didn't. But I do believe you were sent word."

"Who then?"

"Kahir," Benjamin said matter-of-factly.

"He must know you're here."

"That knowledge will do him no good." Benjamin stepped over to a wall and pounded. There was no echo, just a dull thud. "Six-foot-thick stone," he said, "and mother earth beyond that. This chamber is secure from all external influences."

Jack looked toward the flames. "The flue—it leads outside. It's a simple thing to drop down a grenade or something as nasty."

"Possibly. But up every five feet, there is steel grating with spacing bars of an inch or so, and at the top, the chimney tapers to about a foot. Much too narrow for someone to enter with the intent of cutting the rungs. And if the idea of, let's say, some unwelcomed creature triggers your imagination, a fire is going at all times if the room is occupied. The constant chill makes that necessary."

"Gas," Jack said.

"Excuse me?"

"Poisonous gas. Odorless. Nonflammable. Heavy enough to fill this space within minutes. Grating or not, you can't seal it off completely."

"An astute observation," Benjamin said. "That's why we have extensive surveillance. If anyone approaches this complex, my people will know it. And I assure you, our enemy is far too clever to use such crude methods."

"Never underestimate your opponent."

Abrams gave Jack an amused smile. "That doesn't sound like the utterance of a humble journalist."

"When you're in the field, you learn stuff."

"Of course. And I won't press the issue any further. We all have our little secrets."

Benjamin assured Jack of the temple's protections, so having no reason to stay, he departed. Jack wondered why Kahir bothered to send him on such a wild goose chase—the ruse served no purpose. But the question would have to wait—it was time he picked up Justin. After that, he'd drive home and get Anna. It may not be as fortified as Abrams' bunker, but he had a place where he could keep his family safe.

ELEVEN

School had just let out, and Justin Railey headed to his bus for the ride home. He didn't look forward to the math homework Mrs. Johansson assigned to the fifth grade class. He hated story problems. If a train goes this fast, and another train goes that fast, which train gets somewhere first? They were really dumb. Who would bother riding on a train when they could fly in an airplane? Why weren't there ever any math problems about planes or flying?

"Hey, there's the beggar girl's brother," a boy shouted out. Justin saw it was Tommy Hurly—he sat three desks over from him in the classroom. The four boys with Tommy laughed at the slur.

"Throw him a nickel," the kid standing behind Tommy said.

Justin tried to ignore them until a coin hit him on the base of the neck.

"Good shot," someone said.

"Give that to your sister," Tommy yelled. "Don't they beat her if she doesn't collect enough money? Or do they lock her up in the basement with rats?"

Justin faced the boy. "You don't know what you're talking about."

"My brother's in the same homeroom as your sister. He said she's down on Hennepin Avenue begging for dimes and quarters. And that she lives in a cult now. And they have orgies every night."

Justin lost all control! He jumped Tommy and punched him hard, square in the nose. Fast trails of blood ran down the boy's shirt. Justin fought on, pulling Tommy down to the ground.

The others, seeing their friend fall under Justin, struggled to pull the enraged boy off. Justin struck at the first touch, hitting the closest kid in the stomach, who instantly released his handful of jacket. But the other three boys grabbed him, all punching at once. Justin took some hits, but he dished out plenty. His wild swings connected more often than did the blows of the other boys.

Two of the five boys ran off. One held both hands to his right eye as he disappeared out of view.

Justin fought the others like a trapped animal. He stomped hard on one boy's foot, sending him rolling in the dirt. He caught a second with a punch under the sternum, causing that boy to fall to all fours, gasping for air.

The last, Tommy Hurly, who had started the taunting, stood with both fists at the ready, but his eyes moved to his fallen companions.

"You got something to say?" Justin said, also on his feet, confronting his foe. His breathing was labored, and his arm hurt. He had never been much of a fighter and always avoided trouble, but this time, Justin didn't have a choice. He had to stop them from saying those things about Sarah —he had to. "Come on, you had a big mouth a minute ago. Come on— say it again."

Tommy shook his head.

"My sister's not a beggar." He snatched Tommy by the shirt. Justin cocked a fist, but instead of striking, he pushed Tommy down on his butt. "She's not." Justin walked away.

As he left the playground, Justin began to cry. He hadn't gone a block from the school when a short honk sounded behind him. Justin wiped his eyes on his sleeve and turned to see his father's Firebird. He slowed his pace and waited for the car to reach him. Justin opened the door and got in. He stared straight ahead.

"You okay?" Jack asked, having a pretty good idea of what had happened—not by the dirt on his son's pants or by his torn shirt, but by the hard expression on his face.

Justin nodded.

"This has been tough on both you and your mother, but I have to ask you to be brave."

Justin nodded.

"We're not staying at the house tonight," Jack said. "Maybe not for a couple of days. It's important that I know you're safe."

"I understand, Dad." The boy went quiet for a moment, then said, "You'll get Sarah back home—you will."

"That's my boy. Now let's go pick up your mom."

Benjamin Abrams sat studying a language long dead, written on the pages of a massive volume. It was a commonly held belief that not more than a dozen people left in the world had the knowledge to translate the text. For Benjamin, the ancient words came to life with chronicles of the horrifying creatures that ruled the Earth in the time before man. Hidden within these stories were formulas and spells to break down the barriers where these entities still slept.

He would never attempt such rituals himself. They required the capacity to yield and focus more power than he had ever managed. Thaddeus and Anthony longed to funnel a small portion of the great force for their own needs. Tap into the energy pool, as it were, to steal tiny amounts to direct and manipulate without awaking any nasty thing that could destroy them. Somehow, Thaddeus convinced Leonora to go along with the scheme.

By use of the proper methods, Benjamin acknowledged their objectives were possible. He always postulated that the global belief of praying to a deity was a collective unconscious wish to reconnect with the elder gods—a longing to draw from the elemental forces. Unfortunately, the correct rituals had been lost for untold ages. Rituals where the force flowed both ways—by devotion and worship of an entity, the worshippers gained power, while the entity itself grew stronger.

But Anthony and Thaddeus wanted to make sure the flow went in one direction—their direction. And that was where Kahir came in. During one of his many trips to Europe, Anthony learned of a man said to have attained such an ability, yet to what extent was, at best, unclear. Anthony persuaded Kahir to return with him to the United States, but first Kahir had his own demands, which Anthony relayed to the others.

Benjamin remembered their reaction when he objected. "Kahir is too much of an unknown," Benjamin told the group. "He's most likely just another fake, a charlatan, or worse, he's the real thing, but impossible to control."

Anthony chuckled and said that he could "handle" Kahir. Anthony had been wrong.

Now his friend was dead, and that left three in danger, himself included, four if Jack Railey remained involved. Kahir had to be stopped—though any direct action by him or the others might endanger the children. Anthony put together a plan to discredit Kahir in the eyes of the law, and Benjamin aimed to see it through to the end. If they convinced the authorities that the children were at risk under Kahir's care, the police would force him to relinquish custody. It was a simple plan—some may even say naïve, but that was only the first half. Relieved of his disciples, Kahir would be greatly weakened, giving them the perfect opportunity to strike. Benjamin knew Kahir must be expending vast amounts of energy and, with no way to recharge, the war would be won.

Benjamin closed the book and contemplated his next move. Jack Railey had politely told him he was too old to take on Kahir, and the young man was right. Leonora believed Jack was the perfect choice to battle Kahir in his stead, but meeting him in person, Benjamin had his doubts—the man was brutish. He did possess physical strength, and he had courage, but could Jack Railey be trained? Until then, all Benjamin had to do was keep a step ahead of Abhaya Kahir—if it wasn't already too late. Patience and caution had to be the watchwords. To rush headlong into darkness was to rush headlong into failure.

An odd sound shattered his thoughts. From the far corner, he heard what could best be described as a scratching. Benjamin looked at the table and its high stacks of books but found nothing. He rose from his chair and examined the piles. Still nothing.

Over his shoulder came a loud knock. Benjamin jumped at the sudden thud. A second series of knocks had him walking to the door. They were in the prearranged pattern, so he slid the heavy bolt and opened the hatch, creating a narrow gap.

"Yes?" he said with a feeling of dread.

"Your tea, sir." The servant detected Benjamin's uneasy stare and said, "If you prefer it later, I can return to the kitchen."

Benjamin's manner eased. "Now is fine," he said, pulling open the door. "Please, please bring it in."

The servant complied and placed the silver trayed bone china tea set on the table adjacent to the chair. He gave a slight bow and exited the chamber.

"You may retrieve the tray in an hour," Benjamin added.

He closed the door and replaced the bolt. The elderly man made a beeline for his seat, letting out a chuckle at his overreaction to a pot of Earl Grey. Benjamin moved his book and sat. After which, he glanced down at the table, thinking he was more on edge than he realized. He poured himself a cup of tea and took a heavy swallow—the brew was quite refreshing. He'd have to thank his servant properly next time.

Relaxing with his warm drink, Benjamin watched the roaring fire. It seemed to dance for him. Orange flame tongues licked at the half-charred logs, waving back and forth, back and forth, producing weird and wonderful shapes that shifted and changed each second into something new and different. Benjamin even saw a face in the flames. Its blazing eyes stared out at him. A nose formed, then a mouth, which gave him a friendly grin. The face pressed against the fireplace doors. Flame hands materialized alongside and pushed at the glass. Web-like cracks appeared.

Before he realized what was happening, Benjamin was showered with hot flying shards. He threw his hands up to shield himself, but that offered little protection. The glass burned his skin on contact.

A piece of glass embedded itself in Benjamin's palm, producing a hiss as it scorched his open wound. Blood dripped onto the floor as it seeped from around the sharp, jagged edge. He barely had time to pull out the glass—his gaze once more drawn to the fireplace.

Benjamin watched as the face rose on a column of fire—legs formed, and arms sprung out. A flame mouth gave him a wicked leer. The fire demon took a step, burning a path toward him.

The old man stood stunned as the creature drew closer. Then the heat snapped him out of his shock. Benjamin threw his book at the living fire, causing the yellowed pages to burst into flames, leaving nothing behind but a plume of ash—the ancient book now gone for all times. In desperation, he grabbed the teapot and hurled its contents. The brew hissed and boiled away as it withered the creature's arm and part of its shoulder, but the limb immediately regenerated.

Benjamin pushed his chair into the demon's path. The fabric, stuffing, and wood instantly caught fire, filling the air with acrid smoke. Benjamin coughed and shouted for help, but no one could hear him through the thick walls and iron door. He stumbled over and tried for the slide bolt.

The creature released a fireball, which exploded on impact. The resulting force knocked Benjamin down. He shook off the blow and saw the metal bolt melted and fused. His only means of escape had been destroyed.

"Stop," he commanded. From the floor, Benjamin held up his uninjured hand, palm forward. A stream of light shot out and into the demon. The flames that made up what appeared to be its chest faded—the patch turned from bright orange to a darker, dull red.

"In the name of Raagiosl!" Benjamin shouted. "In the name of Iczhiha! I bind you!" The white pulse thinned and became almost solid as it coiled around the fire demon, forming a tight cocoon. Connected to the creature, the backwash of energy Benjamin sensed was immense. Never had he imagined it possible for any one person to wield such power. But this was *his* temple—*his* place of power—here he had strength.

Yet, as the combat wore on, the aged man's strength soon waned, weighed down by the demands of the fight. Between the coils, as gaps opened, the orange light grew and grew with intensity. Heat poured out into the room. Benjamin's heart raced, and beads of sweat formed across his forehead. He strained to keep the coils together, sealing the gaps and containing the fire within.

Knowing little time remained, Benjamin summoned what energy he had left, and willed the cocoon to contract and shrink. He'd smother the evil thing to nothingness. With the constraint at half its original size, Benjamin fought to keep up his efforts until the strain became too great.

In a silent explosion, the white cocoon shattered, and the broken pieces vaporized. The demon stood in the middle of the chamber, larger and brighter. It laughed, then said, "You cannot stop me."

Benjamin knew that laugh—he knew that voice. "Kahir. But how?"

"Simpleton!"

A stream of fire erupted, covering Benjamin's hand, preventing any more acts of defense. He screamed as his skin bubbled and blistered. The smell of burning flesh fouled the air. The creature laughed again, enjoying the old man's suffering.

"None can defeat me."

The demon exploded, sending out waves of flame, engulfing Benjamin Abrams. The chamber, the only place he felt safe, resonated with the sounds of agony.

TWELVE

Last night, Jack Railey brought his wife and son to the three-bedroom apartment under lease by the agency. It seemed the most prudent action until he could devise a more permanent solution. The location was originally a safe house, but after a few years, its security level was reclassified as low. Now used mostly for agents on non-active stopovers, usually for the journey home, these quarters were still very secure.

The morning brought with it a chance to relax and catch one's breath. Jack plopped down on the couch, scooped up the TV remote, and pressed the ON button with his thumb. He had heard Kirby Pucket got beaned by a ninety-mile-per-hour fastball and, as a result, suffered a broken jaw. He wondered how the baseball player was managing. Too bad, he thought, Kirby was the best thing about the Minnesota Twins this year. On the bright side, there were just three games left to end a miserable season.

Five minutes until the sports report, Jack figured he'd catch up on the local news. He hadn't sat down with a newspaper since returning from his last assignment. He glanced toward the bedroom where Anna slept. On a normal day, she'd be up an hour before him—she must be exhausted. Jack decided to let her sleep, allowing her those few more moments of peace, be it only the peace of slumber.

Half-listening, Jack perked up when the anchorwoman read a story of a confined fire at Saint Paul's *Temple of the Silver Night*—cause unknown. She reported one death. A tight knot formed in his stomach. Jack called the television station hoping for more details, but the annoyed voice assured him that all facts had been relayed as thoroughly and professionally as allowed by the ongoing investigation. He tried the St. Paul Police, but they declined to give out any other statements on the case until they could contact the victim's family.

Jack needed to confirm what he suspected deep down in his gut. For the second time in three days, he dialed the number to what the agents jokingly referred to as *The Information Desk* or simply *4-1-1*. Regardless of whether or not specific intelligence was publicly available, the agency possessed various methods to obtain and pass it on to field operatives—even casework from local, state, or federal law enforcement.

The other end picked up with a deadpan, "Station five."

Jack replied. "Seven-seven-four." There was a click, followed by a soft buzz, followed by another click.

It would stun the average American citizen to learn how much of their life had been put under the looking glass. In the United States, agencies such as the FBI, DOJ, IRS, SSA, and innocuous departments like FEMA and HUD, along with dozens more, collect vast amounts of data—personal information including births, marriages, divorces, and deaths. Data collected on taxpayers consisted of salaries, property ownership, assets—stocks and bonds, IRAs and 401Ks. Anyone seeking a license—driver's license, vehicle license, business license—those details were gathered and processed. Criminal records, driving history, phone records, banking transactions, organizational memberships, as well as when and how often someone votes. It's all stored, sifted, and organized—and available with a single call to *The Information Desk.*

A woman's voice took the line. And several deep breaths later, Jack received a response to his query. A response that changed everything.

Anna emerged from the bedroom, her hair disheveled and her eyes a tad heavy with sleep. "Who were you talking to?" She rubbed the side of her neck as she spoke. Even after years together, Jack marveled at how amazing she looked when she awoke, especially now and under these conditions.

"How's Justin?" he asked instead of answering her question.

"Fine. He's still sleeping."

Jack gave her a forced grin.

"What's wrong?" she asked.

"Nothing."

Anna walked over to him and cradled his hands in hers. She gazed deeply into his eyes. She smiled sweetly. "God, you're a terrible liar."

Jack turned away from her.

"What happened?" she said, realizing the severity of the situation. "Please, Jack, tell me. What happened?"

"Benjamin Abrams is dead."

"Dead?" she said in a whisper of disbelief. To Anna, the man was only a voice on the telephone, but her shock was sincere. She understood what it meant for her family. Anna had refused to abandon their home unless Jack explained why. He revealed that Anthony Bane had been killed—though he kept the part about the gargoyle to himself. He told her those attempting to stop Kahir were in real danger, including himself. If things got messy, he wanted her and Justin out of the line of fire.

"Are you sure?" Anna asked.

"It was on the morning news."

"They said his name?"

"No, but…"

"Maybe it's not him. Maybe—"

Jack turned and put his hands on her shoulder to steady her. "It's him." Jack saw a tear in his wife's eye, threatening to fall. He wrapped her in a tight embrace.

After a minute in her husband's arms, Anna said, "You have to leave town. Today. Leave town!"

"I can't do that, and if I did, I'd take you two with me."

"We'd only slow you down. Get your suitcase." Anna pulled herself free and headed for the closet. Jack stopped her by the arm when she tried to slip past him.

"I can't," he repeated.

"Sure you can! You're always leaving for your job."

"What about Sarah? Am I supposed to leave her? Do nothing?"

"The police. They can handle it."

"They've been useless so far," Jack said, knowing the police were powerless against Kahir, and without a way to defeat him, Sarah or any of the other children wouldn't be going home.

"It's their job!"

"And I'm her father." He had never seen Anna so scared, almost to the point of being irrational.

"If you end up like Anthony or Mr. Abrams, and Sarah's still in that cult, how does that matter? It doesn't! I've lost you both. Think what that'll do to Justin."

"Thanks for the vote of confidence. I have been in tight situations before."

"But you had backup. This time, you'll be on your own."

You're not wrong there, he thought. Brigham gave him the death stare when he merely brought up the subject.

"We're not in the desert somewhere," Anna added. "You can't shoot your way out of this one."

Jack stood silent. *Anna two, Jack zero.*

"Go," Anna said. "Let things cool down. Gordon can find you a mission or operation—whatever you guys call it these days."

"How's that any different? It's the same game. I'd just be changing players."

"It's not the same, not the same at all. There's something evil going on, and you seem to be smack in the middle of it. Talk to Gordon. With all the shit happening in the world, there must be some assignment he can give you."

Jack grabbed the remote and snapped off the TV. "He already has."

"Perfect! Disappear somewhere, and you won't get hurt."

The image of angry Iraqis shooting at him flashed through Jack's mind. Of his two options, which was worse? At least with the Iraqis, he could fight back—he knew how to fight back. "The arrangements won't be finalized for a day or so."

"Not good enough. You call and tell them you can leave today—right now."

"You know it doesn't work that way."

"Then hide out until your plane's ready."

"You know *I* don't work that way." He hugged her again. "It will be fine, you'll see."

She buried her face in his chest. "Last night I dreamed we were on a picnic. Justin was in one of his pranking moods. He was tormenting Sarah and her friend Cindy by chasing them with a bullfrog he caught down by the lake."

"Cindy?" Jack said, his expression going stern. "I should call Leonora. She needs to be told about Benjamin Abrams. I expect her reaction to be the same as yours—but not for the same reason." Jack lifted the handset but eyed the keypad. "What's her number?" He didn't miss the slight smirk on Anna's face.

She moved him aside and pushed the buttons.

Jack listened for the ring, but the phone buzzed in his ear. "The line's busy." Jack hit the cradle button. "Give it another try," he said, hoping Anna had misdialed.

More buzzing. "It's no good." He put down the receiver. "I'll go see her."

"No, stay here."

"Weren't you all determined to get rid of me a second ago?"

"That was different," Anna said.

"Leonora warned me about the danger," Jack said. "That's why you and Justin are safe. I owe her the same courtesy."

Anna didn't argue with him—there'd be no point.

Jack kissed her forehead. "Tell Justin I love him."

He made sure the door locked behind him and waited for the reassuring sound of the chain sliding across the other side. During the first ten steps, he must have glanced back five times.

In the parking lot, Jack looked up. Anna waved at him from the apartment window. He returned the wave before speeding off to the de Montia family home. When they left the house, Anna questioned his decision to take both cars. "Just a precaution," he had told her. And at this point—the correct one. While he was gone, if anything happened, she and Justin had a means to escape.

Jack kept an eye on his rearview mirror. At this rate, he was prime for a ticket and didn't need some quota-hungry cop pulling him over. During the drive, he tried to rehearse what he'd say to Leonora, but nothing seemed adequate—which meant telling her the blunt, unvarnished truth.

Up ahead, he spotted his destination. All appeared normal from a distance—the door and windows were intact. A hopeful sign, given the circumstances. Though from his vantage point, the entire rear of the house could have been torn down, and he'd have no way of knowing it.

Jack parked alongside a perfect set of hedges. As he killed the engine, he questioned himself to whether he'd made a rather hasty decision. Would Leonora even be conscious this early in the morning? The woman could be asleep, taking the phone off the hook so as not to be disturbed. If the alcohol she slammed down during their brief talk was any clue, the woman was no stranger to fuzzy evenings and late mornings.

Through the Firebird's window, Jack studied the dark house—he was getting himself in deeper and deeper. *Good ol' Paul Ames always had some quip for moments like this*, he thought. *Probably something stupid —"In for a penny, in for a pound."* Jack shook his head and laughed. "At least it wouldn't be 'Easy as pie,'" he muttered out loud.

Jack jumped out of the Pontiac and proceeded up the long walkway to the front door.

He rang the bell.

No matter his personal feelings for Leonora, he had to admit the house was impressive.

Jack rang the bell again.

He had only seen the property from the curb on those few occasions he drove Sarah for a Friday night sleepover or a weekend afternoon.

For a third time, he pressed the button, but to no avail.

Jack started knocking. He rapped twice, then looked in the octagon-shaped window at the top of the door. No lights were on, and he was about to walk away when an object caught his eye—a purse—Leonora's purse. He remembered the handbag from the meeting at Bane's office. It was lying open on its side a foot past the entrance, with several items spilled out across the foyer.

Jack pounded his fist and yelled out her name. *Why doesn't she answer?* The reason too dreadful to think about, he threw all his weight on the door, which moved but did not give way. Two more forceful thrusts and the formidable barrier broke free from its frame—wood splinters sprayed into the house. He pushed past the broken entryway and knelt by the expensive purse. The items weren't scattered very far, indicating the purse hadn't been thrown but dropped. His gaze scanned the rest of the foyer, locking on the phone in shambles at the foot of an ornate table.

"Leonora!" he called out. "It's Jack…Jack Railey."

He rushed from room to room—the kitchen, living room, dining room, study—all were clear. Jack bolted up the staircase to the upper level. He searched those rooms in order. Besides a sewing room, the rest were bedrooms, each spotless and well decorated. One thing that could be said about Leonora, she had excellent taste. Then came the bathroom. It wasn't the last room on the second floor, but the last room he would search.

On the marble tiles, Jack found a lifeless Leonora de Montia in a pool of her own dried blood. Her crimson-soaked eyes stared up at him. Streaks of red ran from her ears, her nose, and her parted lips, all converging into a death halo.

And Leonora made three. He approached her rigid body. Through Anna's rather colorful tales, Jack had only known *of* Leonora, and as for Benjamin and Anthony, they had been complete strangers. He had seen death many times, too many perhaps, but it always astonished him—you're alive, then you're dead. No deals, no bargains, no do-overs—you're just gone.

Behind Jack, a loud creak pierced the silence. He spun around and found a gun barrel pointing at him square in the face.

"Don't move," the uniformed policeman said. "Keep your hands where I can see them."

"This must look pretty bad," Jack said, immediately shaking his head at how stupid that sounded.

"Stand clear of the body," the cop said, taking a slow step sideways, not letting Jack out of his gun sight.

"My name is Jack Railey. I'm acquainted with this woman."

The officer didn't hear the words or didn't care. "On the floor," he ordered. "Flat on the floor. Hands on your back."

"I'm trying to tell you—"

"I said, 'on the floor.' Now!"

Given no other choice, Jack obeyed the command. Face down, he heard the clicks of handcuffs locking in place. A tug on his elbow was accompanied by the order to sit up. The cop helped Jack lean against a nearby wall. His gun in its holster, the officer read from a Miranda card, then asked if he understood his rights.

Jack nodded, then said, "This isn't what it seems."

"Let's see if I got this straight. My dispatcher receives a call about an unknown white male breaking into this house. I get here. Find the door splintered on its hinges. And an intruder leaning over a dead woman. What does it seem like to you?"

Jack sat speechless, reflecting on what the cop said. He sort of wished he had a broken gargoyle to blame.

"Check the body," Jack said. "It's obvious the woman's been dead for hours. I had reason to believe she might be in trouble, but I got here too late."

From outside came sirens. "You'll have a chance to tell your story, pal. But I suggest you exercise your right to an attorney. You're sure gonna need one."

The hours ticked by, and Jack sat quietly in cell number three, which he shared with one other man, who was passed out and lying in his own urine. The stench was foul, but he had endured worse. His thoughts kept returning to Anna. She was a strong woman, but how would she react to learn that he was in jail? Considering all that had happened, how much more could she bear?

"Railey," a voice called out, "Jack Railey."

Jack stood up. "Over here."

"Your story checks out," the pudgy officer said, turning the heavy key, producing a low metallic clack.

Jack didn't speak as the door slid open.

"Can I give you a free piece of advice?"

On his way out of the cell, Jack shrugged. The advice was coming if he wanted it or not.

"Next time there's trouble, try calling us first. Don't go playing hero. This ain't the movies, and you ain't no secret agent guy."

Jack grinned. "You're right. I ain't no secret agent guy."

After collecting his wallet, belt, shoes, and car keys from the property window, Jack called Anna for a pick up. When he heard her voice, his worries vanished. She sounded relieved, of course, but also a little annoyed—*that* was the Anna he married. Jack stepped out of the glass doors of the police station. He had to shield his eyes until they adjusted. The sun was shining brightly, and there was no wind to dilute the warmth. A great day for September. It would be a good ten minutes before Anna showed up to take him to retrieve the Firebird, but he needed to get out of that building.

Jack's stomach rumbled. In his rush to Leonora's place, he had neglected to eat. Once Anna picked him up, they'd have to stop somewhere for food—the Firebird could wait for an hour or two—his stomach, not so much. And Anna being Anna, it was a sure bet she hadn't eaten anything yet herself.

While standing on the sidewalk, Jack felt a gentle touch on his arm, almost like a soft, light breeze—an accidental graze from a passerby. But on the second touch, Jack turned. He stood there, a wave of disbelief crashing over him. Less than six feet away was Sarah. She appeared so thin, and her cropped hair was mussed. He took a step toward her, but she responded with a step back.

"Hi, Daddy," she said with her hands clasped together in front of her body. The child looked curiously at peace, almost angelic.

"Come home," was the first thing out of his mouth.

"I can't, Daddy. I can't come home."

The temptation to grab her swept over him. But if he failed this time, he might lose whatever trust she had left for him. There had to be some trust, he reasoned. Why else would she be here? Still, it required real effort to restrain himself.

"Daddy," she said, "don't try to stop him. He'll get mad at you."

"Who, Sarah? Kahir?"

"He'll hurt you. Like the others. Stay away. Leave us alone."

Jack wished Anna would hurry. If Sarah saw her mother and brother, she might want to be with them. For an instant, in his mind at least, they were all together as a family.

"You can't stop him. No one can. They all tried, but he punished them."

"Come with me, Sarah."

"I'm sorry, Daddy."

His patience had run out—damn the trust. "No, honey, *I'm sorry*. I'll make it up to you later." Jack rushed dead-on toward Sarah, his hands extended out, making ready for a steel embrace. He'd rescue his daughter now!

Jack's arms surrounded the child, then passed completely and cleanly through her body. His momentum carried him too far forward, and he toppled headlong, landing on the concrete.

He got up and spun around, fearing he had fallen into Kahir's trap. But the girl made no threatening move toward him. She looked up at him with her sad brown eyes.

"Nice trick," Jack said. "What are you?"

"It's me, Daddy. Stay away. Please, stay away."

As Jack listened to the girl's words, Anna pulled up to the curb. The front passenger window rolled down with a hum as she stopped the dark blue Ford Taurus.

"You Okay?" Anna asked. She spoke as if she was ignoring Sarah.

"Hi, Dad," Justin said, leaning forward from the backseat. "We're going to Pizza Hut for lunch."

He turned his head, presuming Sarah had run off, but she was still standing with her folded hands. "Yeah, fine," he told Anna.

She stretched over the seat. "Gonna stand there all day? Let me guess. You forgot your wallet inside."

"No, my wallet's right here," Jack said, tapping his rear pants pocket. He didn't understand how, but only he could see Sarah.

"Then get in already," she said, pushing open the car door.

"Go, Daddy," Sarah said. "Don't come after me. He'll hurt you."

Jack kept peering out the window as they drove off. The Taurus turned a corner, and Sarah disappeared from view. He barely spoke except to agree on pizza.

"Can we have Canadian bacon and black olives?" Justin asked with a huge smile.

"How about some pineapple too?" Anna said.

"With black olives? Yuck!"

A half-hour later, Jack watched his boy and his wife sitting across the booth from him, going over the list of toppings. Justin's excitement at the possibility of a third choice beamed on his face. Anna tried to mirror the boy's enthusiasm, but Jack saw the sadness hiding in her eyes. He deemed it best to say nothing of his encounter with Sarah or what appeared to be Sarah—it made no sense. But then, lately, not much made sense.

As the waitress jotted down their order of a thick crust topped with Canadian bacon, black olives, and banana peppers, Jack pondered what few options he had left. With Bane gone, with Abrams gone, it all fell to him. By the time he swallowed the last bite of his first slice of pizza, Jack had made his decision. He excused himself and left the table. He broke a dollar at the cashier counter and went to the payphone hanging by the entrance, next to a *Street Fighter II* arcade game.

"Carol, it's Jack Railey calling. I need to speak with Brigham."

"He's on the other line. Can you hold?"

Jack pinned the handset between his ear and shoulder, pushed up his sleeve, and glanced at his watch. "For a minute. But let him know I'm on the line."

"You're in luck. He's off now. I'll transfer you."

"Thanks."

"Jack," Gordon Brigham said moments later, "Perfect timing. We've just finished making the arrangements for your trip. Your plane leaves tonight and—"

"That's why I'm calling," Jack interrupted. "I can't accept the assignment."

"Everything's set. We don't have time to get another agent. You're all we've got."

"I'm telling you, I'm not going."

"Consider what you're saying, man! Markus Radford, his team—Christ, Jack, they don't have a snowball's chance without you."

Jack's chest grew very heavy. Markus was his friend. And this was the first mission he had ever turned down. "I'm sorry, Brigham. Please, find someone else. It can't be me." Not giving Brigham the opportunity to respond, he hung up. Jack stood by the payphone for several seconds, then returned to the booth. He told himself it was the right decision—the only decision. When he saw Justin, who had switched sides and was seemingly in heaven with a mouth full of pizza, and Anna, doing her best to hide her worry and pain from her son, he knew he had no other choice.

"Everything okay?" she asked.

He gave a slight nod. "Everything is fine." He lied. Jack took his new spot next to his wife. She held a damp tissue tightly in her fist.

"Something's wrong," Anna whispered.

"It's no big deal." He lied again. "I'm reconsidering us staying at the apartment. It may be better if you and Justin visit your mother." Jack had a sinking feeling that from this point on, the agency apartment was off-limits. His actions were paramount to handing in his resignation, and if Brigham wished, he could bring him up on charges.

"We goin' to Grandma's?" Justin mumbled through a full mouth.

"Does that mean you're taking the assignment?" The pain on her face eased some. "Will you be leaving soon?"

Jack chose not to reveal that he had told Brigham to find a different agent for the mission. "An exact departure hasn't been set," he said, "but, yes, soon." And easier on her nerves not to tell her what he really had in mind.

Anna touched his hand. "It doesn't matter. All that matters is that you'll be far from here."

Jack kissed his wife.

"Oh, mush!" Justin said before biting into his pizza.

THIRTEEN

Jack applied a slight pressure to the turning tool inserted into the lower half of the keyhole. Then, using a wave rake lock pick, he opened the door to the late Anthony Bane's office. It had been a while. Jack feared he might have lost his touch. *Just like riding a bike*, he thought, going inside and relocking the entrance. If only he'd had his picks at Leonora's. The cop wouldn't have found a broken door, and he wouldn't have wasted those hours in jail.

When Anna had dropped him off to get the Firebird, he saw the front door had been boarded up with plywood and several strips of police tape. He caught Anna looking as well, but she said nothing. He got the impression that she didn't want to know. She stayed silent as he sent her and Justin to the apartment with instructions to pack again.

His rushing off to Leonora's was not like him at all. The impulse lacked his usual desire for proper preparation. He didn't make the same mistake this time. On the drive over, he made a detour to his storage locker, where he kept certain gear not suitable to keep around the house. On Anna's *insistence*, he stashed away his guns, and knives, even brass knuckles, but he also kept some items he figured she'd prefer to remain ignorant of. The stop didn't take long, and he retrieved his favorite set of lock picks and a few things that may prove handy.

Jack moved past the reception area and into Bane's office. Some of the computer equipment and display monitors were missing. The picture of Anthony's son, Tony, was gone. It seemed preparations were already underway to make the space ready for its next occupant.

He hurried over to the desk to check for any signs of the files he had been shown on his first visit. Abrams had told him they were *safely stored away*, but Jack still hoped something remained—the littlest bit could be useful. He focused his attention on the desk drawers. The conditions inside stunned him.

During their meeting, he had appreciated Bane's knack for order and efficiency, but all the drawers were in such disarray it didn't seem possible to find anything within them. Jack began rifling through the mess. He couldn't make it any worse. It did occur to him that someone else had trashed them. And considering all that had happened, the idea was quite feasible.

In the bottom drawer on the right, Jack spotted something of interest after all—a 5" X 8" black personal phone book. Most pages were blank, but under "B" was a scribbled entry for Blackburn, Thaddeus.

Jack picked up the desk phone's handset, and thankfully, there was a dial tone. He punched in the digits from the book, and a ringing filled his ear.

"Hello," a shaky voice said.

Bull's-eye, Jack thought. "Blackburn, we need to talk!"

"Who the hell is this?"

"Jack Railey."

"How did you get this number?" The shakiness now mixed with anger.

"That's not important. It's enough to say I got it."

"You're wasting your time. I have nothing for you." Pause. "I suggest you forget this number and leave me alone."

"All I'm asking is—" The line went dead.

Jack tried to call him back but with no response. He realized he had to use other means to find Blackburn—he was the only one left with answers.

He made another call, but not to Blackburn. "I need a location," he said to the short-lived voice on the other end, then read out the phone number. "I'll wait." As he held the line, Jack continued scouring through the desk. Here were the last remaining tidbits of Anthony Bane. He hoped these scraps would serve him better than they did the dead man. "Yeah, I'm here." He wrote down the address. "Thanks."

Jack hung up and stared at the paper. *I killed a fly with a sledgehammer.* He knew that part of town. It was a simple business address. He could've as easily looked in a telephone directory.

Twenty minutes later, he was standing outside the office of Thaddeus Blackburn. He entered. A gray-haired woman sat typing, but she stopped when she saw him.

"May I help you?" she asked, though her expression gave Jack the feeling that those words meant nothing.

"I'm here to see Blackburn," Jack said. He tried to force a grin, remembering the adage about flies and honey. Still, he found it difficult.

"Mr. Blackburn has a very busy schedule. Maybe next week. If you call, say Monday, we might be able to work you in. But I can't promise you anything."

Jack dropped his facade. "That won't do." He marched to the inner office door, and without a word, he tore it open and stormed in, ignoring the woman's objections.

Blackburn stood up. His stance was like a rabbit trapped by a wolf, deciding to run but not having a way out.

"Sit down, Blackburn. We have to talk."

"Yes, yes," the man said, "but as you can see, I am currently occupied." He gestured to the other side of the room.

To Jack's shock and surprise, during his rather abrupt entrance, clouded by anger, he didn't notice the young couple sitting on a far couch. The startled expressions on their faces surpassed Blackburn's—a madman had just burst into the office.

"I'm sorry, Mr. Blackburn," the secretary said from the doorway.

With a flick of his wrist, she returned to her desk. Blackburn's attention focused on the couple. "Please forgive this interruption. I forgot to inform my colleague of my change in plans. If I could have a moment with him."

The young man was bug-eyed and held his wife's hand. Neither had spoken a word since Jack practically tore the door from its hinges.

Blackburn darted around his desk and grabbed Jack by the arm. "I neglected to tell my secretary to call you to change our appointment time. It slipped my mind. Come, let me offer you a cup of coffee. We can set up a new time to meet." Blackburn displayed a smile bigger than Jack thought possible. "I'll return momentarily," he told the couple.

Out in the reception area, Blackburn pulled the door closed behind him. "What the fuck do you think you're doing here?!"

"Tell me what's really going on," Jack said, "not the bullshit you've been trying to feed me."

"You have some balls coming to my place of business. Involving you was a big mistake. I told Bane that—damn fool should've listened."

"I don't give a crap what you told Bane. You gave me no choice. I'm going to ask you questions, and you will answer them, even if I have to interrupt all your meetings from now on."

"Should I call the police?" the secretary asked.

"Good idea," Jack said. "Let's get the police here. They must have their own questions. Especially when I bring up your association with Benjamin Abrams and Leonora de Montia. Considering their current state, I'd bet they'd love to speak with you."

"Take your break, Mrs. Carson," Blackburn sharply said. "I'll handle this."

"I just got back from my break."

"Then take another," he snarled.

She left the two men alone.

"I want answers," Jack said.

"You've made that painfully evident. But this is not the place. Let me meet you somewhere else, anyplace else, in ninety minutes." Blackburn glanced at the office door. His voice dropped to a whisper. "Please."

"I'll give you this one chance. But you should know, if you don't show up, I will hunt you down and extract what I need. Am I making myself clear?"

"You are. Perfectly clear."

"I saw a park two blocks away. You have an hour and a half." Before leaving the office, Jack turned and faced Blackburn. He looked the man directly in the eyes. "Just remember what I said about hunting you down. And I mean what I say."

"I'm sure you do, Mr. Railey. I'm sure you do."

Returning to the apartment building, Jack pulled into the parking lot. He sat a moment, alone with his thoughts. The dashboard clock told him he had a good seventy minutes until he had to meet with Blackburn. Minus the drive to his mother-in-law's place—that left about forty minutes. Forty minutes to make final arrangements and tie up loose ends—forty minutes to make sure his wife and son were safe from danger—forty minutes to say goodbye.

Not wanting to waste any more precious time, Jack headed toward the front entrance. He stopped to look up and down the street for any occupied cars. Jack didn't put it past Brigham to have the place staked out, instructing one of his messenger boys to pick him up and haul his butt to the office.

A man with a leashed poodle strolled by, but all else seemed clear.

Jack hurried into the building, up the stairs, and down the hallway. He slid the key into the lock and pushed the door open. It stopped short at the end of the safety chain.

"Is that you, Jack?" Anna said from the other side.

"Yes, dear." As he spoke, Jack heard the phone ring. "How long has it been doing that?" he asked as Anna removed the chain and reopened the door. Brigham couldn't be all that upset if he was still willing to try the subtle approach. That meant he had a little more time to get things together.

"Since we got here," Anna told him as he came in. "It hasn't stopped for more than five minutes at a time. I did what you said. I let it ring."

"You two ready to go?" he asked, knowing full well Brigham would soon tire of calling and just show up, if not in person, then a dark-suit representative—the one Jack had expected to be waiting for him outside the building. "We have to hurry," he added.

"Justin's ready. He barely opened the suitcase I packed for him. He's sitting on the bed reading a comic book. As for myself, I'm almost done —need to gather my stuff from the bathroom."

"Did you call your mother?"

"An hour ago. I told her we'd be there after stopping by the house."

"House?" Jack said, raising his voice. "I never said anything about stopping at the house."

"I should grab a few things to bring with us. I didn't think it would be a problem. It's on the way."

"You're right," Jack said calmly. "I'm sorry I snapped at you. It was uncalled for."

"We're all under a lot of pressure. Especially with you leaving town and all. I know you'd rather stay."

"We have to go," was all Jack said.

The ride home was a quiet one. He took the lead, keeping an eye on Anna in his rearview mirror as she followed behind him. Justin had his head down, enthralled with his comic book. This extra stop wouldn't allow him enough time to meet Blackburn as arranged. He'd have to adjust his plans.

Jack stopped in the driveway and waited for Anna to park. He got out of the Firebird and walked over to the Taurus. "Get what you need," he said. "Remember, it will be a while before you can return."

"Can I bring one of my models?" Justin asked.

"Sounds like a fine idea," Anna said, glimpsing up at Jack. "But hurry," she added, returning her gaze to her son.

Justin jumped out of the Ford and ran inside and upstairs to his bedroom. Over on his desk was a half-finished G-164 Ag-Cat Biplane Crop Duster. He preferred fighter planes, but something about this model had caught his eye. He gently lifted the plastic double wings. The glue had dried crystal clear. The piece was ready for a coat of enamel paint. He then examined the fuselage. He'd have to attach the wings first and the wheels second.

He eased the unfinished plane into its box. From a side desk drawer, he pulled the bottles of enamel paints he had already decided on three days earlier. Out of the top drawer, he retrieved a fresh sheet of decals.

They'd be the final touch. Justin carefully slipped on the cardboard lid and admired the cover picture. Justin felt pride as he imagined the completed duster sitting between his F-14 Tomcat and P-40 Warhawk. His models were his most prized possession. He had built each plane by himself—had hand painted them and put on the decals. He spent hours upon hours working on the fine details, but now he'd give them all up if only Sarah would come home. A price gladly paid to have things back the way they were.

"You ready?" Jack asked from the bedroom doorway.

"Almost," Justin said, picking up his precious bundle.

"You're handling this whole thing like a champ, son. I'm so proud of you. Sometimes I forget to tell you, but it's important that you know."

"Proud of me? For what?"

Jack moved further into the bedroom. He noticed the dump truck sticking halfway out from under the bed and picked it up. Made of metal, the toy had held up over the years. Jack remembered it as Justin's favorite—before receiving his first model plane kit, that is. "Do I need a reason?" Jack asked.

Justin shrugged.

"When I'm away, you watch over your mom. She'll be depending on you. You'll have to be strong for her."

"I will," Justin said, holding the model box close to his chest.

"You're a good kid, buddy-boy," Jack said, putting his hand on Justin's shoulder. "Let's go. Your mother is waiting." Both father and son returned to the living room.

"I was starting to wonder what happened to my two men," Anna said, trying to ease the situation.

That caused Justin to giggle.

"Put your things in the car," Jack told him, "while I speak with your mother."

Model and paints in hand, Justin obeyed and headed outside.

When the door closed behind the boy, Jack stepped over to Anna and kissed her. Then he held out her car keys. "Take them," he said. "There's no more time." Not exactly how he imagined their farewell, but it was probably for the best.

Astonished, she simply looked at the dangling keys, finally saying, "A clean cut hurts the least—is that it?" A tear ran down her cheek. "I told you to leave town." She wiped her face dry. "And I don't regret it, but I'm going to miss you so very much."

"I'm doing what has to be done."

Anna offered no reply. Instead, she gave her husband a long embrace. Anna thought she might never let go, until Jack said, "It won't get any easier."

"It never does."

"Please, Anna, Justin's waiting." He kissed her, then escorted her to the front door, where he watched her walk those final steps. Anna got behind the wheel. The engine roared to life. Justin waved goodbye as the Taurus pulled out of the driveway. Jack saw Anna's teary eyes peering at him from her mirror.

Even after they drove out of sight, he stood in the doorway, staring down the road. In his mind, Jack replayed that last moment with his wife.

FOURTEEN

Jack arrived at the park with five minutes to spare. Out of habit, he scoped out the area. It was a pretty nice place—lots of trees, perfect grass, and even a clear pond in the center. And plans were in motion for expansion. A nearby building was under demolition, which would add over 50,000 square feet. A crane equipped with a wrecking ball sat outside a long, five-foot-high solid concrete barrier erected to keep joggers and rollerbladers from accidentally entering the debris field. Down by the pond's edge was a large dump truck filled with sand. A small beach was being built up. Several piles of sand had been spread out in preparation for more.

As Jack's focus returned to the green grass, he noticed a family enjoying themselves on a picnic. They had food, a blanket, a cooler full of ice and drinks—the whole bit. He ventured a guess that on summer days, this park must get crowded. Already, Jack missed Anna—he missed Justin and Sarah. He tried to convince himself that this was just like any other assignment, but he had a tough time lying to himself.

He waited in the Firebird, shifting his weight to fight off a cramp. Jack doubted that Thaddeus Blackburn would arrive any earlier than promised, but he had no doubt that the man would indeed show up. He could always spot fear, and it was fear he had instilled in Blackburn to drive home the point he wasn't bluffing.

Jack closed his eyes. He felt tired. The emotional drain was catching up with him. It's one thing to be on an assignment dealing with virtual strangers, but it's quite a different matter once loved ones are involved.

A brief honk caused Jack to glance into his rearview mirror. A silver Bentley pulled up behind him. Jack reached for the Firebird's door handle when a dizziness hit him. He shook it off. Jack hoped he wasn't catching some kind of flu bug. He had to be at the top of his form.

After exiting his car, Jack approached the Bentley. Thaddeus Blackburn lowered the window halfway.

"What do you want?"

"For starters, you can step out of the car," Jack told him. "Let's remove any temptation of you driving off if things become uncomfortable."

"If you insist," Thaddeus said. The window rose with a soft hum. He shut off the engine, opened the door, and stepped out. Thaddeus pressed the red button on his key chain. The Bentley emitted a double chirp as the alarm activated. "You can never be too careful," the man added.

Jack declined to comment, but found a bit of irony in the man's words.

"Do you mind if we walk?" Thaddeus asked. "I'm out of my car as you demanded, but I feel quite foolish just standing here."

"Suit yourself."

They had gone only a few steps when Thaddeus Blackburn spoke. "Now, what is so important that you practically break down my office door? Disrupt my place of business?"

"The truth," Jack said. "How about we begin there?"

"A relative thing—the truth."

"I'm sick of playing games, Blackburn. And in my current state of mind, I'm more than likely to knock you down and keep knocking you down until you tell me what I want to know."

"You'll find, Mr. Railey, I don't respond well to threats."

Jack stopped walking and faced Thaddeus. "I don't make threats," he said in a very calm, very precise voice.

Thaddeus sighed. "I will tell you what I can."

"Begin with how you, Bane, and the others got mixed up with Kahir."

"We couldn't have been any clearer. He kidnapped our children."

Jack gave out a chuckle. "You must take me for an idiot. You keep feeding me that same old line. I think Kahir abducting your children was more of a defensive act on his part. Leonora told me Sarah was taken because she happened to be with Cindy. But like the rest of you, she never said why Kahir targeted her daughter."

"We have never kept that fact from you. Kahir is frightened that we will put a stop to his evil deeds."

"That's where your explanation falls apart. Kahir kidnapped your kids to prevent you from retaliating *because* he kidnapped your kids. It's circular logic. If he didn't take them in the first place, you'd have no reason to get involved with him or his activities. Unless…you were involved with Kahir before then, and things didn't go as planned. Your group and Kahir developed a mutual disdain for each other. Grabbing the children was his means of holding you all at bay. How am I doing so far?"

"Speculation. Pure speculation. What possible business of Kahir's could've been of any interest to us?"

"That's the million-dollar question."

"You forget who's the bad guy here, Mr. Railey. Abhaya Kahir is the enemy. Yours, mine… It's imperative that he's stopped. Those poor children must be free from his vile grasp. If it wasn't for men like me—"

"Don't try to make yourself out as lily-white," Jack said, cutting him off. "We both know that's a load of shit."

"How dare you speak to me in that manner!" Thaddeus shouted.

"Drop the bravado. Answers!" Jack pushed the heavyset man up against a nearby tree. "I want answers now!" Jack's forearm rested on Blackburn's Adam's apple. He applied a tiny amount of pressure—just enough to show he was serious.

"Power," Thaddeus said with a slight gasp. "It all comes down to power. Who has it, and who controls it."

"Better," Jack said, releasing his hold. "But I'm going to need a little more."

Thaddeus Blackburn stood rubbing his throat, but before speaking again, the pulsating whine of a car alarm caused both men to turn their heads the way they came. Even from that distance, they saw Blackburn's silver Bentley had been started and was rolling back and forth in the parking spot. It moved forward, hitting the Firebird's bumper hard, then backward, smacking a two-tone rust bucket as it tried to move out of the space.

The big man rushed to his expensive automobile when it jumped the curve. He stopped as his prized possession raced toward him. Thaddeus turned to run, but he wasn't fast enough, and the Bentley grazed him, knocking him to the ground.

Jack sprinted over to Thaddeus—he was still breathing. Jack took him by the left arm, which caused Thaddeus to scream out in pain. "We have to get out of here," Jack said, looking over his shoulder. The Bentley made a U-turn, driving over the sidewalk, demolishing a coin newspaper stand, and sending a trash can flying. The collision knocked out the alarm. After another slight turn, the car sped toward them.

"I can't make it," Thaddeus said.

"You're not dying today," Jack said. "I'm not finished with you yet." He yanked Blackburn up by the belt. "Move! Or I'll drag your sorry ass."

The car was about to hit them when Jack leaped sideways, pulling Thaddeus along, barely getting them both out of the way. Thaddeus landed on top of him.

"On your feet!" Jack yelled, pushing him off. "On your feet!"

Jack wasn't sure if Blackburn was afraid of death or afraid of him, but the man did as ordered. Jack was surprised at how fast he moved—given the proper motivation.

Blackburn's Bentley performed a sharp turn—too sharp. The side of the vehicle struck the nearby wrecking ball crane, smashing in the rear fender and sending the car into a spin. The only damage visible on the crane was scrapes and scratches in the yellow paint, though the violent hit caused the heavy ball high above to swing.

Jack remembered the concrete wall he'd spotted from the Firebird while waiting for Blackburn. That barrier would serve as perfect cover if got to in time, but it stood halfway between them and the killer car.

"This way," Jack said, grabbing Blackburn by the jacket sleeve. He pulled the man toward the construction site and in the direction of the oncoming Bentley.

"Are you crazy?!" Thaddeus said, jerking away, producing a loud rip as his shoulder seam tore open.

"Do what I say." Jack forced Thaddeus closer to the crane, using its steel body as a shield. The car spun around, and as Jack figured, it had barely enough room to maneuver. In the short circle, the Bentley managed only to strike the crane a second time. The heavy equipment moved some, but at the cost of a torn-off front fender.

As if realizing its mistake, the Bentley reversed direction from the crane about five car lengths. It made a wider turn and headed straight for the two men.

Jack pulled at Blackburn. "Move!"

"I can't. I really can't."

Thaddeus was breathing so hard that Jack worried he'd pass out on the spot.

"Stay with me!" Jack hauled him the last few feet to the wall. "You're going to have to climb," Jack yelled, holding him up to the concrete barrier.

Blackburn waved Jack away. "I don't have the strength."

"It's not that high. Reach up with your good arm, and I'll push you over."

The car finished its turn.

"Try, damn it, try."

The Bentley baring down on them, Jack guided Blackburn's uninjured arm to the wall's edge. The man's sense of self-preservation kicked in, and he fought to pull himself up.

With great effort, Jack shoved Thaddeus over the top, but it was too late for himself. He watched the car coming, knowing he couldn't jump the barrier in time. Nor could he run. Whichever direction he ran, the Bentley would hit him. He had no escape.

When the Bentley drove closer for its final, fatal strike, Jack saw a pair of red eyes staring at him. But they were not looking through the windshield—they were part of the glass. The eyes faded, and the car built up speed. Jack's back was against the concrete as the large silver automobile barreled down on him. Mere seconds remained of Jack Railey's existence.

Then, coming from above him, Jack heard a sharp metallic twang as the steel cable snapped. The wrecking ball dropped, landing on the hood of the Bentley, crushing it into stillness—his life was spared.

After a second to catch his breath, Jack jumped the wall to check on Thaddeus, who was lying in a heap, holding his injured arm. The man didn't look so good—his face was a pasty white. "Leonora was right... about...you...," Thaddeus said, passing out.

FIFTEEN

Jack Railey huffed as he made his way to the Firebird with a groggy and heavy Thaddeus Blackburn clinging to his shoulder. The damage to his car's bumper and rear end was moderate, but not bad enough to impede his ability to drive. His insurance rates were going to be murder next year, but at least he had the means to get the hell away. Jack had passed through a group of onlookers. Someone shouted out for the police to be called. Jack didn't want or need that kind of attention. He'd have difficulty explaining his second visit to the authorities in a single day. First, being questioned in the death of Leonora de Montia, and now, he'd be facing charges for the destruction of public and private properties. He had no time to waste sitting in a cell. The police would not believe he was a victim with a big man hanging from his arm.

And Blackburn was indeed a big man. Jack wondered how anyone could let themselves fall into such bad shape. The man's weight pressed hard against Jack's shoulder, which had to support most of it. Every third step or so, Blackburn let loose a moan. His left arm hung down, limp at his side, his fingers slightly swollen.

Stuffing Blackburn into the passenger seat, Jack drove the man to Unity Region Hospital. After a thirty-minute wait, he got the word that

Blackburn had suffered nothing more serious than a broken arm. It could have been much worse, Jack supposed. Then, the nurse insisted that Jack also receive treatment. Not wanting to appear as a man with something to hide, he agreed. He didn't require any stitches, only a touch of disinfectant and a gauze bandage.

Jack returned to the reception desk and asked if he could see his "friend." Not that he had the tiniest bit of loyalty toward Thaddeus—Jack still had questions he wanted answered. The nurse smiled at Jack and gave her okay, provided he'd hurry—they were about ready to put on Blackburn's cast. Jack assured her he'd only be a minute. She pointed him to examination room three.

Jack knocked prior to entering, though it was a fast knock. He gave Blackburn no time at all to respond. As he burst in, Jack read the surprise on the man's face.

Blackburn sat with his injury stabilized in a gray plastic temporary brace. "I wrongfully assumed," he said, turning away from Jack, "you'd have left by now." The man faced the wall.

"You're not off the hook that easy," Jack snarled. "You, Bane, and the others have been holding out on me. And that's going to end!"

"You're acting crazy. Look at yourself. Charging in here. Ranting like a madman."

"And with good reason."

"Count yourself lucky. You came out of that scrape in one piece."

"I'm tired of this. How'd you like your other arm broken?"

Thaddeus smirked and shook his head. "You among us all should know what you were getting into," he said, his gaze returning to Jack.

"What the blazes are you talking about?"

"You may have fooled Leonora and Anthony, even Benjamin, but Mr. Railey, that innocent, naïve act, won't work on me."

"Did you crack your skull when you fell?"

"Fine, keep up appearances, but allow me one question. Can you explain how a stone statue can kill a man?"

Before Jack could say a word, the door was opened by a nurse pushing a cart with cotton wrap, white plaster gauze, and a basin of water. "I'm afraid you'll have to leave," she said. "We need to apply his cast."

"We'll speak again," Jack told Blackburn.

"It's funny, but I hope you're right."

The expression on Blackburn's face was sincere enough, but Jack didn't trust the man's words.

Jack walked back to the emergency room lobby. He turned the corner but immediately retreated. At the desk were two uniformed police officers. One was speaking with the station nurse. His partner was scoping out the other patients. It didn't take a genius to work out who they were looking for. Jack slipped down the hall, hoping to find an alternative escape route. The next closest exit had an alarm, which would scream out when opened, giving away his location. He quickly moved on. It wouldn't be long until the police were directed to Blackburn's room—his last known whereabouts. Jack's search led him to a loading dock. Luckily, the hospital's food supplier was in the process of making a delivery. Between loads of bread and eggs, milk and coffee, meat and cheese, they left the door open, and he seized his chance.

Out in the parking lot, Jack snaked along the maze of cars until he reached the Firebird. Jack scrunched down and grabbed the handle. For a second, he became very dizzy and lost his grip. Jack fell forward but caught himself on outstretched arms. "This is really becoming a pain in the ass," he said while staring down at the pavement. Jack steadied himself somewhat, opened the car door, and jumped in. He sat low and took several deep breaths until the dizziness passed. Finally feeling better, Jack peered over the steering wheel. He saw one of the police officers had exited the hospital and was talking into a radio mic inside his cruiser. Jack sat up and started the engine. He pulled forward and slowly approached the street.

At the curb, the heavy cross traffic forced Jack to stop. He glanced in his rearview mirror. The cop had put down his microphone and was stepping out of the squad car. Jack stared forward. With no gaps between vehicles, Jack considered pulling out, bullying his way into the flow. But any honking from an angry driver might draw in the officer, thwarting any getaway.

Jack took another quick peek in the mirror, then, realizing he was holding his breath, he exhaled. The officer disappeared through the hospital entrance.

A tapping caused Jack to jump.

His eyes shifted toward the tap-tap of knuckles on glass, expecting to see an officer standing with gun drawn. Instead, an older gray-haired gentleman stood there, gesturing for him to roll down the car window. Jack did.

"Listen, buddy," the man said, "you ain't never gonna get out from here at this time of day. Try goin' around to the rear entrance. It's a whole lot easier."

"Thanks," Jack said, looking back at the swarming traffic. "Thanks a lot."

"Anytime. Made the same mistake myself once. Waited a good twenty minutes before I gave up and went the other way. Have a good day."

"You too," Jack responded. As he drove to the other exit, he pondered his current state of mind. Feeling so wound up—walking on such an edge. It wasn't normal. He had been in situations where his life hung in the balance and had handled them without breaking so much as a sweat. But as of late, he was quick to anger, jumping at the slightest sound, cowering at signs of pursuit, even bouts of paranoia. More than a case of bad nerves, something was wrong, terribly wrong. He needed help.

Jack parked the Firebird and walked the final five blocks. He needed the few extra moments to clear his head. It had been over a decade since he had visited this section of St. Paul, colorfully known as Frogtown. The neighborhood had changed, not in a bad way, just in a different way. A lot of the landmarks he remembered were gone, replaced by an Asian restaurant, grocery store, and clothing boutique. A new mini-mall had been erected along with several fast food places. Dirty book-stores and theaters had been closed down and left as empty shells—some had been demolished altogether. The whole area was a blending of East and West cultures.

As he moved closer to his destination, the strong aroma of garlic, onions, and fish sauce hung in the air. On the corner stood a Vietnamese restaurant. *Never too far away*, Jack thought. Even now, Clifford must still have a taste for hot and spicy chicken. Just as he was about to walk by the establishment, a tall, good-looking Caucasian male emerged holding a brown paper bag filled with takeout. Jack assumed the man had traveled a ways for the food while watching him climb into a gold-colored four-door Saturn. Judging by his appearance, he didn't belong to this neighborhood.

Jack tried to ignore the tantalizing smells as he passed a home where children watched him from the porch. Their eyes displayed a mixture of emotion, of both fear and fascination. A little girl wearing a flowered dress giggled. When Jack turned and waved at her, she ran inside. She reminded him of Sarah, and his heart grew heavy, thinking he had frightened her. He was relieved when he saw her watching him through the screen door, and she giggled again. Jack kept walking.

Two blocks over, he stood in front of an older house. It was small but well kept up. The grass was neatly mowed, and the fence around the lot appeared new. He pushed up the latch, swung the gate open, then walked up the concrete path to the front entrance. At the far edge of a flower bed, off to the right and under a big bay window, sat a foot-high stone gargoyle. Jack did a double take, remembering Anthony Bane. A silly little thing—he had seen many like it in stores throughout the cities. Anna had always said they were ugly. He couldn't agree more.

Jack raised a fist to knock, but didn't get the chance. The entryway swung open, and there stood Clifford Stuart. A man of average height and weight, the last twelve years had left their mark—his brown hair peppered with gray, and the lines at the corner of his eyes added character to his face.

"You could've tipped me over with a feather when I got your call," Clifford said, holding open the door. "Come in, come in. It's good to see you."

"And you," Jack said, entering the house and immediately detecting the scent of sandalwood incense.

Closing the door behind Jack, Clifford led him to the sitting room. He walked with an uneven stride as they passed the kitchen. "Coffee?" Clifford asked, briefly stopping.

"None for me, thanks." Their conversation, what there was of it, was somewhat forced: *Hello, how are you? I'm fine. Thank you.* This was a guy with whom Jack shared many hours, talking, laughing, drinking, and fighting. Now, he barely knew the man. And his future depended on him.

Clifford gestured for Jack to enter the room, which was sparsely furnished with a table, a couple of chairs, and several shelves full of books. The depressions in the carpeting were much deeper by the farthest seat than by the other. On the table, next to a silver-framed photograph, smoke rose from a ceramic dish—the source of the sandalwood aroma. Clifford told him to sit. He did. The chair was surprisingly comfortable.

Clifford had to tap the back of his knee forward with the tips of his fingers to ease himself into his seat. Jack felt a pang of unease watching his old friend wrestling with his prosthetic leg.

"Reminds me of my mortality," Clifford said with a slight chuckle.

Jack forced a smile, but recalled the day he heard about Clifford's run-in with a land mine. It happened in the West Bank of Israel. Clifford got caught in some gunplay with the Palestinians. A brother and sister, ages five and six, ran into the crossfire. Clifford stopped shooting, bolted out, and grabbed them both. He missed seeing the warning flags. Clifford saved the children, and they came out with only bruises. Following a long recovery, he received a commendation and took early retirement. He couldn't stand the idea of sitting at a desk. He'd rather sit in a boat fishing.

The rising sliver of sandalwood smoke drew Jack's eyes to the burning dish and then to the framed picture of a thin woman with straight black hair. She had a sweet smile, yet beneath it, there was a hint of sadness.

Clifford caught Jack staring. "It's going on five years now," he said.

"Excuse me?"

"Five years. Julia died five years ago."

"I saw her obit…" His words trailed off. "I always meant to call, but—"

"But things got in the way," Clifford finished the sentence. "They do. They really do." He picked up the photo. "Remember the day I introduced you two?"

Jack nodded.

"She said you had an aura of danger around you. That peril was never far behind."

Jack grinned. "I worried you were engaging in too much pillow talk with her."

"But I wasn't. She had the gift. A true marvel." Clifford's gaze lingered on the image with fondness. "She saved me, you know. More than once I thought about biting the end of my old service revolver. But she kept me going. She never let me give up."

"It must have been difficult for you when she died."

"That's putting it mildly. But I'll say this—I never think about my gun anymore. That would dishonor her memory." He returned the picture to the table, turning it to face him. After a pause, Clifford asked, "What brings you to this part of town?"

"Information." Jack took a short breath. "What can you tell me about magic?" The question sounded so idiotic.

"You mean pulling rabbits out of a hat or maybe having little red balls disappear?" Clifford hadn't lost his odd sense of humor.

"You're not making this any easier."

"When is anything ever easy?" Clifford said, rapping his knuckles against his leg.

"Black magic. I'm asking about black magic." Jack looked around at the multitude of books. "You study that sort of stuff."

"That sort of stuff?" Clifford said.

"What do you call it, 'New Age'?"

Clifford laughed.

"I said something funny?"

"My apologies. It's that term 'New Age.' The word 'occult' sounds too frightening. 'Parapsychology' is too cerebral. To make it more palatable for common folk, they came up with 'New Age'—two three-letter words of one syllable."

"But every bookstore you go into these days has a New Age section."

"I didn't say the term was useless." Clifford suppressed an impish smirk. "I still find it humorous."

"And foolish?"

Not at all. Many topics are very popular—and harmless—even a kick for some. Astrology, the Tarot, Palmistry—these are just a few examples. They serve as diversions, giving people the illusion of direction in their lives. And, of course, there are those who dabble with the cosmic forces, but the results are rarely significant. Most fool themselves into believing they can effect real change.

"You're talking about magic? The power to make stuff appear from nothing."

"Magic isn't creating something out of nothing. That's impossible. Magic is the study of forces. And those forces can be controlled by direct effort of the human will."

"Can you control them?" Jack asked.

"I'm strictly a bookworm on the subject. True manipulation is quite rare." He glanced at the face of his deceased wife. "But Julia—she had the talent—an exceptional talent."

"She was a witch?"

"Witches practice the craft of Wicca—the old way. Julia would best be called an Adept. She hated labels, but she accepted that description for the sake of discussion."

"Where did she learn? I've heard stories of Tibet."

"There are sects. Monks well versed in the knowledge of the occult. There have been monasteries high in the Himalayan Mountains for twenty-five centuries. While many have been destroyed by the Chinese Communists, some remain. In their seclusion, they have studied life, the universe, other planes of existence."

"Monks? Monasteries? Is it a religion?"

Clifford shrugged. "Each sect has its rituals, and they believe in their particular deities."

"I'm finding this all very confusing."

"Don't feel bad. Every culture has a unique set of beliefs and teachings. The Jews, for instance, have a framework known as the Kabbalah. But for our discussion, let's focus on the Tibetan Monks. They are the oldest group of scholars. They're centuries ahead of everyone else. They've explored ESP, meditation, and altered states of consciousness long before our forebears landed on Plymouth Rock."

"My forebears landed on Ellis Island."

Clifford smiled, then continued. "Their studies are vast. Levitation, incantations, necromancy, all of which are doubted and scoffed at by the uninitiated. Strange and marvelous stories have been told of those mountains. Some true, some bullshit. Tales of disembodied spirits, reincarnated gods, demons, monsters, even ghouls. You name it. But all in all, the monk's primary goal is to explore reality in all its subtleties." Clifford paused.

"Keep going," Jack said, his eyes narrowed. "How do you join these groups?"

"You don't. Just getting to a monastery is nearly insurmountable. If you can cut through the red tape of the Chinese government—" He stared at Jack. "Probably not a deterrent for such an industrious man as yourself."

Jack gave Clifford a slight, knowing nod.

"But trekking up the Himalayas is a whole 'nother ball of wax. And if somehow you do manage, finding the monasteries is the real trick. They're not in the Yellow Pages, and there are no road signs. And on the absolute remote chance, by the favor of the Creator, you stumble upon a monastery—the monks are great believers in the racial purity of their teachings and the lifetime commitment. To put a fine point on it, they wouldn't accept you."

"But with all this secrecy, how did the knowledge leak out?"

"As it's bound to happen, a few of the monks decided they had had enough of the cloistered life—and perhaps craving more power—they ran away. And five will get you ten that some were kicked out for, shall we say, bad behavior. These disillusioned adepts moved to India or Asia, starting less restrictive sects. Knowledge tends to flow out to the masses. But I can't help but wonder what mysteries have never left Tibet. And

I'm not alone. The secrets hidden within those ancient walls could be tremendous."

"You spoke of ESP. That's different from magic?"

"It is. ESP is a more natural ability. Magic, while it does require natural talent, is also a learned skill. Imagine a practitioner as a cosmic athlete. They possess abilities, but they also need to develop and refine them with study and practice."

"What about objects moving on their own? That must be magic." The twinge in Jack's shoulder kicked up. It had to be psychosomatic. The memory of his fight with the gargoyle still bothered him. This whole subject bothered him, but it had no other explanation. Science certainly couldn't explain how stone can walk. Anthony, Benjamin, Leonora—all dead. Thaddeus in the hospital. And he narrowly escaped being mashed between steel and concrete. If he didn't find the answer, he could fail to save himself next time.

"Not necessarily," Clifford said. "The mind is powerful, capable of performing miracles."

"Like animating a hunk of rock? Making it crash around by itself?"

"The scientific name for it is psychokinesis."

"There's a term I recognize," Jack said. "I saw a guy on TV once who bent spoons by barely touching them. But I'm talking on a much larger scale."

"What's 'scale' to a disciplined mind? Or to the eternal spirit? The spark within us all needs to live, grow, and evolve."

"You're saying this is all evolution?"

"Partially. But telepathy, clairvoyance, precognition—to a certain extent, we all have these abilities naturally—the human race always has. And some individuals have them turned on, so to speak, more than others. In our formative years, we manifest these skills, but our young minds can't comprehend what has happened. When children try to convey the experience to their parents or other adults, they are told it's their imagination. Over time, a child believes that to be true, and soon, the ability to perceive the world on a grander scale fades and shuts off altogether. So much the pity, really, but keeping in mind history, I suppose it was necessary—such displays were met with superstition and fear. During the Puritan days, especially in Salem, Massachusetts, innocents were burned at the stake for exhibiting their gifts, even by accident. It's only been fifty or sixty years since this phenomenon has come into the mainstream, though it remains filled with myths and legends of past ignorance. Imagine the number of fakes and frauds that plague the occult world, claiming to be the new messiah, not to mention the nut cases. Then, we have the other side of the coin. Almost all major universities have studies in parapsychology. Real money and real brains are fueling the search for truth. Of course, that's scientific truth with its meters and measurements. But some aspects, certain intangible elements, can't truly be measured. And if a discovery is made, someone comes up with contradictory facts to disprove it. It all boils down to who gives the best spin. And spin keeps the grants coming. And there we have scientific light keeping mankind in the dark."

Jack clinched a fist and lightly banged it on his upper thigh. "How can anyone defend himself against any of this? Guns, knives, bombs, I understand. Here, I'm out of my league."

"The universe is balance," Clifford said. "You can counter a force by applying a second force."

"Fight fire with fire?"

"I suppose that's a novel way of looking at it. By employing one type of energy, you can cancel out another."

"A magical short circuit."

"A touch simplistic, but the right idea." Clifford raised an eyebrow, a spark of curiosity in his eyes. "You haven't yet told me what this is all about. In all the years we've known each other, you've never had an interest in the occult."

"Things change," he replied. "Yourself, for instance."

"Indeed, things do change, but only for a reason. What is your reason, Jack?"

"There's a man. Abhaya Kahir. Let's just say I'm having issues with him."

"Troubles?"

"He has my daughter."

"Sarah?" Clifford said. The last time he saw Jack's daughter was at her christening. Not long after his accident, Clifford broke off contact with most of his friends. Partially a matter of security, mostly though a matter of pride. "And you think this man has arcane powers?"

"Not think. I've seen it…and the results. Three people killed—slaughtered."

"Jack, you've royally put your foot in it—again. Getting shot at isn't enough for you?"

"There's more. Sarah's been out begging for money with a group of children. I tried, foolishly, I might add, to grab her, but they swarmed between us. I didn't make it five feet to her. They whisked her away while I was held back." Jack paused to gather his thoughts. "Then, earlier today, I was on the street waiting for Anna. Sarah came to me by herself. None of the others were with her. When I touched her, I…I passed right through her as if she was a ghost. Was it a trick—just all in my mind?"

"What does your heart say? Trust your feelings. She's *your* daughter."

"It seemed to be her. Yes, it was Sarah. But how?"

"Astral projection—leaving one's body to travel from point A to point B."

"Sarah can't do that. She's a child."

"Age is irrelevant. It's possible that being in an environment saturated in psychic forces unlocked some latent abilities in her. It's even possible she did it without knowing—when asleep, for instance. For her, the whole incident would be like a dream."

"She tried to warn me about some danger, but the danger is obvious."

"Never assume anything is obvious. That's the first rule."

"Rules! There are always rules."

Clifford responded with a puzzled expression.

Jack's face went stern. "How do you get these powers?" Yes, fight fire with fire, that's what he'd do. And he planned to light a big match.

"I don't know, Jack. I don't want to know. That was Julia's domain. I'm just a researcher of myth and lore. I study the theory, not the practice. Perhaps if Julia were alive…" Clifford glanced down at the floor but quickly looked back at Jack. "You're right, my friend. You do have a problem, and it might be bigger than you can handle."

"But I have to handle it," Jack said. "No one else will."

"How did I know you were going to say that?"

"Maybe you *are* psychic, after all."

Both men sat in silence for a moment until Jack asked, "Do you have a name? Is there anyone who can teach me?"

"Teach you what?"

"A way to defeat Kahir and rescue my daughter."

"No," Clifford said, his voice shook some. "No, I can't."

"Please, Clifford, for Sarah's sake, for Anna's sake. I've run out of options. Please."

Reluctantly, Clifford agreed. "All right. I know someone who may be able to help you if you want to follow this course."

"I do," Jack said.

"I must warn you, the price could be great."

"I'll pay any amount. Money doesn't matter."

"The cost won't be in dollars," Clifford said, a harshness evident in his tone. "The price could be your life—or worse."

"Whatever it takes. Nothing is too much to bring my Sarah home."

"Then go see a man named Eric Sanders."

"Just point me in his direction," Jack said, rising to his feet. "I'll do the rest."

SIXTEEN

Jack refused to let the frustration of getting lost stop him. The almost mind-numbing repetition of driving this same stretch of road over and over had started to wear thin. He had followed Clifford's instructions carefully, but this far out of the city—out past the suburbs—the roads weren't so clearly marked.

He turned down a side road. "Damn," he muttered, seeing the stub of an old farm well. He recognized the broken brick and concrete from before. Jack continued on until the way widened enough for him to make another U-turn. After stopping and staring at that irritating patch of blacktop he had just traveled, he sighed and re-read Clifford's directions—again. He scratched his head. "It has to be here somewhere," Jack said to himself, tossing the paper onto the empty passenger seat and heading back to the main road.

Driving about halfway and over a small rise, a large house came into view, shocking Jack. There was no way on Earth he could have missed such a structure. This was the sixth time he'd driven past this exact spot—three times up, three times down—and yet, here he was, seeing a house. It had to be his mind playing tricks on him—a mirage. He expected it to fade away as he drew closer.

It didn't.

He slowly drove up the long driveway—his neck stretched over the steering wheel as he stared out the windshield, taking in the entire mansion. How could this be? There had been nothing in sight for miles. Nothing! Then, out of nowhere, there's a grand estate.

The landscaping was impeccable, with tall trees and perfect shrubbery. Baffled, Jack could have sworn he'd passed only a weed-ridden field. There were no fences or barriers to separate the unclaimed expanse from the pristine property, but straight lines marked where the flawless lawn met the weeds. The square of land had the appearance of having been cut out and dropped into the heart of the wild overgrowth.

Jack sat in his car, lost in his thoughts, then realized he was wasting precious time. He got out and approached the door. He lifted a fist to knock.

Before his knuckles had even the chance to touch the heavy wood, it swung open. *I hate when that happens.* It would be a nice change for him to at least go through the formality of knocking.

An Asian man stood in the doorway, sporting a light green, collarless shirt, which reminded Jack of the Nehru jackets of the '60s. The ends of his sleeves had fine gold embroidery, and the pattern continued up to his elbows. He wore matching pants, and his shoes were black cloth slippers. His face was round, with gentle features highlighted by a warm smile.

"Good afternoon, Mr. Railey," he said.

"Are you Eric Sanders?" Jack asked. Somehow, the man struck him as a natural extension of the grounds and manor.

"No, sir. He is the master. I am Quon, his humble servant."

Jack found himself taken aback by the subservient words, but he had to admire the loyalty. "May I—"

"See him? Mr. Railey." Quon opened the entrance much wider, giving Jack room to enter. "You are expected."

"Clifford Stuart phoned you?"

"We have no phone."

"Then how—?"

"Please, this way," Quon interrupted.

Inside, the man led Jack down a short hall off to the right. Quon stopped in front of a pair of sliding doors. He pulled them apart and crossed the threshold. The day's waning light seeped through the windows, filling the room with a pleasant glow.

The servant gestured to Jack, signaling him to enter. "Make yourself comfortable," he said. "You'll be seen shortly."

Jack stepped in as instructed and turned to thank Quon, but he was gone. Jack figured Eric Sanders must be an older man to need a servant, and with what Clifford had said about magic being a 'lifetime commitment,' it only served to support the assumption.

He moved farther into the space, which seemed inviting enough. There were several cushioned chairs spaced out from a large fireplace and a full bookshelf next to an oak table. Jack spotted a curious little statue on the tabletop. He had no idea what it depicted. Picking it up for a closer look, its weight surprised him. Its design embodied a cross between an octopus and a man. From the neck down, it had a human body, but the head was a complete octopus with its tentacles hanging down past the shoulders.

"Quon will bring us some tea," a firm voice said from behind.

Jack immediately returned the statuette to the table. A twinge of guilt hit him—he was a boy caught swiping a ten-cent candy bar.

Turning toward the voice, he hoped his face didn't reveal his astonishment. Instead of an elder, the man entering the room appeared to be about his own age. He had angular good looks, enhanced by a strong jawline. Steel-colored eyes, keen and observant, seemed to draw in everything around him. He had dark hair and a matching mustache, but his temples were solid gray, though the color didn't add any years to his appearance.

"Eric Sanders?" Jack asked.

"Yes, I'm Sanders," Eric said, motioning for Jack to take a nearby chair. Jack hesitated for a moment. Compared to the lavish mansion and expansive grounds, Sanders' outfit was simple: black pants paired with a white shirt, loosely unbuttoned at the collar. The long sleeves extended to his wrists, flaring slightly before the cuffs. It made Jack wonder if Sanders was deliberately trying to appear humble or if he simply didn't feel the need to impress.

Both men sat, and Quon returned with an aromatic brew. Jack felt anxious to question the man, but this was his home, and discretion seemed the better approach. He took the first cup, keeping a casual eye on his host, sensing this as a subtle test of his patience.

When Quon finished serving Eric, Sanders spoke. "Now, what brings you to my doorstep?"

"Clifford Stuart told me how to find you." Jack reflected on the frustrating journey to this house, passing empty fields along desolate roads—then it appeared just as he was on the verge of abandoning the search. Another test? "Clifford said you could help me."

"Help you how?"

"He said you have certain powers?"

"All have power—of some sort."

"Occult powers," Jack said bluntly.

"And you believe him?"

"If you'd asked me that a couple of days ago, I'd've answered with a definite no."

"And now?" Sanders took a sip of tea, studying Jack with quiet but intense interest.

"Given what I've seen, what I've experienced firsthand…" Jack fell silent, then added, "You have to help me."

"I heard your request. My question was, 'Help you how?'"

"I want you to teach me magic."

"Just like that? Teach you magic."

"You asked 'how'—that's how."

"It's unfortunate, but I have to disappoint you—there is no magic." Sanders paused. "Not in the way you think, anyway. And it cannot be *learned*."

"But I've seen it. It's real."

Sanders folded his hands together in his lap. "I'm confident you have. All I'm saying is that one must possess the power first. What is learned is focus…control. The development and discipline of the human will."

"I don't need a lesson in dogma. A man is targeting me. He's already made an attempt on my life. It's only a matter of time."

Sanders moved little in his seat, his eyes fixed with a penetrating gaze. "Maybe it's a warning—to scare you off."

"It won't work. If he's so knowledgeable, he already knows I'm coming for him. That's also only a matter of time. No, his attack was no idle threat."

"You're sure?"

"Sure as three dead people." Jack saw no change in the man's demeanor—Sanders sat silently and sipped his tea. "You can't be that isolated out here," Jack added. "You must have read about the deaths in the papers. And their killer is still out there."

"You speak of Abhaya Kahir. I tend to keep an eye open for specific types of situations."

"Those three people were part of a group dedicated to stopping him."

"That's not exactly true, Mr. Railey. It's what they told you."

"What do you know about it?"

Sanders did not answer Jack's question but rather asked his own: "Are you seeking a means to avoid Kahir's attacks?"

"Not quite," Jack said. "I want to beat him at his own game."

"Mr. Railey, that's somewhat troubling. What you ask of me is no game. And I assure you, Kahir doesn't consider it a game either."

"Neither do I," Jack said with a slight edge. "The man has my daughter. He's brought nothing but misery and sorrow to my family—my wife, my son. Not to mention all the other families he's hurt. Someone has to do something, and no one else wants to, or they're afraid to or don't know what to do. I've been in a lot of tough spots in my life, and I'm not the type to back down."

"I regret," Sanders said, "that you've wasted your time. I cannot help you."

"It's as easy as that for you. You can't help me—that's it."

"Control of the universal forces is not a trivial matter. To fan the internal spark, a feat few can accomplish, years—even decades—of training are required to first develop the self and the mind. Without such discipline, destruction by the very forces you seek to control would surely ensue."

"Clifford told me there are abilities we all possess that develop naturally for some people."

"He is correct. But most of the *people* you refer to are tormented by their gifts." Sanders leaned forward. "I'm talking about those with true talent, not individuals driven by fame and wealth. While pursuers of personal gain may have a meager amount of power, the ones with real strength don't crave notoriety. Most merely desire a normal life and to keep their special skills out of the public eye. Kahir *himself* does not parade his powers."

"What are you telling me? To give up all hope of saving my daughter? Of defending myself?"

"Don't mistake my words for callousness, Mr. Railey. My concern for your well-being is at the forefront of my decision. Even if I could show you the path to channeling the forces you wish, it would be your undoing. Although armed with that knowledge, Kahir would still overwhelm you. He is no novice."

"Sounds like you're suggesting I'd do better with a gun. Just blast him."

"No. A fool's errand. Such crude attempts are easily detected and thwarted."

"I'm done feeling helpless. I *will* get my daughter home with her mother—for both their sakes. And I will free the other children from Abhaya Kahir's control." Jack noticed a tiny change in Sanders' expression, but it lasted no more than a fraction of a second.

"To overcome a thing," Eric Sanders said, "you must understand a thing. And all things of nature have their positive and negative aspects—light, dark—order, chaos—good, evil. It is a balance. Tell me, Mr. Railey, do you believe in evil?"

"I believe men do evil things."

"Evil as a force—do you believe in evil as a corruptible force?"

"To be honest, I've never thought about it."

"Most men are born with a neutral disposition. But there are those few who tend toward one side or the other. Gandhi. Hitler. Both are modern examples of good and evil. Mahatma Gandhi radiated with the light of goodness. Adolph Hitler displayed the darkness. How would your science explain the difference between these two men?"

Jack offered no response.

"A most difficult question," Sanders said. "As children, both led comparable lives, but as they grew, the changes developed as the power at their core strengthened. Both men died in a similar manner within a mere three years of each other. That is the balance of the universe."

"Then Kahir can be defeated?"

"At a cost."

"I understand."

"Do you? Do you really?"

Jack shook his head. "Not even close."

"It takes courage to admit one's shortcomings. Perhaps I can instruct you after all. Are you truly willing to learn from me?"

"I am."

Sanders stared at Jack as if seeking something hidden beneath the surface. Jack sensed he was being sized up, weighed, and considered as though Sanders were drawing up a catalog of his faults and strengths.

"Be sure," Sanders said. "Once you begin this journey, you'll be forced to shed your ignorance, which, by its nature, has protected your sanity. Your world will change, never to be as it was. Are you certain you wish to proceed, Jack Railey?"

"I am," Jack repeated.

"Very well. We shall begin." With those words, a white glow came from Sanders and briefly surrounded Jack. Sanders rose to his feet, and, thinking he was to follow, Jack also stood.

Eric Sanders walked over to Jack and, with a sharp motion, plunged his fingertips into Jack's chest. Jack was stunned as Sanders' hand disappeared up to the wrist. There was no pain, just a tingling, warm sensation.

Sanders yanked his arm back. In his grasp was a four-limbed creature about the size of a small house cat, but far more slender. It was brown, hairless, with a yellow beak and two circular red eyes. The creature whined with a high squeal. Its three free, spindly limbs pushed and pulled at Sanders' grip.

"My, my, what do we have here?" Sanders said.

"What is it?" Jack asked, still shocked but now fixated on the thing, struggling to make sense of it all.

"I do not know—yet." Sanders waved his free hand, and a clear sphere formed around the creature, and it floated in midair. "I was aware of your…passenger the instant you stepped into my home."

Jack moved closer. The creature jumped toward him, bouncing off the interior of the sphere. Jack recoiled. "I…I remember that thing. I was on my way up to…" Jack's internal security kicked in. He couldn't tell Sanders about the office. "I was running an errand, and I saw something in a bush. I got distracted by a panhandler and turned away. When I looked again, it was gone. I figured I imagined it. Seems I was wrong." A sudden weakness hit Jack, making his legs shake. He collapsed into his chair.

"Quon," Sanders called out, and as quickly, the servant entered. "Bring our guest to an upper room. On the third level."

"The third level, sir? I assume Mr. Railey will be with us for a while?"

"Yes, he will."

Jack opened his mouth to speak, but no words came out. His strength slipped from his body.

"Conserve what energy you have left, Mr. Railey. Go with Quon and rest. We'll talk more later."

Quon helped Jack Railey walk to the upper floor as Sanders studied the bizarre little creature. Although he lacked an understanding of the beast's function, its mere presence—and its physical attachment to Railey—told him a great deal. Sanders had to weigh his next decision—many lives hung in the balance.

SEVENTEEN

Abhaya Kahir sat cross-legged in the meditation chamber. The room atop the tower was lit by nothing except the sunlight creeping along the outer fringe of the single pair of curtains. The only sounds came from the light rustle of fall winds swirling around the spire. Being the highest point of the house, the tower proved susceptible to the slightest breeze due to its age and construction. It shivered under even the meagerest gusts. The wind whistled past the windows and rattled the shingles on the roof. The wooden spindles creaked and groaned in surrender.

His eyes snapped open as a sharp pang of failure struck him. He had reached out with his mind, trying to connect with his spy, his secret ally—a creature created by ancient magics. Though the ritual left him dangerously weak and susceptible to attack, it had been the perfect infiltrator. But his spy had vanished. If it had completed its life cycle or been destroyed, he'd know. Yet, there was nothing—not a trace.

Through a dark rite, Kahir gave his little creature life for one, maybe two days—time enough to find its targeted host and attach. It would sustain itself on the host as it carried out its task. By its nature, the creature's existence would last only until it completed its purpose. But it survived far longer than Kahir had hoped, thriving on that brutish man whom Anthony Bane had recruited for their doomed cause. The man, Jack Railey, became an unknowing pawn, supplying Kahir with the means to further his plans. The creature's endurance stood as a surprising testament to the man's strength. It drew from his energy, tapping the currents of life that flowed within him, constantly renewing itself. Without the fool's vitality, the creature would have weakened—a slow but inexorable decline, one Kahir should have sensed, but didn't.

Kahir closed his eyes again, centering his will, focusing his awareness inward as the possibility of outside interference returned—a sensation that had haunted him for weeks. His enemies numbered many, but none were bold enough to thwart him. Whoever was meddling did so from the shadows, concealed—for now. The only question was whether this unseen foe would remain hidden or draw him into a confrontation.

A knock sounded from one of the two doors that led into the inner sanctum.

Kahir stayed silent as Rajak entered.

"Pardon my intrusion, Master, but the children are about to depart for the gathering. Should I inform them that there will be a service on their return?"

Kahir looked over at the second door, which connected the room to the sacramental chamber. After a brief pause, Kahir said, "No, not this evening."

Rajak's brow rose in surprise. "Are you certain? It has been days since—"

"Don't question me!"

"Forgive my assumption, Master."

"Instruct Shawn to join me," Kahir said. Shawn had proved useful as a hostage to keep his grandfather, Benjamin Abrams, at bay—a pawn, a piece to be used and then thrown aside. And with Benjamin dead, Shawn's role had changed. He possessed raw, untapped power, no doubt inherited from Benjamin. Kahir had respected Benjamin's cunning and strength, but for someone who hadn't lived the years, he also found the man's arrogance particularly galling.

"On his return from the gathering?" Rajak asked.

"No, Shawn will not be going with the others."

After his customary bow, Rajak pulled the door closed.

Kahir's gaze lingered even after Rajak left. He listened as the servant's footsteps faded down the outer corridor. Silence finally settled, and his thoughts drifted, slipping away from the present—away to a time when he had been just a boy, born Rohan Bhat, no older than the children who dwelled within these walls. A time in India, two centuries ago, when everything had begun.

He lived in the tranquil village of Vashisht, nestled in the heart of the Kullu Valley and surrounded by the Himalayan mountains. His family led a humble existence, crafting and selling pottery to their neighbors and to religious pilgrims. But Rohan believed he was different. While others in the community accepted their lives as they were, he always sought more. His intelligence pushed him to think beyond the confines of the village, driven by a hunger that outgrew the prayers and stories his parents passed down—lessons that no longer satisfied him. The world outside the village, with its ancient temples and lost secrets, called to him.

His chance came the day he met an old mystic, a wandering sage, who spoke of deeper truths—things buried in the dark corners of reality. The sage differed from others Rohan had come across. He sought neither wealth nor position, but power—secret knowledge he eagerly shared. He saw potential in Rohan, a rare strength, and took him under his wing.

Rohan showed an eagerness to learn, full of questions and brimming with ideas. But the magic the sage taught him wasn't about simple spells or charms. It was older, a raw essence underlying the universe itself. The sage instructed him in prana, the life energy flowing through all creation. Rohan learned to see it. He could feel it, and eventually bend it to his will.

The path wasn't easy. The rituals were complicated, and his body lacked the strength to handle the power at first. But as time passed, the magic became more natural. Rohan began to see things differently. Where he only saw ordinary people and objects, he now perceived the invisible waves of energy connecting all things. Everything around him —the trees, the people, the stones, the water, the earth beneath his feet, even the air moving in and out of his lungs—seemed to hum with life in a way he'd never noticed before. His world ceased to be a realm of static, fixed elements—everything was alive.

At the age of nineteen, Rohan sat, legs crossed, in a desolate temple deep in the valley, encircled by incense and silence. The sage brought him an ancient scroll, yellowed and frayed along the edges, and instructed Rohan to study the ritual within. It was then the sage revealed a startling truth. Magic wasn't just about control—it demanded sacrifice. Power didn't come freely—it had to be taken.

What Rohan didn't realize until much later was that his mentor hadn't been teaching him magic out of any noble desire to pass on his wisdom. The sage saw him as a simple tool, a way to extend his own life.

The ritual Rohan was learning wasn't to empower him—it was a trap. As the boy's potential developed, the sage's scheme fell into place. He intended to drain Rohan's prana—waiting for the right moment to steal it and prolong his own existence. But when the sage initiated the final incantation, Rohan proved too clever and reversed the flow, turning the magic back onto him. The sage's eyes widened in shock and pain as Rohan siphoned off his life energy, his very essence. The old man tried to fight, but it was too late. Rohan stripped the sage of everything. He stole his strength and drained his vitality. A lifetime of arcane knowledge was now his. Rohan left his teacher nothing more than a lifeless shell.

In that instant, Rohan embraced a force beyond that of a mere mortal. His body surged with stolen power, and magic, once distant and unknowable, was suddenly an extension of his own will. He had killed for the first time—not out of malice, but out of necessity.

His abilities progressed quickly, but with each skill gained, a part of him changed. Friends and family, the valley and the village—everything became foreign to him. As he absorbed more magic, tiny bits of his humanity slipped away. People he'd known since childhood were little better than strangers. The years went by, and those around him aged—he did not. Whispers of Rohan's unholy longevity spread until the day his neighbors, gripped by fear and suspicion, sought to drive him out, and he fled for his life.

Rohan spent the next two decades in Kaza, a village high in the mountains, far from the place of his birth. It required time and patience, but he found contentment in his new life. He did his best to hide his slow aging, blending in with the locals and enjoying the simple pleasures of anonymity. But despite his efforts, the fear was ever-present that his secret could be revealed.

One day, a man arrived from Vashisht. Though much older than Rohan, the man remembered knowing him as a boy—but back then, Rohan had been several years his senior. Shocked, then terrified by Rohan's unnatural appearance, he threatened to expose him as a rakshasa—a shape-shifting demon. Rohan pleaded, begging him not to destroy what he had struggled so long to build. Unable to convince the man, Rohan lost control and cast the spell to absorb his prana, draining him into a shriveled husk. As he withered, Rohan grew younger.

In a panic, Rohan dragged the corpse into his house, set the structure on fire, and fled. He prayed the blaze destroyed enough evidence to make the villagers believe the body was his. Rohan Bhat abandoned his second life and, from that point forward, adopted the name Vivek Patel.

With his new identity, Vivek departed India and renewed his studies of the dark arts. He moved across the continents seeking a greater understanding—studying ancient rituals, forbidden texts, and learning how to shape life itself.

And the cycle repeated—new names, new lives, the next, just as hollow and fleeting as the last. His soul, long eroded by the relentless consumption of magic, turned colder with every passing identity. Each one was a broken fragment of a life he no longer remembered—or cared to. He moved through the centuries like a predator, feeding on the fragile souls in his charge, yet growing emptier and more monstrous. The weight of his immortality crushed any remnants of his former self—a boy named Rohan Bhat.

Kahir's focus shifted to the present—the echoes of his past faded away. He sat in silence, contemplating the cold, unyielding span of the last two centuries—a trail forged that day he first tasted the power that had shaped his life. But enough of idle reflection—there were other pressing matters at hand. Enemies remained, and one demanded his immediate attention: Thaddeus Blackburn, a man who had been a thorn in his side from the start—the pompous fool. Blackburn was an obstacle that begged for removal—methodically, carefully. He had somehow escaped one attempt. However, without his creature, Kahir needed to wait until his strength reached its peak. Then, Blackburn could be dealt with. Kahir would allow none to stand in the way of his plans—not now, not ever.

And then there was the girl. Like her father, she held a strong life force. If he employed restraint, he could perform many harvest rituals, sustaining himself for more than just a single feeding. Perhaps someday, he could train her, thereby increasing tenfold the amount of prana he could reap, but he would not repeat the mistake made by his mentor.

A knock drew Kahir to the next task at hand.

"Please, enter."

"You wanted to see me?" Shawn asked, stepping into the room with a cautious gaze.

"I have been watching you, my son. You are very important to me."

Kahir's lips curled into a slow, cruel smile as he reveled in Benjamin Abrams' final defeat. Shawn, his grandson, came to him of his own free will.

EIGHTEEN

Jack stood alone in an old forest. To his left and right were clusters of barren trees—all twisted and lifeless. The bark of several had been peeled away, revealing the gray, dry core underneath. Before him, a path stretched forward into the endless horizon, while behind him, the darkness went as far as he could see.

He'd been walking for as long as he could remember. Or at least, he thought he'd been walking. No. No. Not walking—running. Something horrible had been following him—chasing him.

Then laughter echoed in the stale air, radiating from all sides. The sound made his heart pound as he ran anew. Ahead, the path continued. He didn't know when or where it might end—only that veering off meant certain disaster.

From up in the trees came a low-pitched growl. There, Jack spotted a hideous creature with glowing brown eyes. It kept to the treetops, tracking him. Jack ran faster, but the thing leaped from branch to branch, easily keeping up with him.

Jack opened his mouth to shout—nothing.

Up ahead, someone called out his name. Though the voice wasn't familiar, Jack knew it was there to help him—to guide him.

"Mr. Railey." The voice sounded so far away. "Mr. Railey." Jack's body shook. “Mr. Railey, it is time for you to wake.” A hand pushed on his shoulder. The shaking brought Jack out of his nightmare.

Jack’s eyelids eased open. He blinked twice, waiting for the fuzzy image to come into focus. Quon stood bedside, holding a glass of clear liquid.

Jack sat up and gave a slight moan as his head throbbed. His mouth and tongue were thickly coated with a tart paste. His stomach was queasy.

“Drink this,” Quon said, handing Jack the tall, half-filled glass. “It will help you regain your strength.”

Jack cautiously took a sip. Whatever the liquid was, it wasn’t water. The lukewarm brew tasted both sweet and bitter. In one swallow, he drank the rest and handed the empty glass back to Quon. Seconds later, Jack felt better.

“What was in that stuff?” he asked.

“An herbal extract, mostly.”

“Mostly?”

Quon gave the man a sly smile. “I set out some things for you to wear. I’m a good judge of size, but if I am in error, do not hesitate to inform me.”

Jack didn’t realize he’d been stripped down to his underwear until that moment. “What’s going on here?” he asked, shocked by his lack of clothing.

“It wouldn’t do to have you sleeping in your street clothes, now would it?”

“Sleep?” Jack checked his wrist—his watch had also been removed.

“It’s on the nightstand,” Quon told him.

Jack caught sight of the watch face. “It’s only been an hour,” he said.

Quon crossed the room and yanked open the curtains. Jack’s eyes widened at the sight of sunshine pouring in. At this time of day, the sky should be getting darker. “I slept through the night?”

Quon smiled. “You slept through two nights.”

“Two nights? What have you people done to me?” Jack stood up, but much too fast for his own good. Becoming dizzy, he eased himself to the edge of the bed.

"We did nothing to you, Mr. Railey," Quon replied. "I will leave any explanation to the master. Please dress."

Slowly, Jack rose and approached the chair with the folded pile of new clothing. He drew the shirt cut from a silky material from the stack. He knew it would be loose-fitting. The design reminded him of a colored karate gi. "I'm supposed to wear this? Where are my clothes?"

"They have been laundered and stored. These clothes will be more comfortable for the work at hand."

"Work?"

"You came seeking answers. But the truth is never easy. It always comes with a cost. Please." Quon handed Jack the matching bottoms. "Your time here is short. You must not waste another moment." Quon started for the door. "Wait here until I return."

"Uhmm, before you go." Jack shrugged. "You did say two nights. Where do I…"

"Yes, I understand." Quon pointed to a second single door Jack had mistaken for a closet. "You will find other amenities within. Soap and a washcloth and towel if you wish to freshen up. A fresh toothbrush and paste. Feel free, as you wish." With that, the man left Jack alone.

After relieving himself and a quick cleanup, Jack took under a minute to get dressed. As he'd expected, the clothes were loose, but that must have been by design. The seams and hems were perfectly aligned, as they should be for a well-fitted piece of clothing. Jack finished tying the drawstring of his pants, then went over and tested the window. The paint along the edges sealed it shut. Even so, a thirty-foot drop led straight to the ground.

Jack returned to his bed and sat. His training had him scoping out the room. It was simple: a bed, a nightstand, a lamp, and a wooden chair. The window was stuck tight, leaving a single way in or out, giving him no means of retreat. The half-bath, however convenient, wouldn't make much of a stronghold. He'd literally be boxing himself in—not the sort of place he liked to find himself. Something seemed off about all of this—he had nothing but Clifford's word that he could trust this Sanders character or that he could even help him.

Jack stopped himself and cleared his mind of doubt. He had nowhere else to go if he wanted to beat Kahir and make his family whole.

Several minutes passed. Quon said he'd return, but he never said when. Thinking that he had been forgotten, Jack walked to the bedroom entrance and opened it.

"Hello," he called out. The words echoed through the long corridor. Jack glanced back into his empty room. Quon's instructions about waiting rattled around in his head, but Quon also said his time was brief, and Jack intended not to waste any of it.

Jack ventured into the hallway and blinked in disbelief. The number of doors was overwhelming—far more than seemed possible.

"Hello?" Jack repeated. The wood floor was cold against his bare feet. Quon had neglected to provide shoes with the fancy duds. On purpose, he wondered.

He headed down the hall, hoping to find the stairs. He remembered Sanders telling Quon to bring him up to the third floor. And by the view from his bedroom, Sanders' servant had done just that.

But this hallway had no windows, and more disturbingly, it also lacked stairs—at least, no visible ones. Maybe behind one of the doors, he hoped. Jack extended a hand toward the nearest brass knob but pulled away, not wanting to barge in on anyone by mistake.

He knocked and waited for an answer.

None came.

Jack twisted the knob and yanked it open.

What he saw defied reason. He had to look twice. He was standing at the entrance to the very space Quon had brought him to sleep—the one he'd just left.

At first, he assumed it was a different room, arranged in a similar manner. But on the nightstand by the bed was his wristwatch.

Jack looked out into the corridor, confirming that he had indeed passed several other doors. He hadn't taken any corners, nor was it possible for him to have gone in a circle.

No, Jack tried to convince himself—*this can't be the same place!* He went inside. Hurrying over, he picked up the silver timepiece and a shudder of disbelief ran through him. On the back were inscribed two dates: June 12, 1980 and April 27, 1985. Somehow, this was where he had awoken a short while ago.

He stepped out into the hall, moved one door to the right, and swung it wide. Again—the same room.

The next three doors made absolutely no difference at all.

Jack entered and sat on the bed.

There, he waited for Quon to return.

Jack followed Quon down the staircase, feeling an odd sense of disorientation. He had a vague memory of going up these same stairs, but now they felt off—like they were leading him in a different direction as if the layout of the house had shifted. Maybe it was his imagination playing tricks, but considering what had happened in his room, there was no doubt—this house was weird.

They arrived at what he guessed was the main level and entered a modest chamber, sparsely furnished with a low-seated table and a woven mat lying flat.

"Please wait here," Quon told Jack. "The master will join you." Quon left. Jack watched the door as it closed.

"Alone again," he muttered under his breath. But this time, he decided to stay put and hope Sanders would be along soon. Barely three minutes passed, and the door reopened. Eric stepped in, carrying a white candle.

"Good day, Mr. Railey."

"Forget the Mr. Railey stuff. The name's Jack."

"Very well—Jack. I trust you had a pleasant rest."

A multitude of images swept over Jack as if he were on the verge of remembering. "Pleasant? That's rather hard to say." He still found it difficult to fathom that he'd slept for two days. Then the memory of that creature and his overwhelming weakness finally resurfaced. "What was that thing you…you pulled out of my chest?"

"There will be an opportunity for questions later," Sanders replied. "Please, sit on the mat."

Jack complied and sat cross-legged. The mat provided some cushion from the wooden floor, though not much. Sanders lit the candle and centered it in front of Jack.

“See how the wick burns?” Sanders said. “See nothing but the flame —no room, no table, no candle.”

Jack turned his head to Sanders. But before he spoke, Sanders said, “Do not look at me. Look at the flame. Ignore everything else.”

While sitting, Jack sensed Sanders’ departure—he was on his own. His stare fixed on the flicker and its bright orange glow. He’d do anything to save his daughter. He’d get Sarah home, no matter what. And with that thought, his mind drifted—how easily distractions could grab hold.

He started over. Jack gazed into the flame—only the flame: the bright and melding colors—the rhythmic motion—even a bit of warmth. The smell of burning wax met his nose. The fire floated, suspended in midair. It encompassed everything.

A slight cramp in his right leg snapped Jack back to his surroundings. His entire body tensed as the hard floor pressed up against his thighs, a dull ache settled into his knees from sitting, and a tightness constricted his shoulders and neck.

“Relax, Jacky-boy.” He cringed, realizing he had spoken aloud.

Jack moved his leg slightly to relieve the pain, then stretched his spine and adjusted his weight to compensate for his position. He mentally commanded himself to focus, but then realized his attention had shifted from the candlelight to the very act of trying to concentrate, which had now become the distraction itself.

He relaxed, allowing his mind to quiet. Jack let go of all thoughts. The glow seemed to expand.

Anna popped into his head—her smile, her bright green eyes, her blonde hair framing her pretty face. It took some willpower, but he forced her image away and returned to the flame. He’d never realized how tough it was to stop thinking about her.

Try as he might to regain control, other diversions pushed into his consciousness, clamoring to be noticed. Insignificant matters of everyday life: changing the oil in the Firebird, doing yard work, cleaning the garage—all the ordinary things put off since arriving home to find Sarah gone. Jack had always prided himself on his discipline. It was disconcerting to realize how much trouble he found keeping his focus on a single task for more than a few minutes. He'd heard that a housefly has an attention span of two seconds. But considering flies live less than a month, a second was a long time. It irritated him to think that, in the grand scheme of things, something as trivial as a fly could do a better job than he could.

Jack's determination doubled. His eyes hardened on the candle as he zeroed in on the many shades of color—the oranges, the yellows, the slight blues. He forced himself to be absorbed by the flame.

The fire exploded, engulfing Jack in a swirling vortex. The sudden eruption sent a wave of terror through him, scattering his concentration. Instinctively, Jack threw his hands up to shield his face. When he lowered them, he saw the lit candle still on the table, as it had been from the start. His fear quickly vanished, replaced by a moment of peace, even euphoria. Jack took a deep breath and refocused. Once more, the blaze surrounded him. He and the scalding fire merged, but there was no pain. His body had become fluid, yet it remained intact.

Within the inferno, a humanoid shape floated toward Jack. A burning hand drew near and touched him. Jack reverted to flesh and blood. "You can take a break now," Sanders said.

"How long has it been?" Jack asked.

"That doesn't matter. You should stand. Stretch your legs."

Jack heeded the man's advice but found walking painful. He stood and managed a few short steps. After hobbling for a bit, his legs responded to his commands.

"What the hell was that?"

"To put it plainly," Sanders said, "you passed my test."

"Test? I didn't come here to be tested."

"You came here for my help. You asked me to teach you how to defeat Kahir. And I told you I cannot give you power—you must already possess it."

Jack studied Sanders, not understanding what he was saying.

"You have that power," Sanders explained, "and you use it more than you know—be it on a subconscious level." The man walked over to the candle. It had burned down to a fourth of its original height. "This exercise was designed to break down any innate barriers and release your abilities. If I may be direct, I had concerns that your strength would be locked at its current state—that you'd have but a minimum of success. It's clear to me now that I underestimated you. You have great potential, Jack Railey."

"You said I use these powers subconsciously, but nothing like that fire has ever happened to me. I'm sure I'd remember."

"Your abilities are likely triggered in situations of self-preservation."

Jack recalled all those narrow escapes where he'd barely gotten out with his ass in one piece. When things were at their darkest, something inevitably pulled his bacon out of the fire—a stray bullet blowing the tire of a terrorist's car, causing it to go out of control, or a wrecking ball breaking free from its cable and crushing Thaddeus Blackburn's Bentley. "I figured it was just blind luck," he said.

"There's no such thing as luck, Jack—merely the manipulation of forces and the direction of energies." Sanders gestured Jack toward the door. "What some people call magic is the controlling of events with the force of one's will.

"Clifford Stuart said the same, but it can't be that simple."

"Can't it? It's a matter of degree that makes a miracle differ from what you regard as good luck." Both men stepped from the room. "'Ignorance is bliss.' Those words hold great truth. Be prepared, my friend—be prepared to lose your innocence. The way you perceive your world is about to change. For better or for worse, I cannot predict."

"Innocence?" Jack couldn't remember when he last saw himself as innocent. "I… I'm not sure I understand."

"Clear your mind. You'll have your answer soon enough." Sanders gave Jack an honest grin. That was the first time since he'd met this extraordinary man that Jack saw him smile. "Come," Sanders continued, "Quon has seen to our dinner. Among his other skills, Quon is an excellent cook."

Dinner? The word caught Jack off guard. He glanced over at the room. The day was gone—it didn't seem possible.

NINETEEN

The next morning, Jack came down from his sleeping quarters just shy of ten o'clock. He had some trouble walking the long hallways and briefly got lost, but eventually, by trial and error, he found the first floor. In the kitchen, Quon served him an aromatic tea and a cinnamon roll. After consuming the breakfast, Quon led Jack to the study, where Sanders stood over a table, searching through a pile of books, some of which appeared as though they would crumble to dust at the slightest touch.

"Did you sleep well?" Sanders asked, not looking up.

"I did."

"Did you dream?" Sanders asked immediately.

"I don't dream," Jack replied.

"We all dream," Sanders said, finally facing Jack. "You might not recall them, but think—did you dream?"

An eerie fragment seeped to the surface of Jack's consciousness. "I—maybe—I'm not sure."

"Try to remember," Sanders said in a serious tone. "I'll have Quon provide you with a journal and pen. You'll use them to record any images, impressions, or feelings each morning. Regardless of how strange or insignificant, try to recall as much detail as possible. Your initial recollections will be vague, but with practice…"

Jack nodded.

"Also, I let you sleep in today, giving your body and mind more time to adjust. But your stay here is limited, so that comfort is no longer conducive to your training. Quon will wake you at 5 a.m. from now on. You'll eat a light meal, then we'll begin the day's work. I presume you are up to it."

"I've had to do worse things," Jack replied.

Sanders' eyebrow raised slightly. "Then let us proceed."

Jack followed Sanders to the same room he had been in yesterday. As he approached the door, a sense of apprehension hit him. It wasn't fear exactly, but an uneasiness that stirred deep inside him.

When the two men entered, Jack found three candles on the table already lit.

"Sit," Sanders said.

Jack obeyed without question.

"As you did yesterday, focus on the flame. But only the center flame. While the others may prove distracting, see just the one—feel it—merge with it." After that brief instruction, Sanders departed.

The bang of the closing door caused Jack to flinch. He looked around the empty chamber, trying to avoid the flickering light. His heart raced, hammering against his ribs, and despite his resolve, a whisper of doubt crept under his skin, planting seeds of hesitation. His gut was telling him to run, but he had never feared an adversary before, and today wouldn't be the day to start.

Jack steeled himself and lifted his eyes to the three licks of fire. He focused on the middle candle, ignoring the other two, but seconds later, they moved into his line of sight. Every time he forced them away, they slipped back, no matter how hard he struggled—each failure deepened his frustration. He battled on with every ounce of will. Beads of sweat formed on his forehead. Jack's strain merged the image of the three into one, but he heard Sanders' words replay: *Only the center flame.*

Jack's gaze tightened on the one candle, but a lost memory surfaced, pulling his attention away. Six-year-old Jack found a baby bird dying in the backyard, having fallen from its nest. He gently picked it up and carried it toward the house, hoping his father could help. But by the time Jack got to the backdoor, the bird no longer moved. He stood there, staring at the lifeless creature until his father came out. The man explained the delicate nature of life, but Jack couldn't understand. The concept of anything so fragile, so fleeting, was too big for his young world. Together, they buried the bird next to the tree where it had fallen. Jack wanted the baby bird to be near its home. It was Jack Railey's first experience with death. He wished they had all been as peaceful.

He quickly refocused on the single candle, noticing the way its flame flickered and shivered between the other two. Its light and heat pressed in on him, each wave of warmth grew more intense. The air thickened with raw power that swarmed over his body—infusing his skin, his muscles, his bones. His mind swirled, distorted by the overwhelming force, until, in a sudden burst, all became clear—he was the flame—the flame was him.

In that instant, Jack reached out with his inner being, touching the very core of the flame's essence—its untamed energy. The fear from earlier seemed distant—a fear of losing himself, of losing who he was, what he was. But as his consciousness stretched outward, his sense of self began to expand. He understood, with quiet insight, that he was becoming something more. A peace settled over him.

"Good," Sanders said from behind him. "You've crossed the threshold into a new world."

Jack was surprised at Sanders' sudden appearance. "But my mind wandered," he admitted. "I couldn't focus. I tried, but I didn't last for more than a few seconds."

"Come," Sanders said. "You'll need to keep your strength up. At this stage, it's important to fuel your body. In time, you'll be able to tap into the universal energy reserves. But for the moment, Quon has prepared you a small morsel."

"So soon? I can give it another shot. I'll do better."

"That won't be necessary."

"It *is* necessary. I barely started."

"You started four hours ago. Please stand."

Jack didn't believe Sanders, but the terrible stiffness in his legs convinced him otherwise. "I'm ready then?"

Sanders shook his head. "You still have a long way to go, and the path becomes increasingly difficult. Do not confuse a step with the journey. You have learned to connect with your inner spark. Now you must learn control. We'll reconvene here in sixty minutes."

"Why wait? I—"

"Your training shall continue—later," Sanders interrupted. "Eat the meal Quon offers you, then rest as you see fit until summoned. Use this respite for yourself, Jack Railey."

True to his word, Sanders returned an hour later to find Jack in the study, reading one of the many volumes he had come across. Jack had considered an afternoon nap, but he wasn't the least bit tired.

Jack closed the book. The text was handwritten, yet very easy to read. It told the legends of Atlantis and its eventual demise when a group of wizards tried summoning the Dark Ones—and to their horror—succeeded.

"Not quite movie material," Jack said, setting the book down on a side table. "But a good piece of fiction."

"Fiction?" Sanders said, lightly touching the cover. "Of course." The study went silent, as if Sanders had something else to say. "Are you ready to continue?" he asked instead.

Jack nodded.

They both moved through the mansion—neither spoke. The room where Jack had spent the morning was closed, but Sanders signaled for him to advance.

Without hesitation, Jack grabbed the crystal knob, turned it, and pulled open the door. As he stepped inside the chamber, he diverted his eyes. The brightness was overwhelming.

Seconds later, his vision adjusted. The number of burning candles seemed uncountable, and the heat poured over his skin. He looked back at the entrance. Sanders remained outside, yet his voice filled the air.

"You know what to do," Sanders said. The words didn't sound like they came from the hall but from all around.

"One candle—one flame," Jack answered,

Sanders replied with the closing of the chamber door.

Jack settled onto the floor mat, squinting against the bright light of the closest candle. His body tensed, fighting the urge to look away. He refused to let his attention wander, determined to stay centered and maintain his focus in the stillness of the room.

But despite his best efforts, the subtle pull of neglected memories transported him to the day Sarah was born. Jack remembered the swell of pride as he watched the tiny infant peacefully sleeping in her bassinet. Along with the immense love for his newborn daughter, the doubts and fears of his new responsibility for this precious little life also resurfaced. And those feelings led him to the birth of his boy. In the hospital room, while Anna nursed Justin, she told him how happy she was to give him a son—he'd never imagined such joy.

Anger—and even hatred—suddenly surged within Jack, anger aimed at Kahir, the man who had torn his family apart. Jack fought to suppress the emotions, drawing on pure willpower. He forced out everything except the flame, and in that moment, a silent explosion erupted inside him. A rush of raw energy fused with him so quickly he could not resist, igniting within him, merging with his soul—a fire burning in his heart and mind. Jack Railey and the fire became one.

The chamber door opened and Sanders entered.

"How long?" Jack asked.

"Two hours."

"Just two? Why stop me? I can keep going."

"That may be, but at this time, it would not serve you. You must progress to the next level." Jack started to rise, but Sanders gestured for him to remain seated. The intense candlelight gave Sanders a brilliant aura.

"Select one candle," Sanders said. "Face it. Concentrate." After a brief silence, as if sensing Jack had properly prepared himself, he added, "Now, extinguish the flame."

Jack turned toward Sanders. "Excuse me?"

"Stay on task. Return to the flame. Just the flame. Use your power to snuff it out."

"I can't do that."

"Yes, you can. The strength is within you. Release it. Accept the flame. Make it an extension of yourself, like an arm or a leg. Command it—it will obey your orders."

Jack's gaze fell back to the candle, his jaw tightening as he pushed aside his skepticism. The orange glow flickered, and the strain made his eyes water, but he kept steady, refusing to break. As Sanders had instructed, he merged with the fire. He commanded it to go out. His brow furrowed as he struggled to smother it, mentally shouting, *Go out, go out!*

"Relax," Sanders said. "You're trying too hard. It takes little effort to raise a hand or move your fingers. The same should be true for the flame. Find your inner peace."

Jack inhaled deeply, stilling his body, quieting his mind—pushing out all distractions, dismissing every emotion. He willed the flame to die. The room plunged into darkness in a puff.

"Focus!" Sanders called out from the void. "Only one candle." The wicks relit themselves.

Jack stilled himself and gave the command once more, and once more dark engulfed both men.

"That will be enough for today," Sanders said over the creaking door. Light seeped in from the hallway.

Jack caught the shift in the man's tone, marked by disappointment—it wasn't the reaction he'd expected. What he had done would have been considered a miracle. "I put the candles out," Jack asserted.

"A simple trick," Sanders said. "You do not have the luxury of tricks. To hone your abilities to a fine edge—that is the true objective. Not to use them in a random, haphazard manner as you have in the past. If we had more time..." Sanders sighed. "Perhaps I was wrong to undertake your training."

"But the candles—I put out all the candles."

"You do not understand—you failed." Sanders stepped from the chamber. His back to Jack, he said, "The day is over. If you need anything, please ask Quon. I must rethink our arrangement." Sanders left Jack alone.

Night fell quickly. Jack tried to sleep but found it impossible. He had borrowed the book on Atlantis from the study, which he had started reading earlier in the day, hoping it would be a distraction. But when he opened it, the words were gone, replaced with a mishmash of squiggly lines and symbols he didn't recognize.

From his pillow, Jack stared up into the darkness. In the silence, he'd spent the past hour reflecting on Sanders' criticism of the afternoon's fiasco. He'd be a fool to deny it—Sanders' words hit the mark, leaving no room for a misunderstanding. He had failed, and though that failure was hard to swallow, it was the truth.

Jack sat up, got out of bed, and walked over to the window. Outside, the moon hung full in the sky, and except for one small cloud, the stars twinkled on an ebony backdrop. Justin had received a telescope last Christmas, and tonight offered the perfect opportunity to use it. Doubt tugged at Jack. It appeared now that he'd been wrong in coming here. But what else could he do? he asked himself. Someone like Kahir lay beyond his experience. As for that matter, so did this Eric Sanders. Neither man fit into his normal scheme of things.

Normal or not, Jack knew what he had to do. He slipped out of his quarters, walked down the hall, and descended the stairs. The house was creepy enough in daylight, but doubly so at night, and he feared he'd get lost in the dark. The mansion had never been easy to navigate—rooms seemed to shift locations, and hallways twisted in ways that had him going in circles. But to his shock, upon reaching the bottom step, Jack stood in front of the candle room.

Thinking he must be mistaken, Jack hit the wall switch. The sudden shine stung his eyes, but within seconds, the familiar sight came into view. Jack peered through the open door. A wedge of light revealed the space was just as he had left it. He was relieved that Sanders hadn't ordered Quon to clean up.

For a moment, Jack studied the candles—he lacked the means to light them. Not willing to give up, he made his way to the kitchen. In a cupboard, he came across a box of blue-tipped stick matches—exactly what he needed. On his return, he guessed it would take at least ten minutes to get the candles lit. Sanders had done it in an instant—and without the use of matches.

Jack's estimate was spot-on. He sparked the last wick and took his place on the mat. Locking onto the first flame, he watched it flicker and sway. He inhaled slowly through his nose—the air thick with the scent of burning wax—and exhaled through his mouth. With every breath, he focused deeper, narrowing his will to a point. Jack spoke no words but aimed a solitary thought into the burning light: *Go out.*

As before, the room fell dark. Frustrated and surrounded on all sides by pitch black, Jack groped along the floor and retrieved the box of blue-tips. He struck a match and relit the nearest candle. Jack looked out over all the charred wicks and exhaled a deep sigh. He relit each and every one.

Calming himself, Jack retook his mat. He cleared his mind and saw but a single flame—he became that flame. Then, as if by a gentle breeze, the flame flickered and vanished in a streamer of white smoke. The ease of it surprised him—like blinking an eye.

Jack directed his attention to another candle, and with no real effort, that flame also went out. He moved on to the next flame and the next and the next. Each flame disappeared on his command. Each one at a time and on cue.

Feeling a presence, Jack said, "You were right. It's like the flames are a part of me."

"They are," Sanders responded. "Everything is part of everything else." Sanders gave a slight wave of his hand, and the chamber door opened. "Return to your bed. Tomorrow will prove most trying."

"You've decided to continue my training then?"

"No. I have not. *You have* decided to continue."

TWENTY

Jack woke thinking he should be tired after his long night, but he was surprised to find himself oddly refreshed. On the stand next to the bed, he found the blank book and a pen. He remembered Sanders' instructions to record his dreams.

He paused to recall any impressions he may have had. Seconds later, a lone image surfaced—faint at first, like something glimpsed through fog. That was all. Jack recorded it as best he could. An enormous gray blob. Maybe it was an animal. Cold eyes also emerged. He wrote that down too, then returned the book to the nightstand.

A knock echoed from the door.

"Enter," Jack called out.

Quon came in carrying a large towel, an unopened bar of soap, and a small bottle of what appeared to be shampoo. "I'm glad to see you well, sir," he said.

"It's Jack. I never got used to that 'sir' stuff, even during…" Jack cut himself off, but a tiny smile formed on Quon's lips as if he knew the unspoken words.

"As you wish." He walked over to the bed and unloaded his arms. "You'll find a shower on the second floor. Please feel free." The man turned to leave.

"Quon," Jack said, stopping the servant. "Have you worked for Sanders long?"

"Worked? I have been with the master for many years. Though I admit, it seems barely yesterday since I crossed the threshold of this house."

"What can you tell me about him?"

"I could tell you much, but I won't. If you have questions, I suggest you speak with him directly."

"I meant no disrespect…"

"And I perceived none. Eric Sanders values his privacy, and I have always honored his wishes." Quon turned. "If you'll excuse me, I have other tasks to see to."

"Of course," Jack said, wondering what secrets the servant kept about Eric Sanders. "Hold on, Quon, don't go just yet… A strange thing happened last night."

"Which was…?"

"You're gonna call me crazy, but I usually have a bit of trouble finding my way around this house. And last night…" Jack shook his head. "Like I said, you'll think I'm crazy." He rubbed the back of his neck. "I headed down to a training room, and I found it right off."

"That hardly sounds crazy," Quon said.

"You don't understand. I always have trouble making my way through the halls and corridors, but last night I ended up exactly where I wanted to be."

"That's quite simple to explain," Quon said with a slight grin. "The house likes you."

Quon left, leaving Jack more confused, but to Jack, in this place, that was par for the course.

After a shower and a bite to eat, Jack walked alone down the hall and opened the door to the candle room. To his surprise, all the candles were gone. Not one stood where nearly a hundred had been in the early morning hours. He stepped into the chamber. His mat had been removed too. A fear filled him. Had Sanders decided to discontinue his training after all? Was this his way of telling him it was over?

"I reasoned you'd do better with a change of scenery," Sanders said from the doorway.

Relief engulfed Jack. "You're probably right."

Led by Sanders, they moved to a different room on the far side of the hall. The room had a glass ceiling that allowed the sunshine to pour down, warming the entire space. There, Jack spotted a mat—his mat. Between it and a second mat was a low-sitting, four-foot-by-four-foot table. Mirroring Sanders' actions, Jack sat. The two men faced each other.

Sanders pulled a perfectly round crystal sphere from his pocket, no bigger than a grape, and set it halfway across the table.

"You want me to read the future?" Jack's tone was of such sincere surprise, it made Sanders laugh.

"Nothing quite that 'New Age.' I'm afraid what I have in mind is slightly more mundane." Sanders glanced at the sphere. It rolled to Jack, then reversed direction, moving past the middle to Sanders. It stopped and again returned to the center. The sphere moved left, moved right, then stopped where it began.

"That's your idea of mundane?" Jack asked.

Sanders did not respond to the comment but directed Jack's attention to the crystal. "This exercise will help you gain better control of your abilities. Move the crystal."

Jack's eyes dropped to the table and onto the sphere. The flame had been a preparation for this clear orb, and now he must become one with it. Unlike the flame, the crystal was cold and dense, and merging with the orb proved tougher than he expected. But his stare stayed locked, as if the sphere held him in place. Jack studied its clarity, analyzed its curvature, and perceived the crystal's hardness. He examined every aspect, and once he absorbed all the subtle elements, he urged the orb forward.

But nothing happened.

He drew on his vast strength and determination, channeling his energy into the crystal, his entire being consumed by the singular goal. But a strong pulse throbbed in his temple, sparking a twinge of pain. He ignored it and ordered the sphere to roll. The harder he pushed himself, the worse the pain grew.

"You're overexerting yourself," Sanders said. "Don't force it. Let your power flow."

Jack almost forgot about Sanders sitting across from him. He looked up at the man and then down to the orb. It still didn't move.

"Do not get frustrated. It's a difficult task. Your mind is like any other muscle. It must be exercised to perform the desired work." Sanders removed the crystal from the table. "And it needs time between attempts. We have concluded this session. Go to your room and rest."

Jack did as Sanders said. He was surprisingly exhausted—considering how good he had felt when he awoke that morning. A short nap would be just the ticket. Hitting the pillow, he drifted off into a deep sleep. But even in his dreams, he did not find peace. The gray figure reappeared in flashes of imagery. At times, it was a fuzzy blur. At others, it had a clearness that exposed its twisted form.

Jack's feet refused to move as the creature approached. Its cold, cruel eyes stared at him, but he could not turn away. There was something familiar about it—this dark, black beast. It drew closer, and Jack knew he had to escape. He tried to force his feet to follow his orders, but, as with the crystal sphere, they too did not comply.

A twisted hand grabbed at Jack. He yelled out and jumped up in his bed.

The image faded quickly, and he strived to capture it in his journal.

What time was it? he wondered.

Jack checked his wristwatch resting on the nightstand. Almost ninety minutes had passed. A sudden wave of nausea hit him. His shoulders were heavy, his movements sluggish, and a faint queasiness stirred in his stomach. He touched his forehead, wondering if he was coming down with the flu. He sat on the edge of his bed—his breathing labored, his heart pounding in his chest. Out of nowhere, the eyes from his dream rose in the air in front of him. Fear snapped Jack's head to one side, but when he looked back, the eyes were gone—it must have been his imagination.

Several moments passed as Jack recovered. The nausea left him, and his heartbeat slowed. He stood up and made his way to the bedroom door. He grasped the knob, but the memory of those floating eyes staring at him forced a glance to his bed. Convinced they were only a remnant of his dream, he continued into the hallway.

The staircase led Jack straight down to the sunroom. He whispered, "Thank you," and went inside, where he saw only one mat and the crystal orb resting in the center of the table. It was apparent that Sanders meant for him to proceed on his own.

Jack sat, then moved to touch the sphere, but pulled his hand away at the last second. Physically touching the crystal might destroy what fragile connection he'd formed with it earlier in the day, and he didn't want to make this any harder than it already was.

He took a deep breath, then a second, and a third. His tension faded, leaving him calm and centered. Jack fixed on the crystal and tried to connect with it—to become part of it, and it to be a part of him. His work with the candles had shown him if he merged with the sphere, he could control it—manipulate it. But the flame was warm and fluid, while the crystal reminded him of the rigidity of ice. Jack brushed aside any doubt and hesitation, and directed his energies toward one simple command—a single word: *Move.* His resolve sharpened, cutting through all distractions until no other thought existed.

Time itself seemed to vanish—the minutes, the hours, passed without notice, as though it had simply stopped. Jack wondered how long he'd been sitting, staring at the tiny crystal. But dwelling on time could shatter his focus, so he shut out any stray flotsam and resumed his exercise. There must be only the crystal—and the crystal alone.

Without warning, the dark, cruel eyes appeared between him and the sphere. Jack recoiled, his body lurching hard, and he was trapped in a vast, suffocating void. The air around him was thick and oppressive, closing in from all sides as if the very abyss itself were alive. His arms shot out, desperate to grab something—anything—but there was only emptiness. A creeping sense of isolation and dread settled over him, and for a moment, he heard a distant clap of thunder. His mouth opened to call out to Sanders, then Quon, but no sound came out.

Jack fought to free himself from the void. He strained against the crushing weight, his muscles tensing and his teeth clenching—but he didn't let up. He focused and pushed back, running on raw instinct and through sheer will, the dark eyes retreated, and the pressure lifted. His breathing eased, and he regained control. Jack blinked and found himself sitting at the low table once more. Looking from side to side, he searched for the eyes—they were gone.

The room remained quiet, and Jack sat alone. All appeared normal—except when he glanced down at the table. The sphere had been moved a good four inches. At first, he assumed he'd bumped the table, nudging the crystal out of place, but when examining the table's position, it hadn't been touched.

He stared at the orb, and as before, he pushed. It didn't budge. Jack pushed with greater force. Again, nothing. He recalled the eyes and his struggle to escape—how instinct had taken over. It was a primal drive that repelled them—repelled them without logic or reason.

Jack's eyelids closed. He relaxed and let everything fade away. In the stillness of his mind, he released his need to move the orb, and instead Jack surrendered to it. Calmly, Jack reopened his eyes and pushed at the sphere.

It rolled. One inch. Six inches. A foot. Two feet.

The orb was about to fall off the far side when Jack mentally ordered it to stop. It obeyed. He commanded it to roll to him, and it did. He directed the crystal to run the same pattern as it did for Sanders. Now its master, he made the sphere roll from one edge of the table toward the other, stopping it at the center, then rolling it the other way. Jack spent the next few hours pushing the orb around the table, striving to have it roll smoothly, with precise speed and in a straight line, determined to perform without flaw.

Sanders entered the room. Jack detected the slight smile on his face as the man revealed a second orb—an exact match to the one already in motion. Sanders didn't speak. He casually set the orb down and left.

Certain of Sanders' intent, Jack focused on the twin orb and pushed—he hadn't known the man for long, but he was gaining the ability to read him.

The crystal began to move, but as it did, the first crystal stopped dead. Jack concentrated on the first crystal. Then its twin stopped. It became clear how difficult it was to juggle these two things at the same time. His skill to manage multiple situations simultaneously had been a source of pride. Now he realized he'd been fooling himself. The moment his focus switched to a new task, even for the briefest instant, the previous something suffered.

His attention shifted between the orbs, and he had no better luck. He spent over an hour trying, and now the sun was starting to set. Jack grew impatient, and in his frustration, he struck his hands together hard enough to make his fingers sting. Like a bolt of lightning, it came to him. He wiggled his fingers—one, then another. He could move them separately, but still together.

Jack placed the two crystals side by side, visualizing them as fingers on the same hand. He commanded them to move forward—together. And they did. He rolled them in reverse—together. He continued this for several minutes and, growing confident in his success, willed the crystals to roll away from each other.

The surprise and excitement of what he had accomplished snapped his control, causing one orb to slip off the edge and bounce across the floor. It was truly amazing—he had moved them both with only the power of his mind. He'd seen people perform psychic feats on TV, but they were always proven to be fakes. One guy, Jack remembered, spun a small folded paper pyramid suspended on the tip of an upturned wire, while the two props were under an upside-down glass fish tank. The con artist did his trick by exploiting the fact that fish tanks are not built with precise alignment—the top edges of a tank don't quite line up, which, when turned over, created a slight gap between one wall and the table. Adjusting the tank so the spacing faced him, the faker was able to blow a discreet jet of air on the hard surface, forcing a breeze under the tank lip. That caused the paper to rotate and create the illusion of mental powers. Jack watched as the fallen sphere continued to roll. Unlike the TV charlatan, this was no trick.

His eyes stayed on the crystal as a hand lowered and picked up the tiny globe. Jack turned his head enough to see Sanders standing in the doorway.

"You must not break your concentration," he said. "Not for an instant."

Sanders placed the orb on the tabletop. But not just the one crystal—he added a second as well. The three crystal spheres sat motionless as Sanders left the room. Soon, all were rolling at Jack's command. And when he mastered the combination, Sanders brought in a fourth. This went on into the late evening until a dozen clear crystals were rolling on the flat top in intricate patterns, all without the aid of human touch.

As the orbs sailed around and around, Jack became acutely aware that his every move—every action—was being scrutinized. He knew it was Eric Sanders observing his progress—assessing whether he remained so easily distracted. Not breaking the flow, Jack carried on moving the crystals. If this was a test, he would not falter. He'd show Sanders that he was worthy of his training. There would be no failure as in the candle room.

Several minutes later, Sanders reentered. This time, he did not produce a crystal but said, "Your thinking is still two-dimensional."

Jack, keeping the crystals in steady motion, responded, "I don't understand."

"While your progress is good, I expected more."

Those words shocked Jack, sending the orbs raining to the floor and scattering in all directions. He couldn't believe his ears. He had the crystals dancing on command, and all Sanders did was tell him he wasn't satisfied.

Sanders held stern, and Jack sensed he was trying to show no discouragement, but his demeanor also made it clear he meant what he said.

"I hoped a man of your nature would have advanced to the next stage of your own accord.

"Which is?" Jack said, knowing it was best to hold his tongue.

"Levitation. You move the spheres right and left, forward and back. Up and down is as simple."

As simple? Jack mused. The expression on Sanders' face was as if he'd heard those inner words of doubt.

"Gather up the crystals," Sanders told him.

Jack stood up to collect the lost spheres, but Sanders raised a hand to stop him. Jack understood. He cleared all other thoughts and pictured only the orbs, but it was beyond merely seeing them—he felt them—all of them. With a single command, each sphere rolled and gathered at his feet.

"Return them to the table," Sanders said. "It's no more difficult than rolling the crystals along the surface. Your limitations exist solely in your mind."

Jack gave out a new command.

One orb bounced—then another—and another. One by one, the crystals rose and hovered around Jack. He had to suspend his amazement—giving in to it would mean losing his hold, and failure.

All the orbs spun clockwise, rising above him and drawing closer together, forming a tight mass. They slowly descended and settled upon the table. The crystals stopped and came to a complete rest.

"Get some sleep," Sanders said. "You'll need to be at your best." And with those words, the teacher left the student.

Jack started off to his room to follow Sanders' instructions, but before going, he looked at the crystal orbs. "I'm coming for my daughter, Kahir. I'm coming for *you*."

TWENTY-ONE

Thaddeus Blackburn lumbered down the long corridor of the Armstrong Hotel, a secluded, rundown, six-story dive that didn't ask too many questions. His breathing labored from climbing three flights of stairs, and he took each step along the hallway very carefully. One of the overhead lights had burned out several days earlier and had yet to be replaced. He squinted his way through the dark zone for a clear path to his safe haven, not wanting to repeat the events from two days prior when he stepped in a pile of human feces. He threw out that particular pair of shoes and now wore ten-dollar Target sneakers.

As he moved forward, Thaddeus spotted another mound. *Not again*, he thought. Last time, his shoe picked up most of the mess. But not today! For a moment, a brief moment, he considered going down and pounding on the manager's door, but remembering the six-foot, 300-pound, biker-looking dude, Thaddeus changed his mind—he'd just walk around the small mound.

Thaddeus gave the crap pile a wide berth, but as he stepped past, it moved. He'd been wrong—it wasn't human waste. A large rat squealed and charged him. Thaddeus kicked at the vermin. It turned and ran, hugging the baseboard, darting into the light.

He couldn't believe the size of the dirty brown rodent with its solid black eyes and long hairless tail. Watching the furry creature squealing and sniffing and digging for tiny bits between the floorboards, he honestly didn't know which was the most disgusting—crap in the hallways or rats anywhere. At least with a careful eye, you could always avoid stepping in shit. Shit never chased anyone down the hall with long sharp teeth.

Ignoring the tightness in his stomach, Thaddeus headed to room 4E —his home away from home. He slid his key into the lock, but it wouldn't budge. The scratching of scurrying rats made him frantically jiggle the key. It finally turned. He shoved open the door, lunged inside, and slammed it hard behind him.

Thaddeus pressed both shoulders against the door, letting out a heavy breath. He stood there, taking in the deplorable state of this so-called efficiency unit—its extensive network of cracks visible beneath peeling paint. Some of the punctures in the plaster reminded him of bullet holes. What a terrible place, but the only one where he didn't have to show any ID and cash was never questioned. There was no paper trail to betray his location. He kept telling himself it was a temporary refuge from Kahir. Thaddeus glanced down at the cast on his arm—his fingers had not stopped throbbing. He would need to move on in a day or two.

Four days ago, immediately on leaving the hospital, Thaddeus called his office and informed Mrs. Carson, his secretary, that he was unavailable until further notice. She asked about his appointments. He told her to figure out some excuse and reschedule. He hung up. Thaddeus then hailed a taxicab and was about to tell the driver to bring him home, but realized that could be a big mistake—a death trap. Instead, he instructed the cabbie to drive him to a seedier part of town. After paying the fair, Thaddeus exited at the corner and waited until the taxi was out of view. He surveyed the street, seeing some likely places to stay, but when he locked eyes with a homeless man, he decided it best to head off in the other direction. It took him four tries to find this hotel. The other three insisted he show his driver's license and sign a registry. This place didn't care. He booked the room, sight unseen.

Still bracing himself on the door, Thaddeus caught a sound from the shadowy side of the room. Fear rooted him to the spot. The noise continued—it was a heavy tapping. Thaddeus barely summoned the courage to flip the wall switch.

Turning on the light and allowing his vision to adjust to the dim glow, he saw a rat running on the sink top. It stopped, sat up on its hind legs, and stared back at him. This rat must have been born of the same litter as the one in the hall. It was huge.

Thaddeus searched the room for some kind of weapon. He grabbed the broom he had bought to clean the dirt off the floor and carefully slipped toward the rodent. It didn't leave the sink and seemed to mock him with its unblinking, soulless eyes. Its mouth moved side to side as if chewing. The handle locked in a stone grip, Thaddeus burst forward, bringing the broom down hard on the porcelain. He missed the rat, which jumped to the floor.

Like a madman, Thaddeus chased the creature, swinging wildly until, at last, he whacked it a proper blow. The rat let out a loud death cry. Thaddeus smashed it with the broom over and over. The squealing grew weaker and weaker until it faded to silence.

The fat man gloated over the crushed rodent. Blood dripped from its mouth. He bashed it one final time for extra measure, then swept the lifeless body. A trickle of blood left a thin trail. Thaddeus cracked the door a foot and nudged the pest out into the corridor. Hey, he figured, if it was good enough for defecation, it was certainly good enough for the disposal of dead vermin. Besides, the resident cats roaming the hotel were sure to make short work of it. Unlike the feces, the rat would be gone by morning—if not sooner.

His eyes scanned the hall, ensuring the deed had escaped any attention. Satisfied and with a smug smile, Thaddeus pushed the door shut with a click, then stood motionless, broom in hand, ready to strike. He drew a shallow breath and listened for any other unwelcome visitors. Thankfully, not a single scurry or the faintest squeal found his ear. Thaddeus leaned his weapon on the wall, pulled a book from his jacket pocket, and walked over to the bed.

He had purchased fresh sheets, two blankets, and a pillow at the same Target store where he got his tennis shoes and broom, always paying in cash. The mattress on the simple box spring appeared to be new—there were no holes or stains. That did, however, considering the rest of the unit, cause Thaddeus to wonder what had happened to require the management to put in a new mattress. Though, if truth be told, he'd rather not dwell on it. Thaddeus propped up his pillow and settled down. He began to read.

Some hours later, something brushed his cheek, waking him. A sharp pain stabbed his fingers, pulling him further into consciousness. Thinking he'd bumped his cast while tossing in his sleep, he moved to sit up. Nothing! He struggled to throw his shoulders—no response.

The cutting burn shot along his entire hand. Thaddeus panicked to free himself, but only lifted his head enough to see the large rat eating his fingertips. It met Thaddeus's gaze, but then resumed its meal.

Thaddeus screamed and tried to lift his hand. He couldn't. An unseen force held him tightly in place. He screamed as the rat pried his thumbnail off. He screamed as the rat tugged at the soft, tender red tissue underneath.

A second rat started to gnaw his pant leg. Its razor-sharp teeth cut through the fabric and continued on to his calf until a dark wet spot spread out as Thaddeus howled in agony.

Two more rats joined the feast, followed by three others, then five more, eight more, twelve more. Swiftly, they came in groups too large to count. They completely covered Thaddeus except for his face. He had to watch as the horde clawed for the best feeding positions.

The mass of rats pressed in on him, their bodies squirming and writhing. He fought to turn his head, but the swarm was too thick—they pulled his hair and bit his ears—they chewed his nose and shredded his lips. Only his eyes moved as he suffered the vermin's teeth picking and chewing at his flesh.

Amid the frenzy and the pain, a shadow crept over Thaddeus's face. Fearful it was a rat coming for the soft tissue of his eyes, he slammed them shut, awaiting the torment. A coldness settled over him, and the rats stopped moving. Thaddeus hesitated, but looked up. He saw Kahir at the foot of his bed. It was then that the rats came for his eyes.

Not quite tired enough to sleep, Jack did feel a tad hungry. He made a trip to the kitchen and was surprised to find Quon still up.

"I have been expecting you," the servant said. He turned to face Jack, holding a plate topped with a roast beef sandwich, which he placed on the table.

"Sometimes I wonder who's the greater wizard—you or Sanders." Jack plopped himself down in a chair and helped himself to the sandwich. He took a bite. It had been several hours since last he ate. He very much welcomed the food.

"We all have our special talents," Quon said. "We need but to unlock them." He walked to the refrigerator, opened the large door, and removed a tall glass of milk. A light white frost-vapor formed on its outside. "It's my understanding," he continued, "that you are readily discovering your own talents."

Jack swallowed his mouthful of sandwich. "I suppose, but…"

"I hear hesitation in your voice. You are not pleased with your progress?"

"Pleased? I'm doing things I never dreamt possible. 'Pleased' is not the word I'd use. Amazed. Awe. Shock maybe." His face eased. "Grateful. Pick one. Though you'd think Sanders would be more satisfied with my progress than he seems to be."

"That is merely the master's way. Please be assured that any doubt he had regarding your matter has subsided. You are an excellent student. He considers his time well spent."

"I wish he'd let me know that." Jack reached for the milk. The exhaustion was starting to catch up with him and his hand struck the glass at a bad angle, knocking it over and sending the contents across the table.

Quon stood up, saying nothing, and went for something to clean up the mess. Jack stared down at the milk. With a simple thought, the liquid rolled back into the glass, and the glass rose up on its base—all as if someone had rewound a scene from a movie.

Returning with a towel, Quon paused, finding not a single drop of spilled milk left in sight. His eyes flicked from the upright glass over to Jack. "The master has not been wasting his efforts on you, Jack Railey."

"If you say so." He, too, looked at the glass. Its contents, only moments ago, had been spread out before him. "Can I have some fresh milk?" he asked.

"Most certainly."

Jack climbed the flight of stairs to the third floor. He was both exhilarated and exhausted. Now, more than ever, he truly believed he possessed the means to get Sarah back home. He would restore his family—make it whole.

At the door to his room, he paused. An odd tingle ran down his spine, compelling him to turn and peer down the dim hallway. He heard a whisper—a faint, soft voice muffled by distance. Thinking the sound was the result of fatigue, Jack ignored it until the soft, unknown words were repeated.

"Who's there?" Jack called out. His eyes darted from door to door, checking if any were open. None were, but a sudden impulse spurred him down the corridor. He paid no mind to the other doors as he walked and quickly lost track of how far he had gone.

Jack's steps ended abruptly, but he couldn't say why. The door facing him looked no different from any of the many lining the passageway. Despite that, it was different—and Jack knew it.

He gripped the knob firmly and turned. It moved freely in his hand. Jack pushed, revealing the chamber within.

Unlike that first day, when every door was a doorway to his own room, this time he found something else waiting. The layout hadn't changed, but the space was much more cluttered. The furniture, what little there was, had been dragged away from the walls. Clothing littered the floor, and a mirror had fallen—its jagged pieces scattered in all directions.

He stood in the hallway. Someone said his name: "Jack." The voice sounded long and drawn out, as if blown on the wind. "Ja-aah-ck," the voice repeated. The wispy echo drew him forward—his gut told him some unasked question would be answered.

After two or three steps past the threshold, everything started twisting and spinning—the walls warped and bent, the bed and furniture stretched to outlandish proportions, and the floor tore open beneath his feet with a thunderous roar. A vast void swallowed Jack, surrounding him with nothing but black.

Laughter followed him down. The low, resonant tone was somehow familiar—it struck a chord in his memory. He couldn't place where or when. Jack gasped as his lungs filled with a rush of hot air, making it difficult to concentrate. The mocking laugh grew louder, and then, directly ahead, the eyes that had haunted him appeared—huge and unblinking, two massive disks blocking his way.

Plummeting fast, Jack shifted his body to avoid impact, but no matter how he positioned himself, they hung in his path—a collision was unavoidable.

Jack covered his face with both hands before he slammed into the eyes. They shattered, like smashing a large plate-glass window—shards flew everywhere. Terrified he'd be cut to ribbons, Jack cried out.

A heavy thud echoed as he hit hard ground, the impact jarring every bone in his body and stealing the air from his lungs. Jack stayed still—he needed to catch his breath. He inhaled deeply, then slowly rose to regain his footing. The mocking began again. Jack turned his head to see a shadowy cave—a blast of heat rolled from the great black mouth. The laughter came from inside. A tightness crept into his chest, but he forced himself to push on. Jack took a step closer to the entrance—the laughter stopped. He froze and watched for any sign of activity.

In a blur, a hunched figure stirred among the shadows. Jack caught a glimpse of its face for only a second. Deformed. Horrifying. The thing didn't seem human, but it scurried about on two legs. A raw, uncontrollable terror gripped Jack—all reason escaped him, his limbs became stone. It was almost too much to bear. He wanted to scream out but couldn't. The creature lunged from the cave—its hand shot toward him. Jack's heart pounded, ready to burst. He met the creature's gaze. Those dark eyes—those evil, dark brown eyes.

Jack snapped awake. He sat up. The moonlight from the window provided enough illumination to show him he was in bed. He didn't recall returning to the room, let alone removing his clothes and slipping under the covers. He did remember being very exhausted from his evening exercises, and chatting with Quon, but after that, everything was a blank. Somehow, he got himself up the stairs to his quarters and climbed into bed—all on autopilot.

He clicked on the bedside lamp and grabbed his journal. Jack hurried to the next available page, his pen ready. The dream remained fresh in his mind—disjointed but clear enough to write down. He started scribbling out the details: falling down a void, the giant eyes and crashing through them, the cave, and the fear—that was a feeling unknown to him—such an intense fear. His hand raced to record every image. But even as he wrote, it all made no sense. The fragments seemed to mean more, but he failed to grasp what. Jack paused over the words. Nothing he had written helped him. He closed his book with a frustrated sigh. The dream wasn't any clearer now than when he'd first woken up.

A quick press of the switch, and darkness returned. Jack surrendered to the quiet, trying to sleep, but sleep proved elusive. Those baffling scenes kept replaying in his head, over and over, as if they were eager to convey a message just beyond his reach.

TWENTY-TWO

Several hours passed, with Jack only able to catch short stretches of sleep. Whenever he drifted off, those eyes returned—haunting, relentless—jolting him awake. That terrifying dream was unshakable. The sky outside remained dark, and he had a little while before Quon would fulfill Sanders' instructions on waking him at 5 a.m.—the man was always very prompt. Jack decided to save Quon the trip and venture downstairs instead. He wasn't hungry, but a cup of coffee sounded just about right.

In the kitchen, Quon told Jack that Sanders waited for him in the west wing study. On hearing that, he forgot about his coffee, his lack of sleep, and the dream. Jack followed the servant's directions, but he'd never been in this part of the mansion. The hallway seemed to wind round and round.

Finding the door Quon described, Jack knocked.

"Please enter," Sanders said from the other side.

The door opened, and Jack caught the scent of what must be frankincense burning. It sparked memories of his missions in the Middle East—a different lifetime ago.

Jack proceeded inside, not believing what he saw—more books. But this space felt like more than simply a library—it evoked the serenity of a sanctuary, filled with unexpected objects, including a collection of statuettes of deities from a multitude of faiths. He even noticed a figurine depicting Mary holding the Christ Child, and beside it, a six-inch bronze Buddha. Along the far wall, on a high shelf, were other curios as well. But those, he had to admit, he couldn't begin to identify—bizarre statues, some a cross between animals and men. A few appeared as figures and forms drawn straight from a nightmare.

Seated behind an ebony desk, Sanders stared at a glass container, no bigger than two feet across. It was square, with no metal clamps or supports. The walls fused seamlessly at the edges, forming a sealed cube. Inside, a strange creature lingered in a state of decay.

Curiosity getting the best of him, Jack stepped closer, peering into the cube.

"You don't recognize your little hitchhiker?" Sanders asked.

"No, I don't." Jack studied the thing. An image flashed—the memory of Sanders' hand plunging into his chest surfaced. "I thought I was hallucinating."

"I shouldn't wonder. When you came to me, your view of this world was confined to that of your senses. The time has come for some answers."

Jack inched forward, and the thing jumped up. It unleashed a terrifying scream and hurled itself at the glass wall toward him. The creature gave one last agonizing cry, fell over, and decomposed as he watched. The rotting tissue peeled from its twitching skeleton, then the bones themselves crumbled to dust.

He looked over at Eric Sanders, who said, "It burned up its final bit of life energy in a vain attempt to feed."

"Feed? On what?"

"Isn't that obvious?" Sanders said matter-of-factly. "On you."

Jack's blood went cold, stunned by the revelation.

"It is, for lack of a better word, a parasite—one that feeds specifically on your essence. Kahir used it as his eyes and ears." Sanders' gaze shifted to Jack as though watching for his reaction. "A man with your history—haven't you wondered how Kahir learned the exact locations and weaknesses of your associates? He did so through you—or rather, the stowaway within you."

Sanders leaned in on the cube, examining the pile of dust inside. "After you met with each of Kahir's enemies," he continued, "it would temporarily detach, then reattach once its task was completed. No doubt the experience was far from pleasant."

Those dizzy spells. Jack exhaled a short breath. *The lightheadedness.* "I figured it was a bad bout of jet lag."

"A construct of this nature can place great stress on the physical body of the host," Sanders said, "by draining its life force. But in your case, due to your rather unique qualities, the effect would be more on your psyche—altering your thought process, clouding your judgment."

Sanders' words hit a sharp and disconcerting note. All the rash impulses, all the bad decisions—they made a terrible sort of sense now.

His strange behavior did start on his first day stateside, after seeing that...that—whatever it is. He snapped at Gordon Brigham in his office, feeling an irrational anger as he heard they had lost contact with Markus Radford and his team. Sure, Markus was his friend and mentor, but he had no cause for his sharp tone.

And later that day, he saw Sarah with the other children begging along the street. He charged headlong with no plan, no objective—driven by an urge he was unable to ignore. He trailed them for blocks, distracted and unfocused.

"I definitely wasn't on my game," Jack said, hesitating, then speaking with a bitter edge. "I kept going off half-cocked. I acted foolishly—recklessly—smashing down doors and ending up in jail." The shock on Blackburn's face when he tore into his office popped into Jack's head—and that poor young couple. "I was out of control," he added. "If it weren't for... Well, it's enough to say I could've been thrown behind bars a second time. Anna, my wife, would've loved that—picking me up from the pokey—twice."

Jack knew without Blackburn's cowardice, he'd have been arrested. But who was he to talk? In the hospital parking lot, paranoia had taken hold of him. The cop on his radio had him checking the rearview mirror over and over, convinced he'd get nabbed. It got to where he jumped at a simple tap on his window. A slight embarrassment washed over Jack. He'd keep the hospital thing to himself.

Sanders motioned for Jack to sit. He did so without hesitation.

"Kahir employed the parasite as a focal point to strike and reap his vengeance—quite effective, actually. By siphoning your untapped powers and eliminating the need to expend his own energy to locate his victims, Kahir killed with remarkable efficiency."

"You sound as if you admire the man."

"Not the man—the strategy. But in this house, you're protected from Kahir's influence. More so on the third level with its added safeguards."

"He used me," Jack said, choking down his anger. Anger only weakened him. He buried the emotion—buried it deep.

"Much like the others would have—given the opportunity."

"The others?"

"Anthony Bane, Thaddeus Blackburn, Benjamin Abrams, Leonora de Montia. They wanted you to join their ranks, hoping you'd develop your powers under their direction."

"But how could they know about me? I didn't even know about me. And besides Leonora, I'd never met those people before this whole mess started. And as for her, I've barely had any direct contact—sure, we were acquainted, but only in passing."

"Your daughter, Sarah, and the de Montia girl are friends."

"Which served as my one connection to the woman."

Sanders closed a large book, which sat alongside the glass cube. "I suspect Leonora de Montia sensed the latent power within Sarah and realized that one or both of her parents must also be gifted. She shared that information with her compatriots."

"Things are starting to add up," Jack said. "Anna told me Anthony Bane insisted on meeting me. He must've assumed it was me, not her, who possessed the abilities he sought to exploit."

"As he and the group aimed to exploit Abhaya Kahir—to their folly."

"So they got what they deserved."

"That's not for us to judge. They paid a terrible price for their treachery. And now other innocents continue to pay. Your daughter included."

"How was I supposed to help them? I knew nothing then."

"They intended to train you in the coarser methods, spurring you on with the grim reality that Kahir has your child. If you succeeded in defeating him, they planned to control you for their own ends."

"They would have found me not so easy to control."

"I believe you to be right about that, Jack Railey, but we have other matters to discuss."

While listening to Sanders, Jack happened to glance at the desktop. He spotted a framed picture of a woman. Jack recognized it as the same photo he saw during his visit to Clifford Stuart.

"My sister," Eric volunteered. "Julia always loved this room. After her death, I made it my special study." He smiled at the photograph. "I think she would've liked that."

"You and Clifford are family?"

"Clifford Stuart is the reason I agreed to meet with you. If not for his urging on your behalf, your stay here would never have taken place. But do not misunderstand me—Clifford merely arranged your introduction. I was under no obligation to accept you as a student. You did that yourself."

"I did?"

"You do not yet comprehend your potential. Even now, with the minor skills I've helped you bring out, you've excelled beyond my expectations. You are capable of great things."

"Is that why you took me on? My potential?"

"Yes, but not that alone. Your cause is worthy and honorable. But I wish we had more time." Sanders' expression went stern. "Quon mentioned your little mishap from last night."

"The spilled milk?" Normally, such a conversation might be considered silly, but Jack saw that Eric Sanders was not at all amused. "It just happened. I didn't mean it to—it just did."

Sanders got up and stepped over to the nearest bookshelf, returning the volume to its usual place. "It's critical you maintain control," he said. "Resist any random impulse to use your power. Without control, you risk harming yourself—or worse, harming others."

"I'll be more careful next time," Jack said.

"Be careful all the time." Sanders returned to his chair. "I've reviewed your journal, and I found it most interesting."

"In what way?"

Sanders answered with just a slight grin. "You're ready for the next phase of your training. But be warned, this will be the most dangerous. And I say that not lightly—some have tried and gone insane at this point. Do you wish to continue?"

"I've come this far," Jack said.

"Then your journey begins through that door."

Jack looked to where Sanders was pointing. To his surprise, a door stood where he hadn't seen one before. How had he missed it when he first entered the study?

He pushed the question aside. If his time with Sanders had taught him anything, it was to expect the unexpected—all was possible.

"Come with me," Eric Sanders said.

Jack rose from his chair and went with his teacher. The door swung open on its own.

Beyond the threshold lay a bleak darkness, broken by the occasional flash of light.

"What's in there?" Jack asked.

"Nothing—yet."

Both men entered. Jack saw the flashes were actually lightning off in the distance—and they were moving closer. The ground was solid beneath his feet, but Jack had the sensation of floating. The landscape—what he could make out—appeared mountainous and barren. Its vastness caused him to almost forget that mere seconds ago, he'd been in a study lined with books. And yet, it didn't seem at all unusual.

"Where are we?" Jack asked.

"Here, you will meet your greatest foe."

"My *greatest* foe?" he questioned, given he'd racked up quite a list of enemies over the years. A crack of thunder sent a tremor underfoot. Jack's attention snapped toward a second lightning burst—more thunder boomed. When he turned to Sanders, there was only darkness—but a voice, Sanders' voice, surrounded him.

"Proceed on your own. Face what lies ahead."

The landscape changed. The thunder and lightning stopped—the wind calmed to a gentle breeze. Jack watched as swirls of color mingled into new shapes and patterns.

The melting backdrop bled away, leaving Jack in a sparsely furnished chamber. Stacks of wooden crates lined a rear concrete wall. There were no windows, just a single door leading to another room. Three people sat talking around a table. He didn't recognize the man or the two women—at least not until Markus Radford appeared. Then Jack suddenly remembered the faces from the assignment folder he'd read over in Brigham's office—an assignment he had refused.

"Markus," Jack said, "it's me."

Markus walked past Jack without the slightest sign of recognition. Not a pause. Not a trace of reaction.

Jack grabbed at Markus's shoulder—his hand slipped inside his friend's upper arm. Stunned, Jack failed to notice the smaller of the two females moving toward him—until she passed right through his body. To her and the others, Jack didn't exist. Or maybe they were the ones not really there. Jack couldn't tell which, nor did he care. What mattered to him was that the team was safe—for now, at least.

He kept watching the small group talk, though their lips moved in silence. At times, the discussion grew heated between the younger agents, but Markus spoke, and order returned. Two more men approached the table as Markus pulled out a map and circled several sections. A bearded Tom Blair emphatically shook his head, then pointed to a different spot.

I've been here before, Jack thought, remembering the deserted bomb shelter on the Iraqi side of the Iran-Iraq border. Markus had secretly set it up when Iraq and the U.S. maintained better terms, and it proved quite handy as a base for their covert excursions into Iran. Markus used the shelter to store his personal arsenal. The company frowned on its agents having their own stash of weapons, so Markus never mentioned it to anyone official. That meant no matter how many teams Brigham sent in, they'd all be searching in the wrong location.

The scenery shifted again.

"Not now," Jack yelled into the air. He threw himself toward his old mentor. "Markus! Markus! Brigham has a team coming for you."

Jack's surroundings blurred—the walls, the crates, the table, the chairs—all became indistinguishable. "You can't stay here! You have to go!" As the world blended into an unrecognizable mass of smeared color and shadow, Jack could have sworn that Markus looked his way.

Doubt and anguish overwhelmed Jack. "Stop! Please, stop!" He had abandoned his friend. "I should've gone—I should've taken the mission. I failed. I failed myself—my friends—my family."

A shriek of mocking laughter rang out as Markus, his crew, and the bomb shelter vanished. Jack clutched his ears and dropped to his knees. The cackle drilled its way into his skull. He squeezed his eyes shut in pain as the torment grew louder. Time stopped. Reality shattered. Something inside Jack snapped. He laughed in unison as madness engulfed him.

On the verge of losing himself, a tiny flicker shimmered in the darkness. Slowly, it brightened into a flame. Its light—its heat—enveloped Jack, giving him the strength he needed to regain his wits. Jack drew on its power to focus, pulling deep breaths into his lungs. He visualized merging with the flame.

"Get out of my head! I won't let you win."

The chaos in his mind ceased, and Jack opened his eyes. A new horizon stretched out endlessly.

A sense of déjà vu hit Jack as he stared out into his surroundings. He began to walk, his steps steady, drawn by an unseen force. The journey brought him across an unchanging, barren landscape. He wasn't sure how far he'd traveled—only that it ended at the entrance to a dark cavern.

The rock wall loomed high, disappearing from sight, but a disturbance in the inky void of the cave mouth made him freeze. Something—no, someone—slipped through the darkness, followed by a low growl. Jack's chest tightened, his air seized in his throat. This cave, that growl—both were from his nightmare. It hadn't been a mere dream at all. Somehow, he'd been brought to this dark place while he slept. An unknown force had come for him—an unseen threat had attacked him.

But Sanders told him the third floor provided extra protection from outside forces. After reading his journal, Sanders apparently understood what was happening and gave him this chance to meet his attacker on his own terms.

Your greatest foe—that's what Sanders said. And Jack knew who that was.

"Kahir!" he shouted.

The growling stopped.

"Kahir, I'm here. I'm here for you!"

A horrific shape sprang from the cavern—a blur of muscle and shadow. Jack couldn't react fast enough. It slammed into him, driving him down into the rocks and dirt. The impact knocked the breath from his lungs. He forced himself off the ground and spun upright in one swift motion. The beast hunched in the blackness between two boulders, leering at him with those all too familiar eyes—cold and unblinking. This monster had been hunting him all along. Jack crouched low, his gaze locked. It had been trying to stop him from the very beginning. He knew he had one choice: fight or fall.

"You want me, you bastard?!" Jack snarled. "Come and get me." Jack grabbed reached for a large rock, then stood up. He turned. The beast was standing, waiting for him to attack. And he intended to do exactly that.

Jack circled to the right, taking in every detail of the grotesque form. In his dreams, he'd seen only fragments—bits and pieces. This was his moment to see his enemy and show it that he no longer feared him. Its features were twisted and warped. Patches of rough, hard flesh hung from its cheeks and forehead in loose layers. Tufts of dark hair clung to its scalp, revealing scabby skin beneath. From between its lips, heavy white froth spilled over its chin.

The abomination erupted with a deafening wail, exposing broken, rotting teeth. More saliva spewed from the corners of its gaping maw. Jack planted his heels as it advanced with a quick but awkward stride. He raised the rock and hurled it, but he missed cleanly, leaving the monster unharmed. It howled and pounded its fists against its chest with the fury of a great ape. Then it barreled toward Jack—who, at the last second, drove a fist into the jaw of his foe.

Jack's legs buckled as he himself fell hard onto his back. The beast must have struck him at the same instant, delivering a blow of its own. Jack kicked his feet out, sliding until a boulder halted his retreat—jarring his body with the sudden stop. As he steadied himself, a jagged object pressed against his side—a stone, long and sharp-edged. He grabbed it. The stone fit well in his grip.

The monster charged, and with his new weapon, Jack slashed—cutting it along the arm and chest. Howling in pain, the beast stumbled back, clutching its wounds.

Slowly, Jack regained his balance. A sticky warmth ran down his arm—fresh blood dripped off his fingertips. His chest also bore a gash—both wounds matched those he'd inflicted on his attacker.

Again, the beast surged forward, letting out a sharp cry. Jack held his ground and, throwing his full weight behind him, plunged the crude blade into the brute's gut. It screamed—as did he. Both collapsed, hitting the rocky terrain. A long minute passed. A brief truce. Then both man and beast waited for the other to act.

His fingers cramping, Jack lifted his stone knife—amazed he hadn't dropped it. He examined his wound, then the beast's. Jack rolled onto his side, gritting his teeth against the pain. The beast didn't move, except for wheezing. Jack readied his weapon, bracing for the final blow. Blood trickled from the deformed mouth—the beast no longer appeared so fierce and even seemed somehow familiar. Jack clasped it by the elbow and helped it to sit up.

"I know who you are," he said sadly. "I've beaten you…and I now understand—I can never destroy you."

The misshapen face started to change. The deep lines dissolved, the distorted flesh straightened. Jack watched in shock as the reflection of himself vanished. He sat alone in the wasteland.

"You do surprise me," Sanders said.

Jack was back in the study as if nothing had happened. But something clearly did. He felt it—the peace, the clarity.

"You faced your darker side," Sanders added, "defeated it, and in the end showed it compassion. We are finished."

"I think I'll go to my room until my next exercise," Jack said.

"No, I mean, it's over. I have taught you all that you wanted. You are ready to confront Kahir on his terms."

Jack worked hard, waited patiently, and sacrificed much for this day. Now that it had come, an uneasiness crept over him.

"Quon will gather your things for your departure."

"That's it?"

Sanders nodded once. "That's it."

TWENTY-THREE

The city seemed so very different. If asked how, Jack Railey would find it a difficult question to answer. The buildings, the streets, the people—all appeared the same as they had before. Yet something had changed, subtle but undeniable. Despite the noise, there was a calm clarity beneath it all—a sense that life pulses through everything, even in the chaos. He waited on a street he had traveled many times in the past, but today it felt like he stood in unexplored territory.

Jack tapped the bridge of his sunglasses with the tip of his index finger. The frames slid back into place, giving his eyes full protection from the daylight. Two weeks cooped up at Sanders' had made them extra sensitive. Still, the warmth of the late afternoon sun was welcome against his skin. It bathed everything in a soft, yellow, pre-dusk glow.

He glanced at his wristwatch—it was the right hour. Jack feared too much might have changed during his absence. Two weeks could be a long time for some things. But he'd be patient. He was in control now. Sanders had freed him from Kahir's creature. His mind was clear. His actions were his own. While he waited, he found a moment to think—how did Kahir learn of him in the first place? The answer was simple—there had been nothing magical about it. Tony Bane. The boy must have overheard his father talking with Benjamin Abrams, or perhaps Thaddeus Blackburn—discussing plans to bring him into their battle with Kahir. Whether it was a careless conversation caught in passing or a deliberate eavesdrop, Tony took that compromising tidbit straight to his master.

A blaring car horn snapped Jack back. He flinched, then straightened. Jack refused to be distracted. It served no purpose getting lost in pointless speculation—none of it mattered. What did matter was being in position—and ready. He stood at the corner of Hennepin Avenue and Fifth Street. The group's route seemed to include this area—most likely because of the large number of people who passed this way.

As the car let loose another honk, a biker sped past it, inches from its front bumper, flipping off the driver without hesitation. The exchange forced a small smile onto Jack's lips—some things will always remain the same. The driver blasted his horn for a good ten seconds, drowning out the very sound Jack was waiting for.

When the car drove off, and the ringing cleared from Jack's ears, the drum beats came—low, distant, but familiar. His hunch had paid off. Kahir hadn't bothered to alter his playbook—having the children out collecting money at the same place, at the same time. But then, why would he? Kahir was likely feeling quite secure. Jack had learned only hours ago that Blackburn was dead. And with his own presence blocked by his stay in the mansion, Kahir must believe all his enemies were defeated or in retreat. That belief was about to change.

Jack held his position as the white-robes came into view, the beats and chants growing louder as they drew near. The rhythms hit him with a sharp clarity—they sounded crisper, more distinct. He made no rash movements while the youngsters wandered among the crowd asking passersby for coins. Jack observed with utter calm as his own daughter raised the collection bowl and gave her pitch to strangers. He detected an odd shift in their demeanor—the group had lost its cohesiveness. They were three smaller groups, spread out and barely working together. Their clapping and dancing were halfhearted, neither in sync with the drum nor with each other. One tiny girl with red hair didn't clap or dance at all. She moved in a manner best described as that of an automaton.

The collection of money no longer sparked any enthusiasm. Jack recalled the bills and coins passing from hand to hand with joy and excitement. Now it had become a simple routine—take money, put in bowl—take money, put in bowl. If onlookers threatened to call the police, the children merely shuffled off down the sidewalk.

Jack changed his vantage point to gain a clearer view of their faces. He advanced some ten feet without drawing attention to himself. Their behavior suggested not just a lack of enthusiasm—they actually seemed drained of energy. Cindy de Montia appeared more withdrawn than the rest as she straggled behind. An older boy brought over a money bowl and shoved it into her hands. Cindy yelled at him and pushed the bowl away. She trudged over to Sarah's side, but said nothing.

The boy scowled at Cindy, then stomped forward and waved the group closer as he spoke out loud. A few nodded in agreement, but most stood with dull, blank stares. He signaled them to advance, and their pace quickened. *Here we go*, Jack thought. They were heading home. No—not home. Sarah's home was with him and Anna, not with Kahir.

The children marched on—all except Cindy. Sarah turned and grabbed her hand. The girl looked ready to pass out at any moment. Sarah pulled her along, running to catch up with the others, who were in a tight group. The leader clapped his hands, and the drumming resumed. On cue, several of them began chanting. The tiny girl swayed and danced, but stopped after only a few steps.

Jack continued to follow, but without sufficient cover, Cindy spotted him. She tugged at Sarah's arm and whispered in her ear. It didn't require psychic powers to know what passed between them. Sarah's head swiveled, her eyes widening as they darted up and down the street. There was no more reason to hide—he had been exposed. Jack stepped into full view.

Sarah's gaze locked onto him, her face flushed with fright. Whether she feared for herself or for him was unclear. Her past warning played over in his memory—*Stay away, Daddy*. The two girls sped up their pace, closing the gap. The next few seconds promised to be telling. Sarah and Cindy caught up with the group, but neither spoke a word. Jack read that as an encouraging sign.

Jack put some distance between himself and the children. He couldn't risk that one of the others might recognize him from his botched attempt at grabbing Sarah those few weeks ago. At Twelfth and Hennepin, a drunk in a business suit stumbled out of a bar, saw the robes, and began shouting. He yelled that they should get real jobs and rambled on about how the streets weren't safe for hardworking Americans. "Little beggars!" the man bellowed. "Get the hell out of here!" He tried to shoo them off with flailing waves of his hands. "You won't steal my money!"

The confrontation seemed to trigger something, snapping the kids out of their stupor. The group spread out, including Cindy and Sarah. They started to chant and dance. One girl rang a bell that she pulled from her robe pocket. The drummer pounded out a strong beat. Their dancing formed a ring around the man. They chanted loudly, taunting the drunk. He burst forward, and the circle broke, letting him pass. He shouted an obscenity as the children regrouped and went on their way.

Sarah led the pack. Her hurried pace forced her comrades to rush along. Cindy glanced in Jack's direction, then spoke again to Sarah, but Sarah shook her head and didn't turn around. Moving quickly, the group approached the estate. At the gate, Sarah pressed the button and waited for the harsh buzz. She held the iron pedestrian door open for everyone to file past. Once alone, Sarah peeked at her father and frantically waved him away.

A pair of large black wings swooped overhead. The raven landed on the top rail. It cried out a single caw, causing Sarah to slam the gate shut and run up to the house, where she disappeared inside. The evil bird flew off. Jack scowled—ugly, dirty raven.

Up in a turret window, a dark form drew Jack's notice. That same cold force from his previous encounter began probing him. He thought to repel it, but instead he let everything go blank—except for the concern and love he had for his daughter. Kahir would learn no more.

Jack kept his distance, but soon—soon, he'd act. Determination tightened his jaw as he locked his eyes on the window.

Jack couldn't say the journey home was a relaxing one, not even a calm one. Seeing Sarah and doing nothing proved harder than expected. It was his only move—his best move. He had to proceed with some restraint—for now. All the same, it left a huge knot, a twisting ache in the pit of his stomach, leaving her behind, but moving too soon could make things worse. Four others had died in a vain attempt to stop Kahir. He didn't fear for himself, but what that monster would do to Sarah in retaliation.

He stopped the Firebird on the road. The apprehension of what awaited him weighed heavily on his chest. His once-happy home appeared so dark—so isolated. Was returning a mistake? Could he be opening himself up to an attack he wasn't ready to defend against? If Kahir came for him, it would be here.

Jack concentrated, focusing on the lonely structure—it stood empty. The sensation struck him twofold—relief...and sadness. Empty also meant no Anna. He missed her—her face, her scent, the sound of her voice. But the fault was his—of that, he had no doubt—staying at Sanders' for too long without a word. He reminded himself that his job often kept him away for extended stretches with little or no warning, but that reasoning offered no comfort. If anything, it made the regret hit that much harder—it wasn't his job this time.

Jack gave the steering wheel a sharp turn and pulled into the driveway. He triggered the remote to open the detached garage. He drove inside and closed it behind him, then cut the engine and sat alone. In the silence, Jack spotted the lawn mower. It conjured images of routine—chores, quiet weekends, barbecues, and waving to the neighbors. He chuckled. His life had never been routine.

He left the garage via its side exit and headed toward the house. What little daylight remained was fading fast, the sky tinged with orange and purple as the sun neared the horizon. Though the pathway was dimly lit, he knew each and every step well, able to walk it in pitch black.

At the stoop, Jack gripped the key tightly and unlocked the front door. He paused at the threshold, taking in the darkness. The emptiness held a strange kind of welcome. His footsteps echoed softly across the entryway, and familiar aromas greeted him—Anna's perfume, that clunky vanilla-scented candle on the coffee table, the pine cleaner Anna always used on the counters and floors. It still amazed him how keen his senses had become. He'd almost swear he caught a faint hint of roasted chicken.

Jack decided to keep the lights off. With the Firebird tucked in the garage, from outside, the place appeared as it did before his arrival—empty. A safe precaution, he reasoned. And with his vision adjusting to the low light, Jack had no need, no desire to destroy the illusion.

He went through the living room, checking for anything out of the ordinary and making certain everything was as it should be. In the kitchen, he did the same, inspecting every spot large enough to conceal something unpleasant. He wanted no surprises.

Secure with his surroundings, Jack grabbed the wall phone's handset and held it loosely. His finger stalled at the number pad. He sighed and tapped the first digit—then stopped. After a long second, he finished dialing. The phone rang.

"Hello," he said. "It's Jack. Sorry to be calling you at home, but—" Jack pulled the receiver away—the yelling hurt his ear.

"Will you just listen to me? I know where Markus and his crew are held up." Those words cooled the venom in Gordon Brigham's voice. … "I can't explain how. … Yeah, I do, but— … I have information and I'm passing it on to you. Use it or not, that's up to you. But consider this—have I ever let you down? … Okay, okay, but last time doesn't count. … Brigham, will you please listen? Your recovery team is looking in the wrong spot."

Jack spent several more minutes convincing his boss that his intel was solid. Brigham spoke little, offering the occasional terse reply, but nothing to suggest he'd either take the lead seriously or dismiss it outright. The call ended, and Jack was left wondering if anything he said had made the slightest bit of difference.

After he replaced the handset, Jack checked the rest of the house, going room by room. He moved cautiously to ensure he was truly alone—that Kahir didn't have a nasty surprise lurking, waiting for him to drop his guard. But deeper than that was the pull of memory. This place held echoes of laughter, of joy, of the lives that had filled it. He wasn't just making sure he was safe—he was reaching for what he'd lost. If this was the closest he could be to his family, he had no intention of wasting it.

He made his way along the hallway, approaching the master bedroom. Surprised by his hesitation, he pushed himself to cross the doorway—the room had never felt so bare, so hollow. His gaze scanned every inch, but settled on the vanity table by the window. Bottles of perfume, a scattered assortment of makeup, and delicate jewelry adorned its surface. He picked up a blue and white marbled hairbrush, pausing at the sight of blonde hair tangled in its bristles. He rolled a few between his fingertips.

"I miss you," Jack said.

How he yearned for his wife—it had been so long. The ache in Jack's chest was almost unbearable. But dwelling on such feelings only clouded his judgment. He had to steel himself, channeling all his energy toward stopping Kahir. When it was all over, he'd be at Anna's side.

He pressed on, entering Justin's room. It was just as his son had left it—model boxes scattered around, a toy dump truck sticking out from under the bed, a baseball glove on the floor. The faint smell of paint and glue hung in the air. He carefully lifted one of his son's detailed airplanes—the B-52 Stratofortress, Justin's favorite, painted in grays and blacks, its tiny decals precisely placed. Justin had spent days on it, obsessed as he was with anything that flew. He remembered how Justin howled with glee after finishing it.

Then came Sarah's room. Nothing had been touched since that night she didn't come home. The walls were plastered with photos of teen idols, and a rack of CDs sat alongside the bedside stand, where the player and lightweight headset rested. The room belonged to a normal fifteen-year-old girl—a happy fifteen-year-old girl. Jack relived the pain of seeing Anna's tears as she told him their daughter was gone. He glanced around, not sure what he was looking for. A pale-blue book sealed with a gilded lock lay tucked half-hidden in an open drawer. He walked over for a closer look. Sarah's diary. He didn't even know she'd kept a diary. Jack forced down the sudden fury—he must not give in to grief, anger, or hatred.

When Jack returned to the living room, the last bits of daylight were finally vanishing. He sat alone on the soft couch as the night completely swallowed his home. Surrounded by darkness, he reflected on the path that led to this point, burdened by the weight of choices and consequences. His time away had changed how he saw the world—how he saw his life. He had always relied on bullets and bombs, but now, he had a different weapon—what Sanders called his inner spark. He hoped it would be enough. Self-doubt was already creeping in. He needed to stay true to Sanders' teachings. They were the key to saving himself—and restoring his family.

Jack's thoughts were ripped away as an alarm blasted in his head. Someone—or something—was here. He closed his eyes and concentrated.

Where are you?

He extended his awareness, casting a wide net into the stillness, hoping to catch the faintest ripple of either movement or thought.

Nothing.

Each breath sharpened his focus as he probed the silence, hunting for any disturbance that didn't belong.

Nothing.

Jack blinked and looked down at the floor in disappointment. He wished he had his gun or at least a sturdy knife.

"Get a grip," he told himself, refusing to surrender to failure—he was stronger than that. He inhaled slowly to anchor himself. Fear of failure was a distraction. It dulled the senses, weakened the mind.

Jack shut his eyes again and visualized himself merging with the walls, the floorboards, the plaster, and the pipes. His consciousness drifted between the studs, passed the rafters above his head, and settled into each dark crack and corner. He wasn't simply searching the house—he was the house.

He stretched out with every fiber of his being. Still—nothing. But this did not mean failure. He detected nothing because there was nothing to detect. What he sensed didn't come from within.

His eyelids shot open. Outside the big bay window, a car drove in front of the house. Its engine's hum grew faint as the vehicle slowed. The darkness hid the make, but the headlights lit the road ahead, revealing its location. Rolling to a halt, the car then turned in and crept along the driveway. The engine idled, then cut out.

Seconds later, a narrow light floated and bounced, slicing the air. It zigzagged wildly, then flickered out. Jack didn't move. He took several deep breaths and watched for the light to reappear. He heard no noise, saw no movement, but he sensed a definite presence—very close now.

The front knob rattled—the frame shook. Then, as it started, it stopped. Brief moments passed in silence. Jack moved to the top of the staircase, waiting. He held the high ground—strategically, the best defensive position. His ears caught the faint scrape of metal against metal, followed by the deadbolt snapping.

The door flew open. A dark silhouette stood framed by an even darker night.

Jack braced himself, unsure what nightmare would step through. The stone gargoyle that had killed Anthony Bane shot up from his memory, but he immediately dismissed it. A creature that powerful could have smashed the barrier to splinters—such a monster wouldn't have bothered with the lock. Maybe whatever it was didn't expect to find him here. That gave Jack a slight advantage. He slipped back, deeper into the shadows, positioning himself out of view while keeping an eye on the doorway.

TWENTY-FOUR

Jack's heart pounded, but he kept his breathing calm and steady. He'd get one shot. He waited, watching the steps, expecting the creature to come up. But it didn't. Instead, it groped along the wall, edging its way through the dark—slow and deliberate.

The overhead light snapped on. To Jack's eyes, it flared with the intensity of an explosion. He lost his edge. He had to act—advance or retreat.

Jack made his choice and charged down the stairs half-blind.

As he got to the bottom step, a single word stopped him cold.

"Jack?"

He forced himself to halt mid-stride, avoiding physical contact.

"Jack, is that you?" Anna said, her words trembling. "You're alive."

His vision cleared to the soft features of his wife's face. Jack rushed to the door and slammed it shut. He hit the light switch, plunging the house back into darkness. Grabbing Anna, he gently but quickly pulled her down to the carpeted steps.

She threw her arms around him as they both went down. The scent of her perfume filled his nose, and in that moment, he appreciated even more how much he hated being apart. He rested his chin on the top of her head, feeling the softness of her hair touching his skin. Her tears ran down her cheek, landing on his forearm.

"It's you," she sobbed. "It's really you."

"In the flesh."

"No one knew where you'd gone. I assumed the worst. Where have you been, Jack?"

"I'm sorry I scared you. A few things popped up that I needed to deal with." How was he supposed to explain a foot-long parasite pulled from his chest?

"I talked to Brigham," she said. "He told me you turned down your last assignment."

"He said that?" The fact Gordon Brigham revealed the status of a mission to his wife shocked him.

"Only after I bugged him every day for a week—he gave in. Turns out, telling me you *didn't* venture off to some unknown country wasn't against national security."

"Still, you must've been pretty hard on him."

"When it comes to my husband, hard is relative."

Jack was happy to see his wife, but— "What are you doing here?" he asked. "Skulking around like a common thief. I might've hurt you. I thought I was clear—you were to stay away."

"You were, and I did," she replied, quiet but steady. "But then I heard you."

Jack blinked. "Heard me?"

"Your voice," she said. "Just—your voice, like you were standing next to me. You said, 'I miss you.'" She folded her arms across her chest, gripping her own elbows.

Her words hung heavy in his ears. Sanders' warning about maintaining control and resisting random impulses echoed sharply, reminding him how the simplest, most innocent actions had consequences.

"I wasn't doing anything special," she continued, "unless you call boiling potatoes special. And boom—I was grabbing my keys. I didn't even think—it was as if I had no choice."

Jack opened his mouth but immediately closed it, hiding his twinge of guilt.

"It sounds crazy," she added, "but I couldn't ignore it."

"At least you didn't bring Justin."

"I left him at Mother's—not without a bit of an argument. He begged to come, but I convinced him it was best if I came by myself." Her gaze moved from Jack. "All our plans—everything we wanted for the children…" Another tear escaped her eye. The reality that their entire lives had been upended had finally broken down her defenses.

He kissed her forehead. "Nothing has changed, not really." *A small white lie.* "You'll see—college is right around the corner. I'll fix this." *The truth.* "But for the moment, you have to do something for me. It won't be easy, but you must do it."

"Anything." Anna touched her husband's cheek.

"I need you to leave."

"Anything but that," she said. "I have you, and I'm not budging."

"Please, for tonight. Drive back to your mother's," he said. "It's not safe here."

"Forget it. I'm staying. I live here too. If it's safe enough for you, it's safe enough for me."

"It's not all that safe for me," Jack murmured.

"Then we'll fight it together. Whatever it is."

"No," he said firmly. "You have to go—before it's too late."

"Too late? Too late for what? You talking this way only convinces me more that my place is here. I was so afraid I lost you. But you're here, and I won't take the chance of you disappearing on me."

"I wanted to call you. I just couldn't." Eric Sanders not having a phone rendered that impossible—but even if he owned a working line, Jack still wouldn't have contacted her. Kahir believing he'd skipped town was a calculated tactic to shield her. It tore him up for Anna to suffer so, but Kahir already had Sarah. Jack didn't dare risk him going after Anna next.

His priority was getting her out of here. Part of him longed to have her at his side, to hold her tight, but that would be reckless. He had missed her more than he'd admit, and the thought of her absence hit harder than he expected. But the best way to protect Anna was to send her away. He couldn't do both—keep her close and keep her safe. It was a painful choice, but the only one he had.

Jack stood, pulling her up with him. "Listen to me," he said, his words heavy. "If you stay, you'll be in danger. I'm begging you—go."

Anna smirked despite the fear in her eyes, a mischievous glint breaking through. "You seriously think I'm going anywhere simply on your say-so?"

He smiled faintly, seeing that stubborn streak of hers—if he weren't careful, he'd be fighting two battles.

"What if I decide not to leave?" Anna said, stepping closer and poking his chest lightly. "You're stuck with me, whether you like it or not."

Jack shook his head, avoiding those green eyes of hers. "This isn't just about us anymore. You need to be somewhere else, away from what's coming."

She touched his arm, her defiant grin not fading. "Fine. I'll leave... but let me make one thing clear. You and I? We're due for a long conversation. You're going to tell me where you've been all this time. We'll call it a debrief. I'm sure you can relate."

"I'll tell you everything later. I promise. Later. Go now."

Anna cocked her head, curiosity raising a brow. "If I didn't know you better, I'd say you're expecting someone."

Jack didn't respond.

"You are! Who's coming? Tell me!"

"Kahir," was all he said.

"That man? Here?" Anna's stare widened with terror.

"Anna, I can't get into it."

"You're scaring me," she said. "What are you planning? Is this why you were gone? Explain it to me."

"If I did, you wouldn't believe it," he said, looking to the bay window. "And we can't stand here while I try to convince you." The clock was ticking. Each moment they stood there arguing edged them closer to disaster.

She tugged at his arm. "My car does fit two."

Jack stroked his wife's hair. "I have to do this. Trust that I'll be all right."

"Please, Jack. Please."

"It's time," he said, opening the front door. "We'll talk later."

Jack led Anna to her dark blue Taurus, ensuring she got in. She gave him a worried glance before starting the engine. Leaning down to the open window, Jack kissed her. For the second time, he watched her drive away. Darkness swallowed the car, and once the taillights vanished, he turned toward the house. Whatever awaited him this night wasn't going away. He didn't feel ready, but thinking back on all his past missions, he never did.

He stepped inside. Somehow, it was even more lifeless than it had been before Anna arrived. But sacrifices had to be made—removing her from danger was all that mattered. Jack promised himself he'd make it up to her. And he would. When this was over, they'd do something normal—all of them together. Taking Anna, Justin, and Sarah out of town sounded good. Maybe Florida. Orlando seemed perfect. Disney World, Sea World, or any other "World" that could help them forget the past month.

Jack's brow furrowed, and he sighed—it was too easy to fall into old habits. He had to keep himself in the here and now. He dared not drift, not for an instant. That kind of mistake, and his fate would be the same as Blackburn's or Bane's. He needed all his wits to find a means to defeat Kahir.

Jack took position in the lowest room—the family room. There, he slid the coffee table aside, pushing it to the wall alongside the TV. He sat on the carpet dead center and began breathing in a rhythmic pattern. Clearing all distractions, he stretched out with his consciousness, expanding it to cover the grounds—from the road out front to the edge of the woods bordering the rear property line. He had never attempted to blanket such a large area, but Sanders told him his limitations were all in his mind—he made it sound so simple.

The minutes slipped by, then the hours, until Jack lost all sense of time. In his mind's eye, he kept vigil over his home and the surrounding grounds—waiting, alert to the slightest flicker of movement in the shadows, any shift in the brush that might conceal a threat. His perception swept over familiar paths and darkened corners, on guard for whatever monster, creature, or foe Kahir would send. Jack held his focus—free of fear, anger, or doubt.

A faint stirring at the tree line caught his attention—a presence large enough to trigger a warning but small enough to hide its true nature. The branches trembled, and leaves rustled, suggesting a creature moving with practiced stealth, blending into the surroundings. He couldn't discern its shape, but it set him on high alert. Then a bitter chill rushed over him, sudden and stinging, as though the air itself had grown hostile. A stabbing force drilled into his skull, boring deep into his brain. Jack clenched his teeth, fighting to keep control until the agony ceased, leaving him dizzy and unsteady.

As the spinning stopped and Jack regained his senses, a light clicking broke the silence. He dismissed it as a lingering effect of the dizziness brought on by the pain. But the sound persisted, and just as he tried to pinpoint it, Jack realized it was something tapping on glass. He turned to the farthest window and saw a face staring in from the other side. Jack blinked, and it vanished into the shadows. He got only a glimpse, but it appeared disfigured.

He rushed over and peered out into the night, but found the view poor. Thick bushes spaced along the windows blocked most of the yard, and the moonlight revealed nothing between him and the woods, which swayed at the faintest gust of wind, making it difficult to tell if anything—or anyone—was actually moving out there. Jack's breath fogged the glass as he leaned closer. He couldn't shake the image of that face, warped and pale. Unsure if it had been a trick of his imagination—or worse—he stepped back and headed upstairs to the kitchen. From there, he eased to the deck window and looked out at the backyard. It was clear. Maybe whoever it was had run off.

Behind him, the floor creaked. That always happened with the weight of a full-grown person. Jack spun around. A figure stood motionless several feet from him.

"Kahir?"

"Don't you know me, Jack?"

The man stepped forward, the stench of death preceding him. As he drew near, Jack recoiled at the sight of rotting flesh—skin sloughing from bone, features twisted and sunken. But beneath the decay, a faint familiarity remained—in his stance, in the tilt of his head, and in the set of his shoulders. Jack's throat tightened. It was him. It was his friend and mentor, Markus Radford.

"You left us to die," Markus said. A flap of torn cheek rippled with each word, exposing both rows of molars.

"Markus, I—"

The corpse shoved Jack with such brute strength, he flew backward and crashed into the large window, shattering it. He stumbled across the deck, and the force sent him tumbling over the railing. Jack clung to the guardrail, gasping, trying to stop his momentum—but his grip faltered, and his fingers slipped.

Jack fell, landing flat on the unyielding ground below. The impact knocked the wind out of him, and it felt like he'd cracked a rib. Cold night air and pain flooded his lungs as he lay there, the moon casting a pale light over the yard.

Markus glared down at Jack, who struggled to stand. "You could have saved us," Markus said, "saved us all."

Jack closed his eyes and concentrated. The sharp ache made it difficult, but he summoned all his willpower. He visualized himself surrounded by a flame—its energy filling his body, healing his injury.

A hand touched Jack's shoulder, breaking into what little concentration he had left. Tom Blair stood next to him. "Why didn't you come for us?" His right eye had been cut out. "I was tortured for days. It didn't matter what I told them. They wouldn't let me die until it pleased them to do so."

"And the others," Markus said.

Jack backed away from the men—and bumped into someone else. A woman stared at him, her expression unreadable. Another figure stepped in beside her. Two more emerged, approaching Jack with a labored gait. Two women. Two men. Markus's entire team. He'd seen them so clearly during that final session with Eric Sanders. "I saw you. You were all alive."

"They raped me," the first woman cried, ignoring his words. Her shirt had been ripped open, displaying her desiccated breast. "Over and over and over."

"As they did with me," the other, smaller woman said. Her cheek had been slashed, her hair burned off.

"Coward," a handless man said while taking a step toward Jack. The others moved closer as well. Jack was surrounded on all sides by the dead. "He deserves the same fate we had to endure," the man scowled. "He deserves to suffer!"

Tom grabbed Jack's arm—the woman with the slashed face grabbed the other. They both pulled hard, sending pain shooting into Jack's shoulders. He strained to break free. The pressure on his shoulder blades increased as he struggled. Each breath stretched his injured rib, causing more agony. Every joint—every muscle—every bone and tendon throbbed. Jack screamed out. He was being torn apart.

The crush of his failure tore at Jack. *Kahir has won. Anna, forgive me. Kahir has won. Sarah is lost to that evil man. Justin. My boy, Justin.*

As his right arm ripped free from its socket, a voice filled the cool night air. "Jack Railey," the voice called out. "Hear me, Jack Railey."

Was it Kahir? The question clawed at Jack. Was this his final gloat as Jack's blood poured out and seeped into the ground? He screamed again as his other arm was torn off by the woman. She laughed and held the limb up high, shaking it in triumph.

"It's a lie," the voice said. "A deception."

He could barely make out the words through the intense pain.

"Focus on me, Jack." A large form materialized in front of him—Eric Sanders stood there, an aura surrounding him as it had that day in the candle room. "Focus!"

Jack met the gaze of the man's image.

"Good, concentrate. Ignore the pain. It is false."

Jack reached out for Sanders.

"These beings do not exist," Eric's words echoed.

"Don't exist," Jack repeated.

Markus Radford, Tom Blair, and the rest shimmered briefly, and in an instant, they vanished. The landscape changed—from the open night to four walls. The ground went from damp grass to tightly woven carpet. Jack collapsed in the middle of his family room. He drew in a sharp gasp and passed out.

TWENTY-FIVE

The next morning, Jack awoke in his own bed. He sat up with a slight headache. All he remembered from the night before was the visitation from a decaying Markus Radford and his cadaverous companions, who had torn him limb from limb. Jack stared down at his hands. He turned them over, flexed his fingers, then wiped the sweat from his forehead. The pain in his shoulders startled him some.

A sharp creak made Jack look up. It was the bedroom door slowly opening.

He jumped out of bed and adopted a defensive posture. But as the previous night's horror grew clearer and clearer, he didn't think it would help. He was in no position or condition to offer an adequate defense.

The door continued to open.

Jack's eyes frantically searched the room for a weapon. But even holding an AK-47 assault rifle, he wouldn't impress an attacker as threatening, standing there in his underwear.

With the door opened wide enough, Jack couldn't believe what he saw. Anna stood in the doorway, balancing a tray of buttered toast, a pot of black coffee, and the morning newspaper. "You're up," she said, her tone somewhere between relief and anger. "You nearly scared the life out of me last night." She marched into the room and dropped the paper onto the bed.

"You came back?" Jack said, taking his folded pants from the seat of the chair where Anna had put them.

"Of course I did." She set the tray down on the nightstand. "And what do I find? You downstairs, sprawled out in a heap. I feared you were dead. That's the second time—please don't make it a habit. It's not something I enjoy seeing."

Jack's eyes narrowed as they settled on the bed. The sheets and blankets had been tugged free—some in a bunch, others hanging halfway off. "You brought me up here?"

"Yeah, and trust me, it wasn't easy. You're a lot heavier than you look."

"Hey, it's all muscle."

They laughed. It felt good. It had been quite a while since the two of them had shared a laugh together.

"By the looks of the bed," Jack said, "I must've kept you up all night."

"Would have, but I slept in Sarah's room. You were mumbling about someone named Markus, and knowing you, I figured you'd be having a rough one."

Jack shrugged an apology, then said, "Didn't I put your butt behind the wheel and watch you drive off?"

Anna poured a cup of coffee. The aroma drifted to Jack's nose. "Appears so, but I don't recall you saying for how long. I couldn't leave you here by yourself."

Jack remembered seeing Sanders' face and hearing his voice. "I guess I wasn't."

"What's that supposed to mean?"

"It's nothing." Jack walked over to the nightstand and dumped a teaspoon worth of powdered coffee creamer into his cup. "Do we have any jelly?" he asked.

"Yes, it's…" Anna glanced down at the tray. "…in the kitchen. Give me a minute."

As Anna left the room, Jack headed to the dresser, taking a sip from the cup. A lump of undissolved creamer clung to his upper lip—he'd forgotten to stir the coffee. He turned toward the tray to grab a spoon but checked himself. Instead, he drew in a deep breath, extended his right hand, and focused on the spoon.

Nothing.

A second breath. Eyes fixed. Jaw clenched. Focus sharp.

He visualized every detail: its shape, the glint of the metal, the handle, the bowl—and willed the spoon to his hand. Then, as he commanded, it rose off the tray and glided toward him. When it was only inches away, he spoke one word: "Stop."

The piece of silverware hovered, frozen in midair at eye level. He pictured it floating, and as form followed thought, it was now suspended before him.

"Grape or strawberry?" Anna shouted up from the kitchen.

A simple question, but sufficient to break Jack's concentration. The spoon fell to the floor. It bounced, then came to a complete rest.

Jack sighed and shook his head.

Anna returned to the bedroom carrying two jars. "Don't look so sad," she said, seeing Jack. "I can get you another spoon."

He set down the cup. "I have to go," he said, grabbing clean socks from the dresser drawer.

"Where?" she asked, watching her husband dress.

"Out," he replied. "Where's my shirt?" Jack slid on his shoes.

"In the laundry basket."

He grabbed a fresh one from the closet—the wire hanger twanged as it recoiled against the clothes rod.

After buttoning it halfway, Jack kissed his wife and left her alone in their bedroom. It didn't escape his notice that Anna hadn't questioned his going, but her silence spoke volumes nonetheless. He had a moment of doubt about leaving her, but he reasoned she'd be safe enough until nightfall—and he'd be home by then.

Jack rushed out, passing the kitchen along the way. He caught a glimpse of the deck window. It overlooked the backyard, intact—as always. The crash of shattering glass replayed in his head. He remembered being thrown through the window, but despite the attack never actually happening, it sure hurt like hell.

Outside, Jack found the Taurus blocking the garage, pinning in the Firebird. Not in the mood to play automotive musical chairs, he jumped in. The keys were in the ignition—a bad habit of Anna's, leaving the keys in the car. The engine started right up, and Jack checked the gas gauge. Anna's other bad habit was running her car near empty. *God, it was good to be home with her*, Jack thought, *even for a short while.*

Over an hour later, Jack steered down a secluded road. The freeway had been tolerable—long stretches of traffic, but no stoppages, with only the occasional semi-truck blocking the left lane. For most of the trip, he kept one hand on the wheel, the other flipping between radio stations, trying to relieve the boredom of the drive, eventually shutting it off altogether. Anna had a weird taste in music.

Not far down, Jack saw the mansion. He'd found it without missing a turn. No backtracking, no detours, no confusion. That must mean Sanders was expecting him—knew he was coming. He took the driveway, which narrowed as he got closer, and the tree line thickened. Jack slowed and eased his car forward. The house stood quiet at the end, as if it had been waiting.

Jack parked and saw Quon already standing at the open door. He stepped out and proceeded along the walkway of granite pavers. At the threshold, the servant greeted him and told him to go to the study—all without Jack having to speak. He continued down the short hallway and stopped at the closed sliding doors. He didn't knock.

"Come," Sanders said from the other side.

Jack entered the room. Sanders was settled comfortably in his chair, absorbed in the yellowed pages of a huge book—its thick, stiff leaves carefully turned to avoid cracking. The worn spine creaked softly under his touch, a contrast to the serenity around them.

"Sit," Jack heard Sanders say, not moving a muscle. No, Sanders hadn't spoken, Jack realized. The words were placed directly into his head—like they had been during Kahir's attack.

Jack sat across from the man and remained silent. He waited. A minute went by. Ten minutes more. Half an hour passed. An hour.

Sanders closed the heavy volume with a loud thud.

Jack studied the cover, unable to accept what it seemed to be made of. His curiosity tempted him to break decorum and ask Sanders—but he hesitated, not wanting to show disrespect.

It was then that Sanders spoke. "This dark book is indeed bound in human skin," he said, answering Jack's unspoken question. Eric Sanders set the tome aside. "It was created in an age preceding the birth of what historians call Lemuria."

"Lemuria? That's a fairy tale," Jack said. "It didn't exist—it's like Shangri-La or Shambhala."

Sanders shifted in his large chair. "Why do you presume Shambhala doesn't exist? Because some expert said so? Never adopt the beliefs of others—seek the truth for yourself. Don't blindly accept all as fact. Learn to distinguish the true from the false—the real from the imaginary. Not recognizing the difference can kill you."

Jack understood exactly what Sanders was referring to. "I failed," he said. "If it weren't for you…"

Sanders raised a single finger, silencing Jack with the gesture. "Kahir attacked you where you least expected—your mind. In my rush to train you, I concentrated on your innate abilities to control the physical world, giving you a means to direct your power. His mental attack caught you defenseless. It was meant to disorient and confuse you."

"Well, it worked."

"You did not fail, Jack," Sanders said. "I failed you. My intent was to give you a way to defend yourself—to save your life. You were beyond reason, inflexible, not open to change by what I or anyone else said. You were determined to face Kahir to retrieve your daughter. I trained you so you'd have a fighting chance—instead of rushing in as a lamb to the slaughter. But I did not prepare you properly."

"You saved me," Jack said.

"And in doing so, I interfered."

"Yes, and thank you."

"Be warned," Sanders said, meeting Jack eye-to-eye, "I will interfere no further."

"I understand," Jack said, "and I'll abide by your decision."

"By surviving—no matter how—you've angered Kahir. His first attempt was thwarted, and now he'll return with greater force. Still, I can tell you this—his efforts only served to drain him. He won't strike, but he will send one of his soldiers, and the assault will be direct—brutal. Be ready. Prepare for a physical attack."

"Doesn't this count as interference?"

"No. It's…advice. Whether or not you use it is up to you." The study door eased open. Sanders gave Jack a slight nod. "Quon will show you out."

On his way, Jack noticed the book on Atlantis lying on a nearby table —the book he started but wasn't able to finish. He flipped the cover and turned several pages. The handwritten words were in English. He glanced over at Sanders, who wore a half-smile.

"Goodbye, Jack," Eric said.

Quon escorted Jack through the quiet halls and out the front entrance. They stood just beyond the open doorway. Quon said to Jack, "I wish you much luck, my friend."

"I'll be needing more than luck."

"Every little bit helps," Quon replied. "Heed what the master has taught you, and have courage. Those things alone could save you. But if you need more, remember all he has said. Eric Sanders is not one to waste words—everything he's told you has value. You merely have to find it."

"Thank you, Quon." Jack took a step away from the mansion, then paused. "I wonder if I'll ever be coming back this way."

"Who can say, Jack Railey? Who can say? Destiny often causes paths to cross more than once in a lifetime." Quon bowed slightly.

Jack climbed into the car and fired it up. A bit distracted, he forgot he wasn't driving the Firebird—the weak sound of the engine caught him off guard. He popped the Taurus into gear and happened to glance in the rearview mirror at the mansion. His foot slammed on the brake. Quon was gone, but in his place stood a woman with long hair wearing a snug white dress that draped down to her feet. She looked sad as she waved goodbye. Jack watched as the woman's form softened, her edges blurring until she melted into the wall. Her outline and eyes lingered briefly, then the mansion returned to normal. Jack exhaled slowly, amazed—but not surprised. The house had always had a way of throwing him a curveball.

During the drive, Jack formulated his plan. It was definitely unorthodox, but it played to his strengths—all of his strengths. Quon's parting words had struck a chord. He found the nearest freeway entrance and headed east on I-94 into St. Paul—he needed to run some vital errands. But first, he had to call Anna to reassure her he was alive and well. Since she'd discovered him passed out, half-dead to the world, he was sure she'd be worried.

The tank running low, Jack took the next off-ramp and pulled into an Amoco service station. He filled up, then found a pay phone and dialed.

To his disappointment, all he heard was a busy signal.

Jack figured Anna was either calling her mother to check on Justin or calling around trying to find him. Being a betting man, option two had his ten bucks.

After giving it a couple of minutes, he dialed again. Still busy.

He should have told her where he was going. *Now that* would have been one heck of a story, he mused.

If only he could get through to her.

Then, out of the blue, a wild idea hit him. It was a long shot—he wasn't sure he was even capable of pulling it off. It would require all his concentration. He had to visualize the house—see each and every detail.

Anna shook out her hand. The button mashing was making her index finger sore. She'd tried calling all of Jack's friends, the gym, even her own mother's house, hoping he'd stopped by to see Justin. No one had a clue to his whereabouts, and most were reluctant to venture a guess. She briefly considered contacting Gordon Brigham, but given the circumstances, she decided it wouldn't be a good idea.

She should've insisted on going with him. But with the way he'd been acting, she was certain he'd say "No." In happier days, with enough persistence, she'd have cracked that stubborn shell of his, and he'd have let her join him.

Lost in her thoughts, Anna glanced out the window into the backyard. The absurd notion that the lawn needed mowing popped into her head. With so much unraveling around her, why, of all things, was she thinking of grass? It didn't take long to figure out. She longed for the return to a normal life—a cook-the-meals, tuck-the-children-into-bed, make-love-to-her-husband life.

A vehicle drove past the house. The roar of its engine gave her a fleeting sense of hope. She craned her neck to check the road and silently prayed it was Jack. But when she saw the red pickup, she knew it wasn't bringing him home. Anna held the telephone handset close to her chest, fighting a tear.

How had everything fallen apart so fast? Why her family? This—*all of this*—that evil man, Kahir—he did it. He was to blame.

The phone emitted a loud whine. She slammed the cradle button, cutting off the sound.

"Jack," she whispered. "Where the hell are you?"

A soft knock came from the front door. Anna almost missed it. The second knock was louder. She hung up the handset and rushed over, curious who would show up unannounced. *Jack? No, he would use his key?* She hesitated, her hand frozen on the doorknob.

"Who is it?" Anna called out. She peered out the side window. The stoop was empty.

Then, from behind her, she heard something drop. A pencil rolled toward her. Anna walked to the table, where she found a pink rose. She recognized the bloom as one from her Morden Centennial bush. Next to the flower lay a handwritten note.

Anna picked up the paper and read the message: *Just wanted to let you know I'm safe. I'll be home soon. Forgive me if I startled you. Love, Jack.* She stared at the note for what seemed minutes. Her eyes moved between the words and the flower—she was sure neither had been there before.

A sudden pounding made Anna jump—this time heavier, more forceful. A wave of dread hit her hard, a cold tightness rising in her throat, though she couldn't explain why. Anna approached, and at the door, another knock sounded.

She opened it a crack to peek out. There on the stoop stood a tall man who looked to be several years older than her, but with a distinguished presence that was somewhat disarming.

"Hello?" Anna said, keeping a firm grip on the door.

"Mrs. Railey?" he asked.

"Yes? Can I help you?"

"Good afternoon. I'm Jonathan de Montia. Cindy is my daughter."

"Oh, I see," she said, knowing how dumb that sounded.

"My ex-wife mentioned you."

"Leonora? But she's…"

"Dead? Yes, she is. She sent me a letter—just prior to her passing. In it, she provided a name to contact if anything happened to her. I learned of the…situation only yesterday. Her message said something about our daughter but lacked specifics."

Anna's mind raced as she recalled when Jack told her of Leonora's death. The news crushed her, each word carrying an unexpected weight. Jack didn't go into great detail—she didn't want him to. Her stomach churned, and the floor fell out beneath her. It was then that Justin entered their bedroom, asking what was wrong. Despite the shock and grief threatening to overwhelm her, Anna didn't let it show—not in front of her son. He needed her now more than ever. She feared she'd break down and cry, but forced herself to stay composed, pushing her own emotions aside. For Justin's sake, she had to be the strong one—the steady presence he'd rely on in the midst of this chaos.

"She gave you my name?" Anna asked.

"Your husband's name, to be precise."

"I'm sorry, but he's not here. You're welcome to wait if you like." The instant the words left her mouth, Anna realized they were a mistake. Given everything happening and the fact that he was a complete stranger, it wasn't the smartest move. "But it might be a while," she added.

Jonathan de Montia glanced at his watch. "I'm running late as is. Can you please explain what this is all about? Where's Cindy? Where's my daughter?"

Several hours later, Jack Railey returned home. It gave him a good feeling to know Anna was waiting for him. That's how it should be —and how it will be again, he assured himself.

He parked the Taurus in the driveway, then retrieved a grocery bag and a small sealed box from the backseat. The late afternoon sun was warm on his shoulders as he walked the path and let himself into the house. Inside, the air was cool and silent—very silent. Out the kitchen window, Jack saw Anna in the yard, her gloved hands delicately working a pair of shears as she pruned patches of dead growth from her favorite Morden Centennial bush.

Stepping through the sliding glass door onto the deck, he called out, "Ready for supper?"

Anna jumped at his voice. But when she turned his way, he caught the relief in her eyes. Anna was trying to put up a front, pretending she hadn't been worrying about him—he wasn't fooled.

"What's on the menu?" Anna asked.

"Two of the sweetest lookin' ribeye steaks."

"Sounds great. I'll be right in."

For a little while, they had some normalcy in their lives. Jack grilled the steaks, and Anna threw together some French fries and a garden salad with blue cheese dressing. The sunshine was fading as they ate out on the deck.

"Beautiful evening," Anna commented. "Hard to believe it's fall."

"That's Minnesota for you. Tomorrow it will probably snow."

They both laughed and continued their casual, carefree conversation, enjoying the moment together without any rush or worry. It was wonderful.

A rustling noise interrupted their talk. Jack looked to the edge of the yard, where something moved in the shadows near the trees.

"Uh-oh," he said, setting down his drink. "We have company."

A raccoon ambled into view, nose twitching, clearly drawn by the smell of cooking ribeye.

Anna inched closer to the railing. "That guy's been hanging around a lot lately. Gave me quite a start the other night." Her eyes fixed on the furry masked invader. "Hey, buddy, you got five seconds to back off before I throw a steak knife."

The raccoon paused, stared at them as if it was considering the threat, then retreated a few steps—only to plop down and watch them from a safe distance.

"Bold little guy," Jack muttered, realizing it was this critter he'd sensed roaming around last night when all hell broke loose.

"Can you blame him?" Anna smiled. "Smells amazing out here."

They sat in silence for a beat, watching the raccoon pretend not to beg.

Then Anna said, "He's not the first visitor we've had today. Cindy's father dropped by—he asked for you."

That stunned Jack. "Me? Why me? What brought him here?"

"Apparently, Leonora sent him a letter before she died. I told him he could wait for you, but he seemed in a rush. He did ask about Cindy, so I tried my best to explain the situation, though I'm not sure how much really got through."

"He must've appreciated any information," Jack said.

"My heart went out to him. He'd been left in the dark regarding his own daughter. And he can't be any happier now that he knows."

"It is true. Ignorance *is* bliss."

"How's that?"

"Just thinking out loud," Jack said. His tone remained calm as he added, "You do realize I'll be driving you to your mother's myself. I don't want you backtracking on me."

"Yeah," she responded as casually, "I figured there was a catch to having this meal together." She touched his hand. "What if I stuck around? I'm tough. I can help you."

"You can't. I have to do this alone. We've already been over this."

"True, we have. But I also found you unconscious. We need to discuss it."

"Discuss what?"

"That you could die, for one thing."

"You must be kidding. Considering my job, it's not much different."

"Different? It's completely different."

"How?"

"First of all, this isn't your job—I came to terms with your 'job' the day we were married. Besides, getting killed in your own home doesn't fall under the typical occupational hazards you usually face. Second, if you remember how the others died, how do you expect to win?"

"Thanks for the vote of confidence."

"I didn't mean it the way it came out. This man, Kahir—you've never taken on someone like him. And now the plan is to fight him head-on. What? It's not good enough that he comes after you?"

"Our next meeting won't be face-to-face either," Jack said. "That's how I'll defeat him. He hides behind his tricks. I'll force him to meet me one-on-one. I've got a few tricks of my own."

"You're talking crazy. How can anyone beat him alone?"

"I'm working on it." Jack paused. "We won't agree on this," he said, "and it's time to make sure you're safe."

"I'll go, but when we get to Mother's, don't leave. Stay with me."

"Not an option," Jack said firmly. "I didn't start this fight, but I'll bring our daughter home. You deserve that. Sarah deserves that. And I'll stop Kahir from hurting other families."

"Tell me you can win. Tell me, and I'll believe you. Say it to my face, and I'll leave you to this thing you're bent on doing." She moved her hand to Jack's shoulder and met his gaze.

"I don't intend to lose—if that's what you're asking?"

"It isn't, but I suppose that's the best I can expect."

"There's no more waiting, Anna. I refuse to run. Kahir might be stronger, more experienced in his ways, but I have my own ways, my own experiences. He may have blindsided me once—it's my turn to return the favor." Jack turned away from his wife. "I have to do things my way," he told her.

"You always do," she replied.

"Grab your stuff. I'll meet you at the car."

Anna said nothing else. He knew she wanted to, but it would've only been wasted on him. She disappeared into the master bedroom, and Jack looked over at the sealed box he had brought in earlier with the groceries.

TWENTY-SIX

Justin sank deeper into the sofa, staring at the television. The new big-screen color TV stuck out among the hardwood floors, oak trim, hung photos, and ugly vases. The house also had an old-timey smell—an aroma that his grandmother had always brought with her on visits, but was only apparent when she hugged him. Here, however, that odor was everywhere.

At night, everything seemed a lot darker than at home. Besides the glow of the TV, the room was lit by a single corner lamp. Justin dragged the light closer to the couch and turned the shade so more light hit him. This old place gave him the creeps. He couldn't wait until he was back in his own room.

It was funny—when he was younger, he thought this house was pretty neat, though he had never spent the night. But a couple of days was plenty to change that. The spooky relic gave out its share of creaks, moans, and groans. Sometimes, lying in bed, he could've sworn footsteps came from the hallway, but he never summoned the courage to check.

A commercial came on right as his grandmother called out to him. "Justin," she said, "would you like some ice cream?"

"No thanks, Grandma," he said, propping his feet up on an ottoman.

"Are you sure? It's Rocky Road. I can put it in a waffle cone."

"Yeah, I'm sure."

Justin was getting sick of seeing some bald guy on the screen complain about having a headache and needing relief—fast. He hit the button on the remote, repeating his tour of all the stations. He paused briefly on each channel until he had come full circle.

Losing interest in the current episode of *Star Trek: The Next Generation*, he considered turning off the TV. Since they'd stopped making new shows, he had seen this rerun at least six times: the good and want-to-be-human android *Lieutenant Commander Data* meeting his evil twin brother, *Lore*. A good episode, but after seeing it so many times, it had lost its edge.

Boredom started to consume the boy, and he wished he had brought more model plane kits with him. He finished the biplane crop duster within two afternoons of arriving—one for gluing, the other for painting. His grandmother didn't own a VCR, so renting movies was out of the question. There were some books on the wall shelf, but he doubted she'd have anything he'd like. He tried to read the titles from the couch.

Then, while sitting, contemplating a fate worse than death—the need to pick up a book—a pale white face appeared in the window. It startled him until he saw it was Sarah. She smiled at him through the glass, then backed away.

"Grandma, Grandma, Sarah's here!" Justin jumped to his feet, bolted to the front door, and threw it open.

"Sarah," he called out, stepping onto the stoop. His eyes scanned the darkness for his sister. "Sarah," he repeated, lowering his voice. "Are you hiding?"

A rustling sound broke the silence, and a shadow ran along the wall, disappearing around the corner out of his view. Justin stretched out his neck to get a better look, but the black of night made that impossible.

"Come out, Sarah. Come out." The door closed, and the latch clicked into place. "It's only me. I promise."

Justin didn't bother with the steps—impatience got the best of him. He leaped down the four-foot drop to the ground. His ankle gave a little, and a slight but sharp twinge shot up his shin. He ignored it.

"Sarah?" Justin limped out his first few strides as he moved around to the blind side of the house. His gait improved, but putting weight on his ankle hurt. Pain or not, he was going to find his sister. She had come to see him—just him. Why else would she be hiding? To the boy, the answer was clear—she didn't want the others to know she was here.

"I won't tell anybody," Justin whispered. "Sarah, Sarah. I won't tell. Where are you?"

The house blocked out what moonlight there was, choking his sight to a few inches. Still, he heard movement in front of him.

"I'm here, Sarah."

Several minutes later, a car pulled up along the street. It sat motionless at the curb for another minute, then the passenger side opened. The interior ceiling dome light popped on, illuminating Justin's mother and father.

"I suppose I'd be wasting my breath," Anna said, not yet releasing the handle, "trying to convince you to stay."

"You suppose right," Jack said.

Anna let the Firebird door swing open on its own as she leaned over and gave her husband a hard kiss on the lips. "Please, please, be careful."

"I'm always careful," he said, smiling.

"Will you be serious?!" Anna snapped. "No," she said. "I'm sorry. If this is our last talk, it's not going to end in an argument. Do what you have to do. I just want you to come back to me."

He touched her cheek. "I intend to." This time, he kissed her. "Go now."

"All right, but do you mind if I don't watch you go?"

"I'll see you later," he said. And with that, Anna got out.

The engine revved, and the Firebird drove off, its taillights shrinking into the distance. She said she wouldn't watch him leave, but she couldn't stop herself. "Be safe, my husband," she spoke out, then turned toward the house.

As she started up the sidewalk, footsteps came from behind her. She spun around—nothing. But, out of the corner of her eye, someone—or something—darted past and disappeared into the darkness.

"Justin, is that you?"

A shadow rose in answer to her question. It was not her son.

The sun had vanished below the horizon, revealing a slightly less-than-full moon. In the clear sky, it hung bright—an imperfect sphere among the stars. The last remnants of twilight faded, darkness swallowed the land, and the long shadows of dusk melted into night.

A raven perched atop a high telephone pole, its black, round eyes fixed on the modest dwelling. It saw Jack Railey drive off with his beloved wife, Anna, and witnessed him return alone. The raven ruffled its ebony feathers, letting out a sinister caw as Jack entered the house.

All the usual sounds of night fell silent, as if time had stopped before the coming battle. The raven spread its wings and glided down from the pole, then, with a powerful beat, soared upward, above the house. At an upper window, Jack stood watching the bird's departure—his plan was nearly ready. Only a few final details remained.

Thinking back to the previous night, Jack's shoulders and arms began to throb. The rotting face of Markus Radford flashed in his mind, sending a slight tremor throughout his body. It was fear. He'd be a fool not to feel it on some level—Kahir controlled great power—four people were already dead. And they, by what Sanders told him, had studied occult lore for years—they understood exactly what they were up against. He, however, lacked such knowledge. He didn't possess the deep insight into the arcane that they did. And that put him at a distinct disadvantage, and Kahir knew it. But it was on that fact that his entire plan hinged.

Night engulfed everything. The moon and stars bathed the world in a pale twilight. The air was heavy with an almost electric charge. An uneasy wind stirred, making the trees sway as if free to move on their own, their limbs trembling like they were afraid.

There were no other sounds. No birds. No animals. No cars. No people. The Railey family home stood alone. Its windows shut tight, the doors locked. The house seemed to be waiting—waiting and listening.

Inside, all was quiet. The hallway light from the upper floor cast a pale glow down the stairs, its yellow hue soft against the walls and carpet. Lamps in the living room had been left on, illuminating the sofa, loveseat, and coffee table. A stillness hung heavy, as if the space itself was waiting for a fight.

A bang rocked the front entrance. The wood shuddered under the impact. Picture frames fell from the walls and broke apart as they hit the linoleum. A nearby potted plant tipped over, dumping dark soil onto the white tiles. A second crash landed—even harder—rattling the entire door. The top hinge tore free from the frame, and the narrow side window exploded, spraying glass daggers into the entryway—some landing as far as the inner staircase.

The pounding stopped. Silence claimed the house. In that hush, the only sound was the tinkling of shattered glass settling on the floor. Peace held for mere moments. Then it began again.

The thunderous slams returned—more forceful now, more deliberate, as if whatever was on the other side had grown tired of the delay. Wood groaned and splintered beneath each brutal impact, the last hinge shrieking in protest. The door warped as the force behind the blows intensified.

Unable to withstand the assault, the thick wooden barrier burst in two, flying inward. The upper half crashed into the iron railing leading to the upstairs, while the bottom slid along the stairwell into the family room.

A piercing caw of victory and defiance trumpeted throughout the house. Massive talons swept aside the remains of broken debris, and an enormous beak pecked at the doorframe, carving out enough space to enter.

The giant raven filled the doorway, paying no mind to the wood and glass it crushed beneath its claws. Its eyes glared up the flight of stairs and down the other, lingering on the shattered pieces of door. The bird listened—waiting—for any sound that might guide it to its prey. It heard nothing but a faint rattle.

Out of the living room, a toy dump truck rolled into the open. The raven cocked its head with curiosity while the truck moved backward, forward, backward, forward, seemingly under its own control—its plastic wheels and steel axles producing a high, soft squeak.

The creature watched the truck spin in circles. It paused, facing the raven, with clear, glossy headlights. The toy steered to the staircase and disappeared beneath the broken plank.

The monstrous bird charged forward and raked its talons across the mangled door. Each slash shredded what remained of the wood, tearing out chunks and splintering slats, forcing its way through.

When the hole widened enough for the raven to attack with its beak, the dump truck charged, crashing into the raven's leg. The toy backed up, then surged forward, ramming the massive limb a second time, drawing a sliver of blood. In anger, the raven squawked and stomped, trying to squish the plaything like a bug.

The truck circled the entryway, its wheels squealing. The creature tried to follow, but its massive form was constrained by the tight space. Frustration erupted in a screech as it slammed a claw, but it was too slow to catch the darting toy. Another strike missed. A third attempt failed as well. Each time, the toy slipped just beyond its range, zigzagging across the floor. Fatigue crept in, and the raven grew sluggish. Then, with a sudden burst of energy, the raven's foot crashed squarely on its target. The dump truck didn't stand a chance—with a loud crunch, it was flattened. Wheels shot in four different directions.

The raven pecked suspiciously at the twisted metal, almost expecting the wreckage to move. It used its beak to tip the debris over when an object slammed the side of its head. A shower of black feathers and broken plastic rained down. The creature spun around to see a model airplane diving from above—this one faster and more precise. Before it could react, the plane struck the bird's left eye. The raven shrieked—a harsh, echoing cry of pain and fury. It clawed at the plastic shards embedded in the soft tissue, knocking them free with its talons, leaving nothing but an empty, bloody socket.

More planes flew at the raven, circling as the creature batted at them with its massive wings. But the cramped quarters made it hard to attack, forcing it to keep any movement tight to its body. The next plane, and the next, and the next, dive-bombed the bird. It managed, but with great effort, to swat each one mid-flight, sending them crashing to the floor. Eventually, all of Justin's models were destroyed—the raven appeared dazed and exhausted.

Things were falling into place. From out on the deck, Jack stepped into full view. Now, to finish it.

The raven spotted him with its undamaged eye and charged through the kitchen. Jack leaped over the railing and sprinted for the woods as the sliding door shattered behind him. He grabbed the leather pouch he had hidden there and darted between the trees. He made his way along his planned route deep into the leafy interior, stopping at a fallen oak where he crouched out of sight.

Jack pressed himself low. He had just caught his breath when a twig snapped—he was not alone. His pulse quickened. Eyes darting to the side, he strained to see in the dim light. He pivoted toward the sound.

Another crack—closer this time. Two glowing yellow eyes stared out from the shadows.

He went rigid.

A jolt of dread hit him. Had he grown careless? Was this one of Kahir's monsters—a beast in case the raven failed? His fist clenched, and he cursed under his breath. He'd gotten cocky—too confident in his plan.

Then the critter rose onto its haunches.

He exhaled—part relief, part irritation. It was the scruffy raccoon that had been lingering around the yard for weeks. Jack hissed and waved it off. The animal blinked lazily, sniffed the air, and ambled into the dark. Shaking his head, Jack refocused, returning his attention to the fight ahead. He listened closely as the bird charged at him in a half-blind rage.

"Something wicked this way comes," Jack quoted softly to himself.

He controlled his breathing by taking deep, steady breaths, matching the rhythm of his heartbeat. During his time between assignments, he and Justin often walked these woods, exploring nature. Justin had always talked about building a fort among the trees, but never did, not having a sufficient clearing. That was about to change.

The steps grew heavier, but slower. Kahir controlled the creature, but the surroundings were unfamiliar, and the bird was literally half-blind. Markus Radford's unofficial first rule of survival was to get your opponent into unknown territory—forcing him to split his battle between you and the environment.

Jack also added a little extra to the "battle-with-the-environment" part of the equation. He smirked, hearing a crash as one of his traps went off. A tension line snapped, dropping a deadfall of jagged scrap and lengths of barbed wire. The impact was sudden and violent, capable of cutting and bruising. A rasping shriek followed as the raven flailed, its wings getting tangled in the debris. The trap wasn't meant to kill or even capture—Jack had something else in mind for that. Since he had no clue as to what kind of threat Kahir might send after him, the traps were designed to slow it and reveal its location.

The raven quickly freed itself, but its movements had grown sluggish. It wasn't just simple hesitation. As Jack planned, Kahir must be expending a great deal of energy—first chasing a toy truck, then swatting at toy planes. Both had Jack using little of his own power, conserving his strength. The additional strain of pursuing him in the maze of trees and thick foliage, along with contending with traps, was all taking its toll.

Jack kept low as the beast drew nearer, gambling that Kahir would be weakened enough not to sense his presence. If he was wrong, he'd die—simple as that.

The monstrous raven stopped only a yard or so from Jack's position. Its uninjured eye shifted, scanning the thickets ahead—slow, deliberate, searching for signs of motion. Jack stayed still, realizing Kahir would surely make him suffer at the hands, or in this case, talons of his creature. It wasn't a coincidence that the man sent a raven to do his bidding. Kahir had picked up on Jack's childhood fear about the bird. And that mistake proved Kahir was not omniscient. Jack was no longer a child, and while he found the dirty scavenger disgusting, he had learned to control his fears.

The bird started to move again, turning away from its hidden prey. Powerful claws scraped the ground with a slow, measured pace. Leaves rustled and twigs snapped beneath its heavy weight as it stirred up the underbrush with each step. Jack didn't twitch a muscle—he watched, heart pounding. The grotesque creature craned its neck in confusion before lumbering off. Markus' second unofficial rule of survival kicked in—get your opponent's back to you.

Gotcha! He opened his leather pouch and pulled out a small olive-green pack attached to a metal strip. His thumb pushed up on the toggle switch, which flipped with a sharp click—a red light blinked on. He sprang up, ran at the bird from its blind side, and slapped the device onto the monster's wing—barbed hooks secured it in place. Jack made a quick strategic retreat, counting down as he moved. At "two," he dove behind the heavy log for cover. On "one," the plastic explosive blew the foul creature into tiny bits.

Jack chuckled at the prospect of Kahir himself somehow experiencing the explosion of his oversized murder bird. It was a dry, humorless laugh—more reflex than amusement. He didn't know the man, had only seen his face in photos, but that didn't stop the mental image from forming: Kahir somewhere immersed in whatever strange rites or dark rituals that led him to think sending a giant raven to kill him was a good idea. Jack pictured him robed, muttering over arcane symbols, or maybe in some meditative state. Then—boom! It must have come as one hell of a surprise. That lifted Jack's mood, just for a moment.

Careful to avoid stepping in bird entrails, Jack returned to the house to find the door completely torn off its hinges. The creature clearly had immense strength to have ripped the planks in half. A direct physical confrontation, powers or not, would almost certainly have failed. But Kahir hadn't anticipated him resorting to such extreme measures—a charge of C4 and a timed detonator retrieved from his storage locker. Jack had taken the gamble—and won.

He walked past the wreckage, his foot bumping the flattened toy dump truck. Model airplane parts littered the floor—Justin's entire collection had been smashed. A large red stain spread over the carpet, radiating from a glob that had once been the raven's eye. The rest of the bird outside was in pieces not much bigger.

The damage continued into the kitchen. Jack's shoes crunched on bits of broken glass, though most of it was blasted onto the deck. Further out, the railing had been torn apart. The creature hadn't bothered to jump over. It had gone straight through.

He crossed the room and picked up the phone, dialing the private number. Gordon Brigham answered on ring two.

"Jack," he said. "I was wondering when I'd hear from you. How did you know?"

"I…I don't understand."

"How did you know where to look?"

"I'm still in the dark here, Brigham."

"If that's not why you're calling, then let me tell you—Colin Reeves found Markus and his team—alive. Exhausted and hungry, but no worse for wear. You did a great job. I'm not sure how you managed it, mind you—an impressive job, nonetheless."

It pleased Jack to learn about the rescue of his friend, but he had little time.

"I need a favor," Jack said.

"Name it."

They kept the discussion short. Brigham agreed to send over a few men to clean up the damage and board up the missing doors, to protect what was left from the weather and the stray looter. It was his home after all.

Jack stepped outside to wait. Near the edge of the yard, the raccoon sat staring at him, a bloody strip of raven flesh hanging from its mouth. It batted a paw before slinking off into the backyard, dragging its prize with it.

"Bon appétit, buddy."

It took barely ten minutes for an unmarked car to show up. The driver told Jack that others would arrive soon with the materials to make the temporary repairs. Leaving the man as a guard, Jack glanced at the damaged property, mentally figuring the odds of his return. He'd faced worse—once. It was time to put the next phase of his plan into action—the most dangerous phase. He'd be playing on a whole new field. His enemy's field.

TWENTY-SEVEN

Under the cloak of night, Jack Railey left the Firebird several blocks away and traveled on foot to the dwelling place of Abhaya Kahir. He went the long way around, staying in the shadows to make sure no one looking from an upper window would spot him. He edged along the stone wall that surrounded the estate, avoiding the entry gate entirely. If Kahir had installed an intercom, he might have included sensor wires to the iron bars as well—a method of detection not as effective with rock and mortar.

The west side gave Jack the best advantage—with the moon in the east, the mansion cast a stretched silhouette, perfect for masking his presence. And with only one high attic window facing his direction, the choice was a no-brainer. He broke into a running start, and inches from the wall, he leaped and grabbed the stone coping. The leather gloves he wore protected his fingers and palms from the rough surface. He pulled himself over and dropped down, landing on the plush grass.

Jack crouched low and scanned the grounds, then darted through the darkness to the house. He kept his body tight to the exterior wall—his pace slow and deliberate. When he reached the front entrance, he paused, listening for voices or any hint of activity. Nothing. Jack tried the door handle. Locked. He kicked himself for not bringing his lock picks.

Breaking down the door was an option, but it would also alert everyone inside—so much for stealth.

What would Sanders say: "Your thinking is still two-dimensional." Jack smiled—old habits were hard to break. He closed his eyes and concentrated. Jack pictured his favorite pick working the pins within the dead bolt lock—positioning them, setting each one. Then he visualized the inside bolt knob rotating.

CLICK.

Jack gripped the handle, said a short prayer, then turned it. The door eased open without a sound. For some reason, he expected it to creak.

He stood at the threshold. It reminded him of the cave—black and foreboding. Jack drew a slow breath and pressed on. His sight adjusted, and it surprised him how mundane everything looked. He didn't expect inverted crosses or sacrificial altars, but this house could have belonged to anyone's family. Jack remembered Anthony Bane telling him social workers had visited several times. If anything had seemed out of the ordinary, they wouldn't have let Kahir keep the children under his care. *Under his care*, Jack thought. It was almost laughable if it weren't so absurd.

As Jack pushed farther inside, the normalcy fell away, replaced by something wrong and hollow. An absolute silence enveloped him—an emptiness where the small noises of life should have been. No groan of old wood settling, no distant drip from a kitchen sink, not even the ticking of a clock—just a thick, unnatural void that pressed in on him from all sides. Despite the dead quiet, he knew Sarah was here. He felt it deep in his gut—the same way he'd always sensed danger before a shot rang out.

He slipped carefully amid the eerie stillness, searching for the stairs to the second floor—the means, he hoped, to the children's sleeping quarters, and to his brave little Sarah. Jack thought of her stubbornness, the fierce fire in the way she refused to back down—she was every bit her mother's child. That bastard Kahir had brought enough pain to his family. It was time to end it. He had come for his daughter, and if anyone stood in his path, they'd regret it.

Jack stopped—his anger was growing. He had to stay focused—

distraction could get him killed, a lesson he'd learned all too well. Years ago in Iran, he'd been preoccupied by being separated from Anna while she was pregnant with their first child, and missed seeing the sniper barrel. Markus Radford took the bullet meant for him and nearly died. Jack's guilt had been overwhelming, and eventually drove him out of the field and into a desk job. But now, he had to force down the surge of emotion and stay sharp. He couldn't afford the same mistake tonight.

He made his way through the living room. Off to one side, a sitting nook with folding doors had been left open, the floor inside covered with a scattering of pillows. Then Jack passed under a decorative arch and entered the dining area. A large oval table, surrounded by wooden chairs, was clean and highly polished.

Two more doors led out from this section of the manor, both closed—one at the rear, the other to the side. Jack walked around the table to the rear door and opened it, finding the kitchen beyond. It was spotless, like the rest of the house.

He was about to try the other door when a creak came from behind. Jack didn't have a chance to turn as a powerful hand grabbed him. Instinct kicked in, and he tore himself free, but his shoulder throbbed where the fingers had dug into his flesh. He backed into the kitchen, where moonlight from the window revealed his attacker. To Jack's surprise, it was the short, bald man he had seen collecting coins and dollar bills from the children when they returned from their begging.

The stout man lunged with surprising speed and locked Jack in a fierce bear hug that pinned one of his arms. They staggered backward as Rajak's weight drove into Jack—the men crashed into the counter. Jack swung his free elbow, driving two hard blows to Rajak's ear, followed by a quick fist to his kidney. Rajak squeezed harder, forcing the air from Jack's chest in a sharp gasp. Jack twisted and strained, landing another desperate punch. Rajak growled and tightened his hold.

His ribs about to break, Jack groped along the counter for a weapon. All he found was an iron cooking skillet. He gripped the heavy pan and struck Rajak on the top of his head. The blow loosened the vise-like hold, and fresh air rushed into Jack's lungs—but not without some pain. Before Rajak retightened his grip, Jack bashed him on the bridge of his nose. The man collapsed to the kitchen floor. But rather than blood, a glowing light-blue fluid oozed from his ears, nostrils, and mouth.

Rajak lay motionless, sprawled where he had fallen, giving no sign of life. Jack caught his breath and fought through the pain in his ribs until his body eased some. As he passed the fallen servant, a hand sprang up and seized the cuff of his pants. Jack raised the pan and brought it down hard—then again, and again. The kitchen rang with the sound of metal meeting flesh. He poured all his rage into the blows and didn't stop until the man's head was reduced to a pile of blue slime.

The glowing gunk covered the floor, the pan, and Jack's glove and sleeve. He recoiled in disgust—beneath the outer husk, there was nothing but the goo. It seeped from his neck, the blue glow flickering, pulsing, fading, then dying out. The lifeless hand released its grip and fell into the puddle.

Silence settled over the house once more until Jack let the pan fall. It clanged. He peeled off his sticky gloves and tossed them beside what remained of Rajak, then retraced his steps into the dining room. He stopped, rubbing the nape of his neck—he hadn't seen anything that disturbing since Eric Sanders pulled that parasite from his chest.

The dining area remained empty, and he noted with unease that the violent struggle had drawn no attention. Jack crossed the room, keeping a wary eye over his shoulder to guard against anyone—or anything—sneaking up on him. At the other door, he took the knob, turned, waited a moment, then pulled it open while standing clear. After a second, he cautiously peeked inside. He had found the stairway leading up.

Jack ascended to the next level, where a multitude of doors lined a long, dim hallway. He quietly entered the first room. It had a simple layout with four beds, but something was wrong. He checked the closest. Empty. The other three were as well. Moving on, he discovered the same silence and vacancy beyond each door. Room by room, he searched them all, but found no children.

Then, from the hall, Jack heard light footsteps and a soft giggle. He turned in time to glimpse a child darting past the doorway. Jack rushed out as a tiny foot disappeared up another flight of stairs.

Alarms were going off in his head—he was being herded to an upper room. *Well,* Jack thought, *who am I to disappoint?* He followed the child, keeping several paces back, not wanting to appear too eager—overzealousness could spoil a good plan.

Jack made it to the last stair leading into a large, open attic. Pitch darkness surrounded him, but he figured he'd soon be given directions—all he had to do was wait. When he heard more footsteps, Jack started toward them, keeping close to the walls until he touched a sliding door. He opened it, and the light of a flickering fire cast a sudden glare, briefly blinding him. The room was illuminated by oil lamps hanging from several mounted iron brackets.

He entered.

Immediately, Jack was surrounded by the watchful glares of many children, catching him completely by surprise. He hadn't sensed their presence.

A whisper rose from the children, but within seconds, the sound swelled into a loud chant.

"Kahir!"

"Kahir!"

"Kahir!"

Jack studied the young faces. They were cold—empty of emotion.

"Kahir!"

"Kahir!"

"Kahir!"

The chanting stopped.

"I know why you have come." Those words echoed from a darkened corner. "You will fail—as did the others."

The children parted as Kahir stepped into view and approached Jack, with the hood of his red robe lowered. He wasn't what Jack had expected—smaller, frailer, with matted black hair and dull dark eyes, he seemed unthreatening. *How could this man wield so much power?* Jack warned himself how dangerous it was to judge someone solely by appearance.

"I can stop you," Jack said. "And I will. You sent that bird of yours after me, and I blew it to hell. I can control my fear."

"Ah, but you possess many fears," Kahir said. "As all Westerners do—boasting of your collective greatness, yet in truth, you are but children hiding in the dark, with no idea of the real world. You are all so frail, easily hobbled by the things and people around you."

"You about done?" Jack said, goading Kahir on. "I'm not used to hearing a sermon when I'm working."

Kahir clapped.

The door at the far end of the chamber opened, and both Justin and Anna entered. They walked in a stiff, almost mechanical manner. Their expressions were blank—their gazes vacant.

"Abduction is so crude," Kahir said. "So mundane. But effective. I do this to show you the futility of your actions."

"What've you done to them?" Jack said, easing his hand to his back waistband.

"Nothing…permanent. I prefer my guests calm."

"I swear," Jack said, every word measured and sharp, "if you've hurt them—"

"They're unharmed—for now." Kahir snapped his fingers. Anna gasped sharply, blinking as she struggled to focus on Jack.

She opened her mouth, but no sound came out. Her lips trembled with the effort. "Jack," she forced out. "Jack, what's happening?" Her gaze shifted to Sarah, and she attempted to step toward her. But with a second snap of Kahir's fingers, Anna's expression went blank once more.

"Taking them was a mistake," Jack said in an oddly calm tone.

"A simple precaution," Kahir said. "Underestimating you has proven a mistake I intend not to repeat. You've thwarted my attempts on three separate occasions."

"I count four," Jack replied. "But let me tell you the real reason—you're terrified."

"Of you?" Kahir laughed.

At that moment, Jack pulled his Beretta into view. He cocked the hammer and pointed the barrel squarely at Kahir's head. "Yes, of me."

Kahir snorted, unimpressed. "You Americans—you put too much pride in your guns and bombs. They are nothing."

The gun flew out of Jack's grip and was sent skidding to the far side of the room. Jack kept a straight face—everything was going according to plan. Sanders had told him that Kahir would defeat a physical attack.

And Jack figured Kahir expected just that. It was a gamble, but Jack hoped any attempt to stop it would only weaken him—and it was already working. The strain of controlling the children, holding Anna and Justin at bay, and having to contend with him was starting to show on Kahir's face. He had to push Kahir to expend even more of his power, but he also had to ensure that any wrath was directed at him, not at Anna or Justin.

A crazy idea struck him—and crazy was the thing needed right about now. It required him to get closer to Kahir while putting some space between him and his family. He had to play against Kahir's ego.

"What kind of man enslaves children?" Jack said, easing to the left. "A coward, if you ask me." He kept drifting sideways and snorted a chuckle. "It's laughable that Bane and the others were intimidated by you. It was only their fear that gave you your power over them. I don't fear cowards."

Kahir remained stoic, but Jack sensed his ire growing. He edged farther from Anna, keeping her and Justin at a greater distance.

"You had to use me to do your dirty work. Anthony Bane. Benjamin Abrams." Jack scoffed. "And Leonora de Montia. You didn't even have the guts to kill a woman face-to-face. You're pathetic."

Jack launched himself at Kahir and swung. His fist missed by a few inches. A second swing. This time Jack landed a solid blow.

Kahir barely flinched. "Barbarian," he said. "And you call me pathetic? Very well. It seems brute force is your greatest weapon. So be it." He gestured with graceful ease, and blue bolts—threads of lightning—flashed from his fingertips. The energy coiled and bound Jack's wrists. For better or worse, Jack's plan had worked.

"Such petulant actions are no threat," Kahir added, clenching his fist. The coils tightened and closed.

The pain drove Jack to his knees. A heavy force dragged him forward, and he heard a crackle like hot water pouring over ice. His fingers darkened to gray as they turned to stone. Thin fractures spread up his hands and along his forearms to his elbows. He strained to regain his balance but was unable to lift himself upright. The weight of his granite limbs pinned him to the floor, and although they were unyielding rock, electricity surged through them, seizing every nerve, tearing every cell.

Kahir wanted him to suffer for his interference and irreverence—wanted him to beg. But Jack held his tongue, denying Kahir the satisfaction, even as he wondered how much longer he could endure the torment.

Then a flame from an oil lamp on the nearest wall caught Jack's eye. He focused on it, willing himself to relax and push the pain aside. He concentrated on the glow—its color, its warmth—hoping to draw strength from it. But the flame answered in a different way. It burst from the lamp with a roar, streaming outward as fire surrounded him, twisting and swirling. Jack controlled his fear and let the blaze merge with him. The entire room flared with light. The children screamed, and even Kahir seemed startled by the sudden transformation.

Jack watched the rock encasing his arms melt away in the heat. He flexed his fingers as flesh and blood returned. Rising to his feet, still wreathed in fire, he sensed Kahir preparing to strike. Jack did not give his enemy a second chance. He willed the fire forward, surging toward Kahir and engulfing him before he could react.

The flames left Jack and coiled Kahir, but the sinister man did not burn. Instead, the energy stolen from countless innocent lives drained from him, drawn into the spinning inferno. As the fire faded, so did Kahir's life force. His face withered, and his body thinned and sagged.

Kahir cried out, more in disbelief than in pain, watching his fingers shrivel. He stumbled backward—his legs failed to support him.

"Come to me, my children," Kahir wheezed.

The smallest child inched forward, but Jack grabbed the red-haired girl and pulled her to him. She batted at Jack with her little fists, kicking as he lifted her off the floor. A skinny boy darted past, and with Jack already struggling, he couldn't catch him.

At his master's side, the boy knelt. Kahir held the child's head between his palms. The boy shook, then screamed.

"Stop!" Jack yelled.

The red-haired girl wrenched free from his grasp and scrambled away, hiding behind the other children.

In Jack's mind, he snatched the youngster from Kahir's grasp. The boy floated several feet upward and flew clear of the old man. Kahir, drawing on the meager amount of stolen energy he had absorbed, fought to retain control. The child hovered motionless above the floor between the two men.

Caught in the psychic tug-of-war, the boy wept. Jack hated that he played any part in his suffering, but if Kahir regained his strength, the child would die, and the others would share his fate. Given his weakened state, Kahir needed to feed on his followers to restore himself. Jack had no doubt Sarah would be first—Kahir's idea of revenge.

"Help me, my children," Kahir called out. "I need your power to defeat this infidel—this man who means to destroy all we have accomplished."

Kahir propped himself up and launched into a chant. A few children spoke his name. The dark guru invoked words of a forgotten tongue, and more voices followed—young voices in a weak refrain of "Kahir."

The pull on the boy intensified. Jack had to concentrate to maintain his hold. He couldn't use the flame—doing so risked breaking his focus. Jack realized Kahir didn't require physical contact to leech power. He had to find a way to break their connection, but getting to the children was not possible while struggling with Kahir.

Then it hit him—maybe getting to them all wasn't necessary.

"Sarah," he strained, "Sarah, stop. Don't help Kahir. See your brother, your mother—he's hurt them. He will hurt you too. Sarah, listen to me."

The girl's chanting faltered. She looked up at her father, then at Justin, then at her mother.

"Sarah," Jack repeated, "help your family—help me."

She turned back to him. Jack detected a shift in his daughter's eyes—a flicker of recognition. Small, but real. He was getting through to her. But that momentary lapse in focus had cost him. The boy was almost within Kahir's grasp.

Jack fought to counter Kahir's pull, but he succeeded only in stopping the advance. The strain was unbearable. The pounding in his temples warned that he was at the edge of his limit.

"See your mother," Jack said. He had to try harder to connect with her. "She loves you, Sarah. I love you. Help us. Don't give in to Kahir."

Sarah broke away from the group, taking Cindy's hand. Cindy

touched the closest child, taking him with her. He, in turn, grabbed the next girl's hand. One by one, the children fell silent as they stopped chanting Kahir's name.

It was working! Kahir weakened with each child that broke free from the worship. On the verge of total exhaustion, Jack mentally drew the floating boy toward him. The youth drifted down and settled gently on the floor, then dashed to the others huddling near the far door.

"Daddy!" Sarah ran to Jack and threw her arms around him.

The moment had finally come. Sarah willingly came to him of her own accord. She was free! But as Jack looked at the other children, he couldn't say the same for them. Their faces were vacant, unreadable. Were they beyond reach—beyond help?

"Your emotions make you weak," Kahir said, his words strained but defiant. He had slithered close to Justin. "See how you lose your advantage." Kahir seized the boy and sent a long blue spark into his temple. "I will kill the waif—painfully." A soft cry escaped Justin's lips.

Jack dared not move. For Kahir to use what little power he had left on torturing a child meant the man was desperate—and, like a wounded animal, very dangerous.

"I hate you," someone shouted. It was Sarah. "I hate you."

The words struck Kahir, and he winced. Justin relaxed—but only for a moment. Kahir's face twisted with contempt, and he sent another blast into Justin.

Justin screamed.

"Stop that!" Cindy shouted. "I hate you!"

Kahir grimaced. It was his turn to suffer—to feel the agony he'd inflicted on so many.

"You see?" Jack told the children. "He's powerless. He needs you. Think—think about your families, your mothers and fathers. They love you. They miss you. Think about all the pain he caused them. Think!"

It began as scattered chatter, growing stronger as more children joined in. Some of them began to cry.

"Your efforts are wasted on those weaklings," Kahir growled. "They obey me."

"The words of a petty dictator," Jack said. "I've heard it all before. But I think things are about to change."

Kahir fought to draw more power from Justin, but without a willing victim, his method was useless. He could steal no more energy.

The children's murmurs sharpened into a chorus of anger.

"I hate you," Sarah said again.

"I hate you," Cindy echoed.

The little girl beside Jack added, "I hate you too."

"I hate you," all the others said together.

"I hate you."

Soon their words merged into a single roar.

"I hate you."

"I hate you."

"I hate you."

"Look at him," Jack said over the rising voices. "See how weak he is without you."

Kahir lost hold of Justin.

The children continued their new chant. Louder. Relentless. "I hate you—I hate you—I hate you."

Kahir grew older by the second—his true form. Like his creature, Kahir was a parasite—a leech. A truly foul being.

The circle of children closed in on him, their chant rising in unison. The sound reverberated throughout the chamber—an ocean of fury and defiance. Kahir staggered, his withered frame trembling under the weight of their words.

But Sarah got too close—just one hesitant step, hardly more than a shift of weight. In a blur, Kahir's bony fingers shot out and clamped onto her wrist. She sobbed as a pale light poured from her into him.

"No!" Jack stumbled forward. "Sarah!" He sensed a surge in Kahir's energy as the monster fed.

"You see, foolish one," Kahir hissed—cold, merciless. "Even your daughter's hatred nourishes me."

Jack tensed, every muscle poised to fight. He feared what Kahir would do to her in retaliation—yet his gut said *wait.* He watched helplessly as Sarah's face grew pale, her strength fading. Anger surged. Jack wanted to attack, to make Kahir pay for the pain he had caused both his children—but he stayed still.

"Her power is strong," Kahir said. "I'll feed on her for years. But you, my brutish friend, shall—"

A sudden crash shattered the chaos. Kahir jerked violently, and his grip on Sarah broke. He collapsed into a heap, and shock flashed across his face. The life-energy drained from Sarah surged back, and she gasped for air, slumping into her father's arms.

Above the fallen Kahir stood Justin, holding a brass lamp by the handle. It swung slightly with several dark strands stuck to its side.

"You talk too much," Justin said. He had the most serious expression on his face. Justin dropped the lamp, and it rolled across the floor before coming to rest beside Kahir.

An eerie hush swept the room as the children watched their former leader transform. His hair grayed, withered, and dissolved. Then his skin dried and tightened over his skull. His lips cracked and split, revealing rotting teeth. A skeletal hand rose in one last desperate attempt to feed on the nearest child—then it dropped. There was no further movement from Abhaya Kahir.

"Is it over, Jack?" Anna asked, coming up beside him. Freed from Kahir's control, she hugged her husband. "Is it really over?"

"Almost," Jack said, watching the children slowly recover—the last of the mental cobwebs lifting. "But this we can manage."

Anna's breath stalled as alarm lit her face. "Where's Sarah?" She turned frantically from side to side.

"She's over there." Jack pointed to the front of the room, where Sarah stood by Justin. The two children walked over to their parents.

"Can we go home?" Sarah asked.

"Soon, dear," Jack said. "We have to call someone to come for the others."

Morning broke to a street filled with squad cars and parents reclaiming their lost children. Anna watched as Jonathan de Montia drove up. He didn't even bother shutting off the engine before bolting from the vehicle over to his daughter, Cindy, pulling her into a tight embrace. The happiness on her face was unmistakable. Still, as with many of the children, she would need some counseling. In time, all wounds would heal.

The remaining children—some wearing oversized jackets, some wrapped in blankets—were escorted from the house to the gate. The concrete path was cracked, forced upward by years of frost and thaw. Along the way, the lawn had thinned to patchwork, broad swaths of bare earth showing where scraggly, knee-high weeds had taken hold. The flower garden on the southern side had collapsed into abandonment, choked with tall grasses and wild shrubs tangled with moss and fallen leaves.

A woman holding the hand of the tiny red-haired girl came up to Jack. "Do you know how this happened?" she asked. "Do you know who saved my little Katy?"

Jack shook his head. "I'm not too sure."

"The children don't remember any of it," the woman told him. "Whoever it was, I'd like to thank them."

"Me too," Jack said, pulling Sarah and Justin close. They all watched as the woman and child walked away.

At the gate, Jack's gaze drifted to the house, seeing its true state with Kahir gone. The once-grand Queen Anne no longer dominated the block as it slumped behind its stone walls. The gray barrier was splitting in places, mortar crumbling to pale dust, and rust streaked the black iron gate. Chipped paint clung stubbornly to the gabled porch, peeling in wide curls from the posts and railings, and one column leaned as if it might topple at the slightest touch. Shingles had slipped and warped, exposing dark underlayers, and the ground-floor windows were clouded with grime, their frames swollen and split.

His eyes traveled higher, toward the tower. The narrow windows were empty sockets, the interior swallowed by shadow, with deep cracks forming veins from the ground to the turret. The dead structure stood, but only out of habit.

Anna smiled and gently put an arm around Jack's waist, hitting the handle of the Beretta tucked under his shirt. "You brought your gun?" Her smile disappeared.

Jack gave her a slight grin. "It's not loaded."

"How did we get here?" Anna asked him. "How did you do this?"

"I'll explain it to you sometime."

"I've heard that one before," she said, and kissed him. "Let's go home."

EPILOGUE

The fluorescent lights buzzed quietly above the rows of stainless-steel tables, casting a harsh glare on the cold floor of the Hennepin County Morgue. Two men stood near the wall, shoulders stiff from the long night. Their voices carried over the hum of refrigeration compressors, casual in tone, masking the weariness that had settled deep in their bones.

"I could really go for some coffee," said the first, stretching a hand to the sink, turning off the water. "Maybe even a bite to eat. Been a long night."

"Yeah," his coworker replied, bringing one arm up, bending it at the elbow, then letting it drop. "I could use the same. Coffee, something warm. Something that doesn't taste like rubber. But I guess the vending machines will have to do."

They exchanged a brief smile. The kind born of mutual exhaustion and the understanding that comes from long hours in a setting where life and death intersect. For a moment, the morgue seemed less a site of finality and more a shared workplace—just two men waiting for a snack before returning to their duties.

"I'll meet you in the lunchroom," the first added. "A body came in. I need to prep it and get it in a drawer." He grabbed a pair of latex gloves and pulled them on.

His coworker gave a short nod, acknowledging the interruption. "Go ahead, I can wait. The coffee will always be there, I suppose."

The first man moved to the table where the corpse lay in its plain black body bag. He paused, hand hovering over the zipper, feeling the weight of routine and the hours of the night pressing down on him. The metal teeth clicked as they parted, opening the bag.

And then he stopped.

Inside was a body unlike any he had encountered in the morgue. The skin was dry and leathery, shrunken tight over bone, the color a muted brown, and mottled in spots. The limbs were stiff and unnaturally bent, giving an impression of age and decay preserved far beyond its death.

"Holy shit…," he muttered, stepping back. "Looks like a mummy."

His coworker leaned over his shoulder, curiosity overriding his own fatigue. "A mummy? Right."

"I'm not joking," the first replied, his voice low, edged with disbelief. "Dried out…shriveled. There's something damned peculiar about this."

There was a pause as the two men studied the corpse. The silence lingered, punctuated only by the gentle drone of the cooler units.

"You've seen worse. Remember that guy whacked by the train? How many pieces did they bring in? And not on the same day."

"I'm just saying a little warning would have been nice."

Despite the unease that crawled up his skin, the first man's hand moved forward almost of its own accord. He reached out to touch the body.

As his fingers made contact, a sharp jolt shot through him. He gasped and staggered, his knees threatening to buckle under a wave of weakness. His grip on the table tightened as he fought to stay upright.

"What the hell—?"

"Hey, you okay?" his coworker asked, concern creeping into his voice. "You don't look so good."

"I—I don't know," he stammered. His hand released the table as he tried to slow his breathing. "I just…it shocked me—right through my gloves. I feel dizzy all of a sudden—"

The coworker stepped closer, steadying him with a hand to the shoulder. "I tell ya, these ten-hour shifts are killers," he said firmly. "Let's get that coffee. The stiff can wait a few minutes. I'm sure he won't mind."

The first man let out a shaky breath, relief washing over him. He gave a small, grateful nod. The immediate pain of the electric shock had passed, and the tremor in his limbs eased enough to allow him to follow his coworker toward the door.

The two men walked side by side, their boots making soft, echoing sounds down the hall. Voices lowered as they discussed coffee and food in tones that were more or less normal. The body, for the moment, was forgotten.

Once they were out of earshot, a subtle, almost imperceptible energy swept the room. The overhead lights flashed and hummed, creating patches of darkness that rippled over the tables and drawers. The eyes of the body opened.

A glint of awareness flickered behind the leathery lids. The skeletal fingers twitched, stiff at first, testing the stillness that had confined them. Slowly, deliberately, a hand rose, curling toward the ceiling as if seeking release from the stifling bag that held it.

Before the fingers could extend fully upward, a blast of energy erupted from somewhere unseen. The body, once dry and brittle, was hit by a bright, forceful surge. Ash and dust flew across the table and floor, leaving nothing behind but the faintest trace of its existence.

From the shadows in a dark corner of the morgue, a figure stepped forward. Eric Sanders emerged, his gaze fixed on the scattered remnants. He walked over the dust—pausing—looking down at what had once been Abhaya Kahir.

"I promised Julia I wouldn't take revenge on you," he said, his words controlled, precise. "I promised her that I wouldn't give in to the darkness."

"I kept my promise," he continued, as if reassuring himself. "Jack Railey did all the heavy lifting. I'm here to...make sure things stayed settled."

AFTERWORD

This novel was first published in 2002 under the title *Messiah*. Written and released on a tight timeline, I always felt the story was rushed. Given the opportunity for rerelease, I have spent the past year cleaning the prose and expanding some character moments, adding detail that brings the story closer to my original vision. The core narrative remains unchanged, though this edition reflects the benefit of time and perspective.

ABOUT THE AUTHOR

Keith Ferrario enjoys horror movies, writing, and traveling. When it comes to writing, Keith's greatest influence for stories and writing style is the old black-and-white monster movies he still enjoys to this day. His love of horror goes back as far as he can remember. As a boy, watching *Shock Theater* and *Creature Features* on late Friday nights, he became a fan of Boris Karloff, Lon Chaney Jr, and Vincent Price. Shows like *Dark Shadows*, *The Outer Limits*, and *Kolchak: The Night Stalker* and comics like *Tales from the Crypt* and *The Vault of Horror* pushed him farther down this dark path.

Also by Keith Ferrario
Dark Carnival
Deadly Friend
Monster

For more information:
www.keithferrario.com
keith@keithferrario.com

www.ingramcontent.com/pod-product-compliance
Lightning Source LLC
LaVergne TN
LVHW090559110826
845146LV00001B/185

* 9 7 9 8 8 8 8 4 6 0 1 8 4 *